Siding
with Plato

Michelle Manning

Clink
Street

London | New York

Published by Clink Street Publishing 2015

Copyright © 2015

First edition.

ISBN:

Dedicated my Grandma, Helen Czuleger and the most incredible friends a girl could ask for.

"Love is a serious mental disease."
Plato

Chapter 1

"No, no, no, not again!" Brooke Aarons said when she caught sight of the flashing blue and red lights behind her. She pulled over to the side of the highway and quickly tried to recall an article she'd read in *Psychology Today* once about dealing with police officers.

She watched from her side-view mirror as the man in uniform approached slowly. When she noticed him studying her car, she remembered a section of the article mentioning an officer will base assumptions about the driver on the car alone, titled "What does your car say about you?" *Well, that's great*, she thought. *Mine says I'm poor and I hit things.* She rolled down the window of her ancient, beat-up Jeep Wrangler, thinking how neither was entirely untrue.

"Is there a problem, Officer...," she glanced at his silver name tag, "Hurley?" That was another thing she'd read: using the officer's name could help avoid the ticket. Sure, all evidence pointed to the contrary, since it had never worked in her favor before, but it didn't stop her from trying. Besides, she was in a new state. Things could be entirely different over here.

"License and registration, ma'am," he said with a Southern drawl so thick she assumed he was kidding. She laughed a little until she noticed his face was stone cold.

It's okay, she thought. *It's not too late to salvage this. Pretend you were flirting. Every other girl does it.* She rested one elbow on the windowsill and tried to look innocent. "Was I going a little fast? I'm so sorry you had to even get out of the car in this heat. I mean, it's got to be a hundred degrees out."

This would totally work. She may not understand the psychology of a cop, but he was still a man, right? How hard could they be to figure out? She pulled her blond, wavy hair over to one shoulder and fanned herself. "And that uniform looks awfully hot, Officer Hurley."

While debating if that was overkill, she pushed her thrift-store aviators up onto her head so she could bat her eyelashes, but instead they caught in her hair, then slid off and dangled in front of her face.

"Oh, look at us. We have the same sunglasses," she said, trying to lighten his mood. "We match." She could feel him assessing her.

"Ma'am, have you been drinking?" he asked while she was still trying to untangle herself.

"It's 12:30," she said in a shocked, shame-on-you tone.

"Well, I'll be. If you can read a clock, I'll wager you can read a road sign, too," Officer Hurley said. "Mind answering my question now?"

His patronizing tone made her want to hurl-ey. "No, I have not been drinking."

"Good. License and registration then, please."

What a waste of boobs you are, she told herself. Not that she was hugely blessed in that area. Flirting like a ditz was out, but she still wasn't about to accept a ticket. She considered for a moment that maybe he was the type of guy who needed to feel like the hero. Damsel-in-distress act?

"Actually, I'm so glad you stopped me," she said, picking up her portable GPS and holding it upside down for effect. "I'm completely turned around." Playing lost sadly came easy, since it was usually the case anyway. "I want to be on the 10 freeway and…"

"You're on it," he said sharply, not hiding his annoyance. "The I-10 is the road you just broke a Texas state law on."

The 10 was practically the only road she'd been on since her drive began, and considering the speed limit had only gone up since she reached Texas, she knew this one was a bit of a long shot. Car trouble?

"Yeah, about that. I think my speedometer must be a little bit broken. I swear it felt like I was going sort of fast, but it said 75 miles per hour."

"Well, it would have to be a-lot-a-bit broken, since I clocked you at 92." He held out his hand. "I'm not going to ask you again, ma'am." The man was impossible.

She reached across the car and pulled her registration out of the glove box. Right before handing it over, she had an epiphany. Reverse psychology? What the hell—she had nothing to lose.

She looked up at him again, making her big green eyes look as sorry as possible. "You're right, Officer Hurley," she said, holding out what he requested. "I messed up. I completely agree with everything you're saying. I was obviously going too fast, and I'm so glad you pulled me over to tell me. Just write me a ticket. Even though I'd hate to see you waste more of your time standing in this unbearable heat, I have to pay for my crimes. I *want* the ticket."

"All right then," he said, snatching her license and registration and turning back toward his car. "Wait in your vehicle, ma'am."

Shit.

She leaned her head back against her headrest. *Highway Patrol, six. Brooke Aarons, zero*, she thought. How was she going to pay for this one?

She flipped her GPS over so it was right side up. Her parents had given it to her as a going-away present in hope of combatting her horrible sense of direction. Unfortunately, she hated being told what to do so she switched the voice off, which usually resulted in her missing a turn anyway. So as far as she could tell, not much had improved.

Only two exits away. Three straight days of driving, and I get a ticket two exits away. Way to kill a Saturday afternoon, not to mention the most monumental day of my life!

While she waited for Officer Hurley to come back with the impending speeding ticket she'd be paying for, she looked ahead toward the city of Austin, Texas. As she studied the skyline, she realized she could already see the football stadium from the highway. A wave of excitement came over her. Everything she'd been waiting for was right in front of her, and she was practically inches away.

"California, huh?" Officer Hurley said when he reappeared at her window and handed her back her driver's license.

She looked at him and raised her eyebrows instead of answering.

"Where you heading?"

"The university," she said pointing ahead. "I'm starting school there Monday."

"Freshman?"

She nodded.

"Well, I hope you're not majoring in theater," he said, still not changing his expression.

Jerk, what if I was? She chose not to respond to his comment, thankful she hadn't tried out her crying routine. Theater was never in the cards for her, as today proved, but that was fine with her since she already knew exactly what she wanted to do.

"All right, Miss Aarons." He started in on his memorized explanation of understanding where to pay and where she could attend traffic school and blah blah blah. She signed her ticket and started to roll up her window while he was still standing there. "Please obey all posted speed limits signs, and get that *speedometer* of yours checked…"

He made it clear he didn't believe her story, so she made it clear she didn't appreciate the B.S. concern. She stuffed the ticket in the glove box and screeched back onto the highway.

When Brooke found out she was accepted to the University of Texas, she couldn't have been more excited. UT had an amazing psychology department, and despite how everyone and their mother (especially *her* mother) advised her not to major in psych, she was doing it anyway. She'd always had a fascination with trying to figure people out. She loved analyzing what people did and trying to guess what made them do it, or simply why they were the way they were.

She already considered herself a master of the subject, though the interaction with Hurley showed her she still had some work to do in dealing with authorities. She could stand to get a better grasp on the psychology of men in general, actually, but only if it came up in her studies. This Jeep was hauling ass away from her seemingly small-town life in Camarillo for a reason. She had no intention of letting anything distract her from acing her classes, graduating, and starting an exciting life somewhere else, anywhere else. Boys were the first thing she listed as a distraction, so no matter how excited she was to break into a whole new scene, she promised herself a potential relationship would not be on her radar. Too many times she'd seen people talk about all the things they wanted, only to go falling in love and lose sight of them. That wasn't in the cards for her.

Chapter 2

Brooke made it to her exit, and, with a little help from her GPS, turned right onto Guadalupe Street. All sense of exhaustion from the long drive was replaced by excitement once she started seeing signs for the University of Texas. She drove toward campus, made a right on 27th Street, and found the building she'd be calling home for the next year, Almetrius Duren Hall.

The brick dorm was six stories high and had a courtyard filled with trees and benches. It was love at first sight. After finding a parking spot close by, she pulled her two huge bags out from the backseat and dropped them on the ground.

It took all of her strength to push her door closed as it made its usual ear-piercing creaking noise. She didn't care that her car was old. She decided as a kid she was going to own a Jeep Wrangler and never looked at another car. A '96 model with chipped red paint and a few dents was the only one she could afford when she was sixteen, but she still loved it. Her parents had even offered to help buy her a more reasonable car, but she refused. She really enjoyed doing things on her own, even if it was just for the challenge of seeing if she could pull it off.

She took a minute to send her mom a text, letting her know she'd made it okay. Her mom replied instantly: "Yay!

Glad to hear it. Have fun settling in and remember if you do drink, always keep your hand over your cup and never set it down. Love you" followed by six or seven farm animals.

Brooke smiled at her mother's predictable paranoia and weird use of emojis before putting her iPhone back in her bag. She had no doubt her mom probably said the same things when she dropped her at day care with a juice box, but when high school, more specifically high school parties, came into play, it sent Kathy Aarons into a whole new mode of panic. Not that she ever really needed to worry about Brooke. She had motivation to break free. And that day had arrived.

Everywhere she looked, people her age were pulling bags out of their cars and pushing carts toward the building. She picked up her bags, slung one over each shoulder, and sighed with a huge smile at the thought of finally making it here. Not just to the building or even college, but to freedom, to a place where her life could finally begin. The rush of it all made her barely notice the weight of her bags as she practically sprinted to the check-in desk inside.

"Hi, I'm Brooke Aarons. I'm in this building," she said excitedly when she reached the desk.

"Well hello there," the woman said, trumping her enthusiasm. "Welcome to Duran!" For a moment she thought the woman might jump up and hug her. While the thought of all the blush that would no doubt wind up on her shirt if that happened made her tense up a little, the thrill of being there got her past it. The woman chatted away about all the building rules and regulations then slid a piece of paper toward Brooke and told her to sign at the bottom. Brooke clicked a pen and glanced at it for a few moments, then paused.

"Wait, *what's* this for?"

"That there is an agreement to not eat the paint," she said, smiling like it wasn't weird.

"I'm… I'm not going to eat the paint."

"Wonderful! Just sign at the bottom."

Brooke looked around to verify that she was actually in a college dorm, then considered for a moment whether maybe she should have been placed in the honors hall if this needed to be explained here. She held back her comments and signed.

When Brooke exited the elevators on the fifth floor, she looked right then left, debating which direction room 501 would be. After deciding it was definitely to the right, she walked to the end, which only proved her sense of direction was wrong one hundred percent of the time. She turned around to go in the other direction and saw a girl walking toward her with a bag slung over her shoulder.

"530?" the girl asked.

"No, no I'm 501. I went the wrong way."

"Oh, okay. Well, we're still neighbors! I'm Stella." She held out her hand and Brooke shook it.

"I'm Brooke. Nice to meet you."

Stella was tall and thin with short bleach-blond hair and heavy black eyeliner that somehow worked on her. Brooke got the sense she pored over every fashion magazine and tried every trend. Sure enough, she spotted a *Vogue* sticking out of Stella's purse.

"Well, I'll get out of your way so you can get in." The girls shuffled around each other in the narrow hallway, trying not to knock each other's bags. The difficulty of it made them both laugh a little.

"Feel free to come down after you get settled," Stella said. "Thanks. You too. You're the first person I've met." "Same here." They both smiled politely then went on to their rooms.

Brooke found room 501 and unlocked the door to find

two twin beds. One was raised like a bunk bed with a desk under it, and the other sat against the wall facing the desk. "Fancy," she said to herself as she looked around at the barren room.

The truth was she kind of loved it like that: completely plain but full of possibility, and all hers for the taking. Well, hers and a randomly assigned roommate. She set her stuff on the floor next to the lower bed, opened one of her bags, and pulled out her sheets. Her roommate hadn't arrived yet, but hopefully she wouldn't mind the bunk bed.

After she made her bed, she started pulling her clothes out of the bags. Aside from her car, the only other material possessions Brooke was obsessed with were her clothes. Every dime she had wound up hanging in her closet, but she had to admit she had a pretty good wardrobe. She certainly wasn't as trendy as Stella seemed, but Brooke coveted the few classic items she had.

A few minutes later she heard a key going into the lock and saw the doorknob turn—her roommate, no doubt. A girl walked in with a backpack and a rolling suitcase and seemed excited when she saw Brooke standing there smiling.

"Hi, I'm Sophie," the girl said, catching her wheel on the doorway and struggling for a few moments before finally making it fully inside. Sophie was about 5'2" with mousy-brown hair pulled back into a low ponytail and not a trace of makeup on. She looked much too young to be in college, but Brooke just chalked it up to her light pink jeans and white Keds.

"Hi, I'm Brooke. I guess we're roommates! I hope you don't mind I took this bed."

"Oh. No problem. I have some issues with high places," she chuckled as she looked nervously at the bed and set her suitcase next to the ladder, "but I guess I've got to get over that some time, right?"

"Oh no, if you want to switch, it's no big deal."

"No, no, no. I'm fine, really."

Sophie was really sweet, Brooke thought. Kind of shy, kind of dorky, but she liked her.

They made some small talk for a bit, but when Sophie pulled out a bible, a snow globe with a unicorn inside, and a curse-word jar, Brooke froze. *Oh shit*, she thought, happy to have kept the word in her head. She couldn't remember if she'd said any words that would cost her yet but decided she should make an exit before she wound up emptying her pockets. It would happen soon enough anyway. She started to head back toward Stella's room and found Stella heading in her direction. They both smiled at how little time it took for them to go looking for one another.

"Did you meet your roommate?" Stella asked.

"Yeah, she's sweet. I have a curse-word jar in my room. You?"

"Mine offered me coke and told me a funny story about how she stole from her last roommate after her mother kicked her out."

"You win." They both laughed, realizing how little they'd prepared themselves for the living situation. "Have you had a chance to check out the campus much?"

"No, I missed orientation. I was still in San Francisco."

"I missed it too. Long drive from Camarillo."

"So Cal, huh?"

"Are we going to have a problem, Nor Cal?"

"We'll give it a shot. Besides, I'll be down in LA soon enough, or maybe New York."

"But you figured you'd stop off in Texas first?" Brooke asked, trying to figure her out.

"Well, UT is a great school. Plus Austin has amazing shopping." Brooke looked at her like that hadn't fully answered her question. "And maybe I have a thing for Southern boys."

They both laughed. "Whatever. I'll get serious later in life," she said, brushing it off. "We're in college!"

"See, I knew we could get along," Brooke said, thrilled to find someone with her same enthusiasm. "But back to this shopping situation…"

"Oh, girl, I could show you around."

"Speaking of which, I have no idea where anything on campus is."

"Me neither," she said pulling her schedule out of her back pocket. "But there is no way I'm going out there in this heat," Stella said. "I saw maps in the lobby, though. We could find which buildings our classes are in."

"I guarantee it won't make a difference come Monday. But sure, it's worth a try."

As they rode the elevator down to the lobby level, Brooke and Stella quickly bonded over their mutual love of fashion. Stella was way more risky when it came to trends, and a little more risqué too, as far as she could tell, but Brooke admired her for it. She could have a thing or two to learn from this girl.

They grabbed two maps off a table in the lobby and sat down on a bench.

"Okay, where's your first class?" Stella asked.

Brooke pulled her schedule up on her phone. "9 a.m., Psychology 101. Um, in the Seay building."

"Okay," Stella said, tracing her finger on the map, "that's Speedway and Dean Keeton. Oh, that's close. And I'm right across the way at the same time! Ugh, my first class is biology."

"Not your major, I take it?"

"God no, I would never. The majority of my classes will be spent with handsome future businessmen, not nerds in lab coats."

"Talk to me in ten years when you're pining for a hot doctor. So where's your next class?"

They figured out they both had a half-hour break between their classes, and Stella pointed out that there was a coffee shop attached to the Perry-Castaneda Library. It was near where they'd split off for their next classes, so they made a plan to meet up and grab coffees.

When they had found where all their classes would be, they decided to head back upstairs. They fell into sync behind another girl walking toward the elevator.

"I wonder how much of my stuff klepto has already swiped," Stella joked while they were waiting.

"Hey, at least you can cuss about it," Brooke said as she caught herself staring at a tattoo on the girl's right blade.

The girl looked back when she heard them talking, and Brooke made eye contact accidentally, so she smiled.

"Sorry," Brooke said, "but does your tattoo say, 'Ask me about my tattoo'?"

"Yes it does," the girl replied proudly.

"Okay, then I have a question."

The girl laughed. "Long story short, I desperately wanted a tattoo, so I kept coming up with all these ideas then imagining how I would tell people what it meant, because, you know, everyone has to have a meaningful explanation or else it's stupid, right? But then I realized I didn't want to be one of those people that just gets one with the hope people will ask them about it, so I'd just make fun of them instead. Plus, now if someone asks, I can make up whatever I want. Does that sound completely nuts or make sense?"

Brooke stared at her for a few seconds. "Actually, it makes perfect sense."

The elevator made a ding, and the doors opened. The girls all walked in, and both Brooke and the girl reached over to hit the number five. Brooke was pleasantly surprised to see she was on the fifth floor too.

"Yeah, well, at 15 I thought I was the most clever person

on the planet. I'm Darci, by the way," she said. Darci was tan and gorgeous with long, stick-straight dark hair, and she was tall and thin like Stella.

"I'm Brooke."

"Stella."

"So did you both get crazies for roommates or something?" the girl said, smiling politely. She must have overheard them talking.

"I don't think we can call mine crazy," Brooke said, "but she got a drug addict," gesturing toward Stella as if having the worst would give her bragging rights.

"Wow, I really lucked out. Mine's kind of awesome."

The elevator doors opened, and they all stepped out. "I'm actually in this room right here if you want to come in," Darci said.

"Kate, my roommate, is out running an errand, but she should be back soon if you want to meet her too."

Both Brooke and Stella were glad to have a reason to postpone going back to their own rooms, so they happily accepted Darci's offer.

The room was arranged identically to Brooke's. Darci had taken the bunk, and her roommate, Kate, had the regular bed. Already Kate's bed was made up and decorated with throw pillows, and her desk had cute blue and brown organizers and framed pictures on it. Darci's side was a little more simple with just a red comforter with a pillow and her laptop, but somehow their room felt very homey already.

Brooke walked around the room, looking at a few of the photos on Kate's desk, but when she heard boys' voices coming from the hallway, she couldn't resist peeking through the peephole.

"Wait, there are boys on our floor?" Brooke asked. "I knew the building was coed, but I didn't think we'd share floors."

"Hell yeah. I circled this dorm on my application like ten times for that reason. Are they cute?" Stella asked, desperate to know.

"The backs of their heads look nice." Brooke stepped away and let Stella take over.

"They're all facing that bulletin board," Stella whined quietly so they couldn't hear her.

"Open the door," Darci said, adjusting herself. "Let's meet them!"

"Are you kidding? I'm a mess," Stella said. "I'm not going to meet them looking like this." She paused so she could make out what they were saying. "I think they're talking about a party tonight!"

"Oh yeah, I saw a flier on the board about a foam party tonight," Darci said. "It's 18 and up, so we don't need ID." Brooke took over the peephole again and saw a girl carrying a bag of groceries coming around the corner. One of the guys turned to look at her, and she smiled and said hi but kept walking. When she pulled out her keys, Brooke realized she was heading for the door she was peeking through. She backed up quickly so she wouldn't seem like a creep.

"Oh, hey!" the girl said when she opened the door and saw Brooke and Stella.

"Hey, roomie. I made friends!" Darci announced. Brooke and Stella introduced themselves.

"Oh, yay! Nice to meet you guys. Are you roommates too?" Kate asked, sounding genuinely excited to meet them.

"If only," Stella said before describing her first encounter with her actual roommate.

Kate was probably 5'5" like Brooke, and her brown ponytail had natural blond highlights. She was just in jeans and a plain white T-shirt but somehow pulled it off like she had specifically picked out the perfect moving-day outfit.

Kate set the bag of groceries down and started unloading things into the mini fridge. "You guys hungry or thirsty?"

The girls refused anything, but Brooke couldn't help but notice how well she stocked the little refrigerator. She instantly got the sense that Kate was the kind of girl who couldn't wait to pack lunches for kids one day.

"So, Kate, how do you feel about going to a foam party tonight?"

"What's a foam party?" Kate asked.

"Yeah, I've never heard of this either," Brooke said. "It's like a big party in a warehouse, or somewhere, that they fill with tons of foam. I've heard about them but never been to one," Darci answered.

Kate looked disturbed by the visual. "Sounds sketchy."

"Sounds fun!" Stella countered. "Those cute guys in the hall are going, and so are we!"

"Do you know what the foam is made out of, though?" Brooke asked. "Is it safe on fabrics?" She waited for an answer, but they all turned and looked at her like she had just said something weird. "Never mind." She had to work for everything she owned, so she couldn't help being a little overprotective of her things. But it was probably best to ease new people into her OCD.

"Only one way to find out!" Darci said with a smile.

Chapter 3

Brooke and Stella met back up in Darci and Kate's room a few hours later to get ready for the party. They mixed lemonade with some Fleischmann's vodka Darci had talked her older brothers into getting her as a going-away present. It tasted horrible and was like trying to swallow syrup.

"My brothers are so cheap," Darci remarked when they all started coughing like it was going to come back up.

Darci had done her fair share of drinking in high school, and so had Stella, Brooke learned. She'd had a few drinks before, mostly just beer at high school parties or sips of liquor she'd stolen from her dad's supply for her friends. She thought whiskey was the worst thing she'd ever tasted, and definitely not worth getting grounded over when her dad discovered his entire bottle had eventually been replaced with apple juice. But all experiences were pretty few and far between, so she hadn't really built up a tolerance.

After her first time drinking vodka, she'd thrown up so many times she begged her friends to take her to the hospital. But not wanting to get in trouble, they just made her ride it out on her own. She took a moment to appreciate finally being in a city rather than a small town with a small pool of people to choose from. Brooke had also tried tequila, and oddly enough that seemed to go over okay. Mixed with pineapple juice, it was actually good, but that was really the extent of her drinking experience.

Kate seemed to have a similar amount of history with drinking. As long as she couldn't taste the alcohol, she said she was fine, but in the case of Fleischmann's, she was struggling, as were the rest of them.

At first they all tried to act like they were seasoned drinkers, but as they loosened up a little, Brooke and Kate admitted their inexperience, and Stella and Darci told stories of how they'd both thrown up in their own purses before.

When they finished getting ready, they all took a minute to check themselves in the mirror. Brooke wore a black miniskirt, strappy wedges, and a strapless green top with big, gold earrings. Her long hair never stayed perfectly straight no matter what she did, and with the Texas humidity adding fuel to the fire, she just decided to let it go wild. She looked over at Stella, who had just added a neon collar necklace to her ensemble.

"Stella, I'm having serious style envy right now. Too bad I could never pull off high-waisted shorts."

"I'd have to be high and wasted to want to," Darci said as she pulled her red halter top, which was noticeably lacking a bra, a little lower. "No offense, though. They're cute on you."

Stella just shook her head and laughed it off.

"I think we all look amazing," Kate said as she zipped up the side of her cute blue minidress. "Now let's get out there and find ourselves some boyfriends!" She raised her cup, but no one else followed suit. "I mean, some hot guys who will buy us drinks?"

"There it is," Darci said as she lifted her cup along with Brooke and Stella.

They walked out of the dorms like they owned the place,

despite the fact they'd all lived there less than a day. Then they hailed a cab and told the driver where to go. When they heard music blasting out of a building on Warehouse Row, they knew they were at the right place.

Their hearts were racing, the excitement was palpable. "Ready?" Brooke asked, taking a deep breath.

"Let's do it!" Darci yelled.

Fifteen minutes later they were sitting outside on a curb down the street, still dripping wet from the foam.

Darci: "Somewhere in the world there's a neglected porta potty that smells better than that place."

Brooke: "Ten bucks says we all wake up with pink eye or something tomorrow."

Darci: "Fifty on some form of herpes."

Stella: "My skin is still burning."

Kate: "I stepped between two people having sex on the floor. My leg was caught between their bodies. It was so slippery." Kate buried her face in her hands as if it would erase the feeling, and Brooke patted her on the back.

Stella: "I mean, I saw a few hot guys in there."

Brooke: "How could you tell they were hot? You couldn't see anyone from the chin down."

Stella: "Well, their faces were decent anyway. I got a phone number!"

She held up a Post-it, but the ink had bled all over the paper.

Stella: "Oh. Oh well."

Kate: "Who brings Post-its to a party?"

Brooke: "It's the business card of an 18-year-old. Although, that guy looked about 40."

Darci: "Someone gave me ecstasy."

"What?" they all exclaimed. Darci pulled out a little blue pill and held it out to show the girls. Kate smacked it out of her hand.

Kate: "Don't take that!"

Darci: "I wasn't going to!"

Kate: "They should really monitor who can post on that bulletin board. And if those guys from the hall are actually enjoying that party, I vote we avoid contact."

Brooke: "Done. Pass the bag."

When the girls had run for their lives out of the most disgusting party any of them had ever attended, they found themselves in front of a liquor store down the street. The kid working the counter looked about sixteen and seemed like he couldn't care less about being there.

The girls sensed they'd gotten his attention when he suddenly tried to act cooler at the sight of them walking in. They decided to seize the opportunity and try buying some alcohol. They didn't want to risk being asked for ID with a credit card, so they scraped their cash together and found the cheapest thing on the shelf. It was a box of wine called Franzia.

After standing with one of the freezer doors open for a few seconds, a braless Darci was the one who went to the counter. She leaned forward, pushing her boobs together. Behind her, Stella was bent over, pretending to reach for something on the bottom shelf, and Kate and Brooke playfully inspected the Slim Jims.

The poor kid didn't stand a chance. He rang them up without a peep, and the girls bolted out the door before he could realize what he'd done. They removed the box so it was just the bag full of pink wine with the nozzle and took turns passing it around.

Brooke held the bag in the air and twisted the knob until enough filled her mouth. Then she passed the bag to Kate, who did the same. They talked about parties they had gone to at each of their high schools, dating horror stories, their families, how they grew up, and what brought them to UT.

Brooke gathered that Kate Holden came from one of those homes where her mom was the perfect homemaker, her dad was the guy who coached all of his kids' little league teams, and all of her siblings were gorgeous and on track for successful careers. She was an education major and wanted to teach preschool after she graduated.

As the only child, Stella Price admittedly made her parents' life hell while she was in high school. She was also a little boy crazy but really smart. After finishing her undergrad, she wanted to get her MBA and eventually open her own high-end boutique, then segue into a career as a stylist for the stars.

Darci Moore was undeclared but not unambitious. Within their conversation alone, she decided she was going to be a lawyer, then an event planner, then a journalist, then a stripper, then back to a lawyer after stripping paid for law school. She had two older brothers, and after her parents divorced, her dad moved to a different state, so she was really only close to her mom.

Brooke told them about her dad, Bruce, who was the editor in chief of their town's newspaper, which had come in handy for Brooke when she caused a four-car pileup and he didn't run it on the front page; her mom, a children's book illustrator; her older sister, Sarah; and her younger brother, Josh. She even mentioned Sarah's boyfriend, Dan, since he was practically part of the family anyway.

In no time at all, they established who was who in their *Sex and the City* foursome. Brooke was a Carrie, Kate was a Charlotte, and both Darci and Stella fought for the coveted title of Samantha, since nobody wanted to be the Miranda. After six rounds of rock-paper-scissors and neither one caving, Kate and Brooke finally intervened, declaring them both to be co-Samantha's.

When they'd made a pretty big dent in the bag of wine,

Stella suggested a game called Would You Rather. They went back and forth answering questions that forced them to decide between being smart and ugly or pretty and stupid, or have legs but no arms or arms but no legs. A few rounds in, Stella proposed, "Find the one and be madly in love or," she thought for a moment, "find ten million dollars?" They all contemplated for a moment.

Stella: "I'm going to say finding the one. And hope he happens to be one with ten million dollars."

Darci: "With ten million dollars, I could buy me some love."

Brooke: "Pretty sure that's illegal."

Kate: "I'm going with love. No question about it, I want to find the one."

Brooke: "Psh. Show me the money. I don't buy into that whole *the one* crap anyway."

Stella: "Well look who's a cynic."

Brooke: "I'm not. I'm just saying, what's the point of believing in that? It's not like we're all handed some guarantee that one day, preferably before thirty, we'll meet this certain person out of billions and it'll all work out. It doesn't make sense."

Kate jumped up like she was confused and appalled by Brooke's answer.

Kate: "Isn't that what people say about it, though? That it's crazy and irrational and it doesn't make sense, but suddenly you meet this person and your whole world gets turned upside down and everything is perfect?"

They all stared at her.

Darci: "This stuff's like three percent alcohol. How is she so drunk?"

Stella: "Maybe it's a sugar high. Have you ever had too many Capri Suns? This is like a giant one."

Brooke: "Oh god, did she get a hold of the ecstasy? Kate, spit it out. Spit it out, girl."

Kate: "Oh, shut up," she said as she plopped back down on the curb. "I'm just curious what you believe in if you don't believe in that."

Brooke: "Okay, well I believe there's a best person for some people maybe, definitely some that are better than others. But no, I don't think there is one exact, perfect fit specifically made for everyone. And I think it's just ridiculous to believe you'll serendipitously cross paths one day in this huge world and it'll all work out. But then again, I think it's just as crazy to believe that one perfect fit out of billions could just so happen to grow up in the same tiny town as you, like so many people back home convince themselves. Suddenly, whoever sticks around just becomes *the one* and we're all supposed to believe it. It's not real."

Darci: "So graduating from high school in a small town is like when the lights come on in a club and everyone looks around to see who's decent enough to go home with?"

Brooke: "Exactly. Actually, I don't know. I've never been to a club. But that sounds about right."

Kate: "So Brooke, you're not even going to try looking for the right guy for you?"

Brooke: "Nope. I'm going to be home, rolling in my fat pile of money, popping champagne, and rapping. I'll be able to rap when I'm rich."

Stella: "Don't you have to start out poor or living on the streets or be in a gang to be able to rap?"

Brooke: "I am poor until I find myself a job out here, and look at us. We're sitting on the street drinking booze from a bag."

Darci raised the bag and polished it off. "Damn it feels good to be a gangster."

A little while later, they hopped out of a cab back by campus. When they'd just about reached Duren, they saw

23

an all-blond group of girls laughing loudly and stumbling toward them. Brooke and her friends glanced at each other, wondering if any of them knew why this weird-looking bunch was approaching them.

"Hi!" one of them said loudly, making a one-syllable word into three. Her look-alikes shuffled around her to create a barrier between them and the dorms. "We're not supposed to do this," the girl said in a thick Southern accent, "but we noticed you girls walking, and y'all have Kappa Phi written all over you."

Brooke looked at the other girls, seeing if any of them would bite. Relieved they seemed bothered by them too, she looked down at her body and back up to them. "No, we don't."

The girl laughed obnoxiously loud, and her look-alikes did the same until she stopped. "I'm Madeline McCuller-lance, president of Kappa Phi Omega, by the way. You can just call me Maddie." She waited for them to respond or seem excited by this, but when it didn't happen, she went on. "So seriously, y'all should rush! Everyone knows Kappa Phis are the hottest girls on campus. Y'all are so lucky you ran into us like this."

Maddie put on a concerned face and placed a hand on her chest. "I'm sure y'all feel like small little freshmen nothings right now, but that'll all change if you become a Kappa. And when you get to be juniors like us, you'll be running this place. I know. You can't even imagine, right?" Maddie and the other girls were clearly drunk as they stood there posing like someone had a camera.

Something caught Maddie's attention in the distance, and her expression went sour. "Ugh, the only thing is…" She leaned in, and Brooke could smell the alcohol on her breath, "and I'm telling you this because I see potential—don't go gaining the freshman fifteen. I'm so serious. No matter how pretty your face is, there's nothing we can do for you if y'all don't take care of yourselves. I see it happen all the time, and it's so sad. Okay, like, look at those girls."

Maddie blatantly pointed at two girls walking toward the dorms with a pizza box. Neither was a size zero, but they were by no means fat. "Hey, girls!" she yelled in their direction. "Y'all wanna be Kappas?" They both stopped for a moment, looking interested. "Then lay off the late-night snacks!" She smiled proudly as she and her friends all started laughing as if her comment was hilarious.

Brooke watched the two girls turn instantly self-conscious and walk faster, looking down at the ground. She hated that she even looked like she was associated with this group.

"See, stick with us," Maddie said. "We would never let that happen to y'all."

Brooke could see Kate, Stella, and Darci were just as disgusted as she was, so she turned to face them as if she planned to discuss Maddie's proposal right there. "What do you think, guys? Would you rather be like them," she paused to think for a second, "or have no arms, no legs, and your hair lit on fire?"

"I'll take door number two," Kate said without hesitation.

"Yeah, with those options, I'd find a way to light my own hair on fire, sure." Stella agreed.

"No need to stop and drop. Just roll!" Darci said, smiling at Maddie.

Brooke turned back to the Kappa Phis. "Shoot, it seems we're not interested, um… what was your name again?"

Maddie squinted her eyes at Brooke, shocked that someone would dare talk to her like this.

"It's Maddie," one of her minions said.

"Fatty?" Brooke replied.

"Maddie!" she yelled with a foot stomp.

"That's what I said. Fatty," Brooke said, trying her best to look apologetic.

"Get it right. It's Maddie McCullerlance!"

"Oh, it's Fatty McButterpants!" Brooke struggled to keep a straight face as Darci and the girls started cracking up behind her. "Sorry, you must have a lisp or something. I can't understand you."

Maddie got so close to Brooke's face that the smell of vodka made her sick.

"You know my name, bitch. And you might want to look it up, because I'm the last person you want to fuck with."

Brooke just shook her head. This was a waste of her time. "Okay, cool. Good luck finding people to join your club," she said as she and her friends moved to walk around Maddie's group. Making fun of someone's appearance was something Brooke could never normally do, but watching Maddie with her Barbie figure tease those girls made her wish Maddie would know what it felt like for just a second to be on the other side of it.

"Oh no, Brooke," Darci said when they were walking in the door.

"What?"

"You got some Kappa on you. Oh shoot, you have Kappa all over you. Oh man, I think you even stepped in some Kappa!"

Brooke laughed. "You're a piece of Kappa."

"Who, me? You're full of Kappa."

As Maddie and her friends stormed off in the opposite direction calling them a list of names, Brooke and the girls couldn't help feeling satisfied with themselves. Immature, yes, but completely satisfied. As if they hadn't already become fast friends, nothing bonded girls quicker than a mutual hatred of other girls, and there could be no better subjects than Maddie and her crew.

Chapter 4

Monday morning, Brooke and Stella walked together to their first class and reminded each other where to meet afterward. Brooke walked in, took a seat in the classroom, and pulled out her notebook. A boy with sandy blond hair, a blue polo shirt, and plaid shorts came in and sat next to her. They didn't speak, but when she noticed him shuffling through his bag for a few minutes, she cleared her throat and looked at him to convey it was slightly annoying.

"Hey," he whispered, "I can't believe I did this, but I think I forgot a pen. Do you have an extra?" She reached down into her purse, pulled out her spare, and handed it to him. "Thanks," he said. "I'm Nolan, by the way. Nolan Greenwald."

"Brooke Aarons."

"Nice to meet you. Are you a psych major?" His Southern accent was slight, but still detectable.

"Yeah."

"Cool, I'm not. I just have to get a science course out of the way, and this counts. I put it off the first two years, so I guess it's about time, right?"

Anyone who had to get a course out of the way would hop in a 101 class. No one would take higher than a 100-level course unless it was their major, so she knew he wouldn't be as fascinated by the subject matter as she would.

"Yeah, well I hear this professor is really good, so it shouldn't be too bad." As if on cue, the professor entered through a side door and walked to the front of the classroom.

"Good morning, class. I'm Professor Bornstein. Welcome to Psychology 101." He had to be 6'4" and was the skinniest man she'd ever seen at that height. He looked like he could have been in his nineties, and already she could see sweat beading on the top of his almost completely bald head. He walked slightly hunched over with his hands clasped in front of him, and even though his voice shook when he spoke, Brooke already knew she was going to love listening to him. Everything she read about Bornstein made him seem so worldly and brilliant, but when he spoke, he couldn't have sounded more humble. Brooke decided that when he tried to make a few jokes that didn't get a response, she would always make the effort to laugh.

When she liked a teacher, it showed. Her work in that class would always stand out above the other students and above her other classes, too. She felt the need to never disappoint teachers she liked, and since she determined Professor Bornstein to be one of them, she made up her mind to be his star student.

"Now, first order of business. Turn to the person next to you. Introduce yourself, and exchange numbers." They all looked confused for a moment. "When you're sick and miss this class, that's the person you're going to call. When you forget to write down the homework, that's the person you're going to call. And when you're too hung over to show up…" He paused for laughter but was only met with silence and Brooke's forced chuckle, "that's the person you're going to call. No excuses for late assignments and no retakes on tests."

Brooke looked at Nolan, and they both pulled out their phones. They typed each other's names and numbers in and agreed to let the other know if they were ever planning on missing so they'd know not to skip too.

"We'll be meeting every Monday, Wednesday, and Friday at 9 a.m. for a fifty-five-minute lecture, and we'll be covering a wide variety of topics to give you a taste of everything the exciting world of psychology has to offer. So if there are no questions, let's begin." He clapped his hands together and began his lecture. "How long does it take to form a first impression of someone? Anybody want to take a guess?" He paused only momentarily. When he saw no one was brave enough to answer yet, he went ahead. "Three seconds. In about three seconds, our brains decide something about a new acquaintance. We form an opinion based on their clothing, their mannerisms, their demeanor, their body language, and so on and so forth. And whatever it is that we initially decide about that person, it can be nearly impossible to undo."

Professor Bornstein then went on to describe an experiment that a few psychologists at NYU had performed, exploring the process of how the brain forms a first impression. Brooke took notes until class ended then packed up her things when Professor Bornstein dismissed them.

Brooke and Nolan walked out of class together in the direction of her and Stella's meeting place. She spotted Stella looking for her, called her name to get her attention, and walked toward her.

"Hey, how was it?" Brooke asked.

"It was *biology*," Stella said, as if that answered the question. "How was yours?"

"Great. I love the professor. This is Nolan, by the way. He's in my class."

"Cool," she said, not seeming interested enough to stay and chat with him. "Ready to go?"

"Yup. See you Wednesday," Brooke said to Nolan as she and Stella walked toward the Java City coffee shop.

They each grabbed a coffee and sat down at a table next to the window so they could people-watch.

"What about him?" Stella said, pointing to a guy sitting at a table outside the window.

"No, I'm not into the whole dirty stoner look. Him?" Brooke asked, nodding her head toward one of two guys walking by.

"Yeah, he's cute," Stella said. "But the guy next to him looks like a theater major, and he'd be all yours on our future double dates."

"Good point. But it's so hard to tell between theater majors and hipsters these days," Brooke said with sarcastic concern.

"Oh, look at those guys!" Stella said, nearly pressing her face against the window as a group in UT Football shirts walked by. "Okay, that's a group I want to get to know."

"Jocks? Ew, Stella, please tell me you're kidding." Brooke rolled her eyes when she saw she wasn't. "They're all idiots who get a free ride because they can run their oversized bodies into people."

"Not a football fan, huh?" Stella laughed.

"I hate football," Brooke said as she took a sip of her coffee. She practically felt the place go quiet.

"Shhh! We're in Texas!" Stella whispered. "You can't hate football here. People have been killed for less." As a group of people walked by their table, Stella flashed the school's sign with her pinky and index finger extended and yelled, "Go Longhorns!" The group enthusiastically responded by yelling the same thing back then gave each other high-fives.

Stella looked at Brooke in an I-told-you-so way, and Brooke just rolled her eyes again. She glanced out the window once more and couldn't help noticing one very good-looking guy in the group. He was taller than the rest of them, and even though he had a hat pulled over his face, she could see him flash a perfect smile from all the way outside. She didn't realize she was staring until Stella broke her focus.

"See something you like?" she asked.

"Nope." She reached down and pulled her phone out of her bag to check how much time they had left before their next class. She noticed a text message from Nolan. *Wow, I guess he's already planning to skip out on Wednesday*, she thought.

She opened the message and read: "Your friend is amazing. Maybe we could all hang out sometime?"

Brooke laughed and showed Stella the text. "Quite a first impression you make."

Before they left Java City, Brooke asked an employee at the counter for an application. Her money was already running out after having only been there three days, and with that ticket hanging over her head, she needed a job as soon as possible.

Brooke and Stella parted ways, and she went on to her next two classes. She had Communications 125 next, which was another Monday-Wednesday-Friday, then Physical Geography 130, which only met Mondays with a short lab on Fridays. Those classes went pretty well too. She liked her professors enough and was glad to be getting those general eds out of the way.

Tuesday she had Principles of Behavior 110 then Anthropology 115, but between them she had time to drop off her application at Java City. The manager didn't look much older than Brooke, but he seemed unnecessarily serious.

He stared at the piece of paper for about three seconds before he asked, "Do you know anything about making coffee?"

She laughed confidently. "Who doesn't know how to make coffee?" She couldn't even figure out the one-button Keurig at her parent's house, but he didn't need to know that.

"Good. You're hired."

She mentally high-fived herself then became instantly concerned about actually having to do the job now.

"Training will be during your first shift. How's Thursday?" Tuesdays and Thursdays she was out of class by 4 p.m., so she agreed to be there by 4:15. He held up an orange apron and visor and welcomed her to the happy team of Java City.

The only thing sure to dwindle faster than her bank account was her clean clothing supply in this heat, so Brooke talked Kate into designating Wednesdays as laundry night, since they were both done with class by 3. She figured she could learn a thing or two from Kate, since she admired her mini-homemaker skills and wanted to pick up on a few of them. Darci and Stella were both done at 4 on Wednesdays, so when she told them about their plans, they decided to jump on board.

"I have news!" Darci announced after each of them tossed in a load and took a seat on top of their washing machine. "I found a guy who can make us fake IDs!"

They all started questioning her in excitement as Darci gave them the details on prices and how long it would take to get them. They fired one question after the next, without a break in the conversation, until they knew everything Darci did. The conversation merged into what they should do that weekend just as the door to the laundry room opened and three guys walked in with their bags of dirty clothes in hand.

"Sorry, fellas, they're all taken," Brooke said, recognizing them as the three boys she'd seen through the peephole.

The guy with the buzzed brown hair spoke first. "How long are you going to be?"

"We're rushing tomorrow," the guy next to him said. He was a little shorter with dark brown curly hair and almost looked too young to be in college.

"Omega Chi," the third guy said, as if they had asked which frat. He was the same height as the curly-haired guy but more built. He seemed like the type who would walk around talking about weightlifting and protein shakes. Omega Chi was the best fraternity on campus, or so the girls had heard, but none of them paid much attention to the Greek system, especially after their first encounter with sorority girls.

"Why would you want to be in a frat?" Darci asked. "Having trouble pickin' up on the ladies?"

"No!" Of course the bulky one was the first to defend his manhood. "That's never a problem." Darci rolled her eyes when he winked at her.

"It just sounds fun," the first guy answered, "and Omega Chi throws the best parties on campus. We went to this nasty foam party last weekend and just figured a frat's the way to go here."

Kate suddenly perked up. Knowing they hated that party too made them eligible again. "But are you sure you want to be frat guys? Aren't they usually…"

"Douchy?" Brooke chimed in. "Disgusting? Using the word 'frat' as a cover for a small-penis support group?"

The guys all started shouting their arguments back, and Brooke started to laugh.

"I'm kidding. We're just asking, because you guys seem cool enough and not like you belong in a *frat*. Except you," she said, pointing to the bulky one. "That kind of makes sense."

"Whatever," he said. "Don't act like you guys won't be begging to come to our parties when they're all anyone's talking about."

"Yeah, speak for yourselves," Stella said. "I'm listening."

"What are your names?" Kate asked after rolling her eyes at Stella.

"I'm Bryan," the guy with the buzz cut said.

"Kyle," the young-looking one said.

"I'm Garrett," the bulky one said as seductively as he could muster.

"You're on this floor, right? I think we saw you guys the other day," Brooke said, choosing not to mention how they'd practically followed them to a party.

"Yeah, we have the three-person room across from the elevators," Bryan answered.

"Cool. I'm at that end of the hall," Brooke said, pointing in the wrong direction, "and Stella's at the other end, and Darci and Kate are roommates in 513."

The guys hung out for a while, and they got to know them, even after the girls told them Wednesday nights the laundry room was theirs. Kyle reminded Brooke of her little brother, Josh. He was from North Carolina, funny, sweet. She hoped a fraternity wouldn't diminish that. Bryan was a cool guy too. He seemed pretty genuine and really smart. He was from Houston and always knew he wanted to go to UT for its pre-med program. Garrett, on the other hand, completely embodied a frat boy, just as Brooke had sensed. He just gave off the impression he was in constant pursuit of sex in any form. He seemed pretty harmless, though, like he would be fun to mess with, since he took himself way too seriously. He'd moved to Austin from Florida and was majoring in business.

"So what are you guys doing Friday?" Garrett asked. "Omega Chi is throwing a huge party."

"G.I. Joes and Army Hoes," Bryan contributed.

"And it would really help us out if we could bring four gorgeous girls," Kyle said. They all couldn't help but enjoy the compliment a little.

"What do you say, girls?" Stella asked, looking back and forth at them.

"I'm in!" Kate said.

"Only because we don't have those fakes yet." Brooke looked to Darci to see if she'd go for it.

"Uh, free booze? Of course I'm in!"

"I guess we'll see you Friday then," Kate said, smiling and holding a gaze with one of the Greek hopefuls.

Chapter 5

Brooke walked over to Java City after her last class on Thursday. She'd convinced herself not to stress over the whole coffee-making thing. She may not be able to talk a police officer out of giving her a ticket, but if group projects and lab partners over the years had taught her anything, it was that she could easily convince someone else to do all the work when she wasn't into it. She figured she'd save her hard work for her career, not silly minimum-wage jobs that would be nothing more than a paycheck. That was until she met the guy she'd be working with. His name was Jeff, and he was dumber than a Ferbie. The obvious physical comparison, with his messy hair with eyes halfway closed and his mouth slung open, wasn't doing him any favors either. If their first shift together proved anything, it was that she'd be on her own with this one. She somehow made it through her shift, headed back to her dorm room, and crashed.

The next morning in Professor Bornstein's class, Nolan took his seat next to Brooke as he'd been doing all week.

"Don't ask, Nolan."

"Did she say anything about me?"

Obviously listening wasn't his strong suit. "No."

"Well, did you put in a good word like I asked?"

She laughed. "I've known you for five minutes. What am I supposed to say? 'Go out with this guy—he can't remember a pen, but he sure can sit in a chair'?" He had pestered her all of Wednesday during class. It drove her crazy when students were rude in her favorite teachers' classes. Maybe she couldn't force Nolan to laugh at Professor Bornstein's jokes with her, but she wasn't going to let him be one of those jerks who talked during his class.

His foot paid dearly for the distraction when she finally stomped on it to make him shut up. It was a drastic move to pull on a practical stranger, and physical violence was never the answer— or so she'd been told—but as far as she could tell, it worked. She did make a mental note to work on her short temper, though.

The second Professor Bornstein walked in, Nolan let his sentence trail off in a whisper, tucked his feet far under his chair, and didn't speak again until class was over.

"Fine, you don't know me well enough to *want* to put in that good word yet, but that's why I suggested we all hang out." He picked right up when class was dismissed, as if fifty-five minutes hadn't just passed. "I'm good buddies with a guy on the football team. I bet you'd like to hang out with one of the players, right?"

Brooke twisted her face in disgust at his comment. "And you just proved you don't know me well at all." Was he really trying to pawn his meathead friends off on her? She told him she had plans with the girls that night just to get him off her back for the moment, but she knew the issue wouldn't be dead.

Brooke and the girls didn't know much about frat parties, but they knew themed parties called for costumes. After they were all finished with class for the day, they'd gone to an army surplus store to find things for their outfits. They brought their purchases to Kate and Darci's room, then pulled out the scissors and didn't stop until the garments were unrecognizable.

Brooke slid into a tiny camouflage skirt, fishnets, and a dark denim corset she had no clue why she'd ever bought until now. She also tied a thin piece of material around her arm, put on a camouflage hat, and pulled on some heavy black boots.

Stella was in black shorts, with a piece of material—it was big enough to cover her strapless bra but just that—tied in the back, plus her signature hoops, black eyeliner, and black wedges. Kate wore a low-cut black tank top with camouflage shorts, tall black boots, and fake dog tags she'd gotten for an old Halloween costume and brought for just such an occasion. And Darci was in a dark green cargo vest she left open to show her black lace bra and a pair of black booty shorts with red stilettos and lipstick.

The looks they got as they were walking out of the dorms were more than they could handle without laughing, but they were sure they'd fit in. When they got to the Omega Chi house, they were speechless. It was actually amazing. It must have taken these guys all night and the next day to decorate and build everything.

There were stages and platforms and lighting fixtures all over the courtyard, and everything was painted in camouflage and covered with nets and shrubbery. It was unbelievable.

The two-story building made a square around a huge courtyard, and it was packed. Inside on one of the stages stood a random cage with a pole in the middle—which Brooke could only assume was put there for attention whores and drunk girls—but other than that, they were shocked that this was actually what a frat house could look like.

They grabbed red cups and filled them up, then spotted Kyle, Bryan, and Garrett in full costume sitting by the fire pit and went over to say hello.

"Guys, this place is pretty awesome!" Brook said. They didn't respond. Instead, they all just sat in a daze, staring at the flames and slowly drinking their beers. "Why are you sitting here? Aren't you guys going to enjoy the party?"

"Enjoy it?" Kyle replied. "We built it! We don't have the energy left to enjoy it."

"This is pledging," Bryan said. "They make you do things. We built this place on no sleep and meals of ketchup packets for the last 14 hours. Now everyone else gets to have fun while I can't even lift my arms." He shakily brought a can of beer toward his mouth but had to lower it before he could take a sip.

"Okay, we're going to go party now," Stella said, unsympathetic. "Come find us if you guys decide to wake up."

The girls left them sitting there and started walking across the courtyard to explore more of the house.

"Hey, gorgeous." Brooke felt someone put an arm around her shoulder.

"Whoa, excuse me there, total stranger. Personal boundaries."

"I noticed your body. What's your name?"

Who actually says something like that? Brooke thought. "Are you drunk, or is that your pickup line?"

"You tell me." *Oh, and he's a smart one too*, she thought.

She turned to look at him, and the smell of BO coated in Axe body spray practically assaulted her. He was tall and tan with big muscles and jet-black hair, but in no way was that combination attractive on him.

"Gross," she let out as she started to pull away. He tightened his hold.

"Hey, baby, I'm just trying to get to know you." He leaned down to her eye level. "I'm Stan. You'll probably hear the guys around here calling me Stan the Man, though. What's your name?"

"Brooke!" Stella yelled as she continued to walk. Brooke gave her a look.

"Hi, Brooke," he said, getting even closer to her face. *Physical violence is never the answer*, she reminded herself as she twisted her way out from under his arm.

"Okay, 'bye."

"You'll find me later tonight," she heard him say as she ran to catch up with her friends. "No, I will *not*," she said to herself.

Brooke caught up with the girls. "Watch out for that one."

"Yeah, he looks aggressive," Kate said, scrunching her face in disgust.

"His odor is aggressive. But I guess every frat's got to have at least one of those to uphold their reputation." They heard chanting behind them. "Go, go, go, go!" They turned to see Stan chugging from a beer bong.

They steered away and all at once spotted Maddie and her look-alikes, all bleached blond and dressed entirely in pink camouflage. Heaven forbid they actually camouflage into anything. As if Maddie could feel them looking at her, she turned, spotted them, and started whispering to the girls around her.

Darci smiled. "Should we go say hello?"

"It's only polite," Brooke said.

All at once the girls opened their arms and yelled, "Fatty!" across the courtyard as they ran up toward them. They all chimed in with, "It's so good to see you again!" and "We've missed you!" in their best mocking tones.

Maddie and her group turned to square off with them. They were covered in so much glitter that it was practically blinding to look at. "What do you think you're doing here?" Maddie said with her hands on her hips. "You freshmen losers are *so* not welcome!"

"I didn't see any signs," Kate said.

"Oh really? You see that picture in the center of everything over there? That portrait of *me*? I'm Omega Chi's Sweetheart, and *I* say you're not welcome here."

"Aw, look at you," Brooke said, glancing at the picture before turning back. "Tell us, how many blows does it take to get to the center of a frat house?"

Maddie smacked Brooke's drink out of her hand and onto the floor.

Unfazed, Brooke just shrugged. "Hm, well I guess I should thank you. So many calories." One of the girls behind Maddie looked in her cup as if she was devastated by the information and set it down. Brooke and the girls just smiled at them then turned to walk away.

"Hey, Brooke," Maddie called. "I'd be careful if I were you. Everyone has a soft spot, and you *really* don't want me finding yours out."

"Okay. Thanks for the heads-up," Brooke called behind her then looked at Kate with a big fake frown. "She spilled my drink."

Kate just laughed and looped her arm through Brooke's. "C'mon. We'll get you a new one."

"Hey, what's over here?" Darci asked. They followed her into a room with a pool table and a bar.

"What'll it be, ladies?" a handsome guy behind the bar said.

"*Hello*," Stella said to the girls before focusing her attention on him. "It's our first time here. Surprise us."

He poured out four orange-colored shots he called The Longhorn and laid the glasses out in front of them. The girls all threw them back with a gulp.

Darci: "That's so delicious."

Kate: "I didn't even taste alcohol."

Brooke: "You've never drugged anyone before, right?"

Stella: "Don't listen to her. Keep those coming."

And he did.

The next morning, light filled Brooke's room and she opened her eyes, trying to remember how exactly she got back to her bed. *So far so good*, she thought. She didn't feel horrible. But what was that smell? She stretched out her arms then pulled the covers off. Swinging her legs over the side of the bed, she tried to stand as she heard someone cough out air. She lost her balance as the surface she was trying to stand on rolled over, then hit the floor, looked over, and screamed like she'd never screamed before. "Oh my god, no, no, no!" she yelled as she crawled backward until she hit a wall.

Stan rolled over, "Hey, babe." She screamed again. "Not exactly how I like to be woken up in the morning, but I'm sure you'll figure that out soon. Why am I on the floor?"

"Why are you in my room?"

"What kind of man would I be if I let you walk home alone?" She wasn't buying his fake gentleman act.

"Nothing happened!" That one wasn't a question. It just had to be true.

"Yeah, I'm aware." *Oh thank god*, she thought. "But you can still make it up to me."

"Gross, gross, gross!" She scrambled to her feet so she could look like she had some authority. "You need to get out, right now! Out!"

"Easy there." He rose to sit on her bed and rubbed his eyes.

"I need a shower," she said to herself, pacing around, horrified by how close she'd been to him.

He reached out for her arm. "Want me to join you?"

"Don't touch me! Ugh, I'm gonna be sick," she said as she paced back and forth faster, waiting for him to get up.

He reached up toward her again.

"Hey, what's wrong, baby?"

"Get out!" she screamed at the top of her lungs. "I'm dead serious!"

"I love how feisty you are."

"Please, I am begging you to get out!" She picked up his T-shirt from her desk chair with two fingers as if it were contaminated material and threw it at him. He caught it with his face, and she raced to the door to hold it open for him.

"Okay, okay, calm down. I'll call you later. And I'll let you make up for what you missed out on last night." He winked at her as he left the room while she held the door open.

I'm never drinking again! She closed the door behind her and rested against it, trying to breathe. Thank god Sophie wasn't there. She couldn't handle any more judgment than she was already giving herself.

She cracked the door open to peer out. When she heard the elevator ding, she counted to ten, making sure he was gone. Then she raced down the hall and started banging on Kate and Darci's door. When she realized it was unlocked, she burst through in a panic.

"I just had the worst… oh! Hello!" She realized there was a guy in Darci's bed. "Um, should I come back?"

"No, he was just leaving. Right, umm…?"

"It's Adam."

"It really doesn't matter," Darci said with a yawn. "I was just trying to be polite."

Brooke watched as he climbed down the ladder mumbling, picked up his clothes, and walked out the door as he was still dressing. "*So* did he ask you about your tattoo?"

Darci rolled her eyes and climbed down.

Kate rolled over and stretched. "Oh my god, how many of those orange thingies did we drink? I feel horrible."

"Oh, I didn't, until I found Stinky Stan in my room!"

"Ewwww!" they both said in disgust together.

"Kate, where's your sanitizer?" She pointed to her desk, and Brooke squeezed the entire contents out, rubbing it onto her arms and legs. "Ugh, he made my whole room smell like an armpit. I need some strong perfume. Is Stella in her room?" They all thought for a moment.

"Last I saw she was still with the bartender. I'll text her," Darci said.

Stella responded a few minutes later: "Still at the frat house. Get me out of here. This place in daylight is terrifying!"

"On our way!" Darci wrote back. "Let's just go grab her. We'll come back and change clothes after."

They piled into Brooke's Jeep, all disheveled, and drove over to the frat house. They had taken the top off because it was such a nice day, and they laughed at all the stupid girls doing the walk of shame out of the house before they realized they were no better.

"You're sure nothing happened with that Stan guy, Brooke?"

"Positive. No clue why I fell for that 'I'll walk you home' bit, but I do have a vague memory of him going in for a kiss before I pushed him off my bed and he hit the floor."

"New rule, Kate said. We leave together or at least check in before heading out."

"before heading oBrooke added said. addeding ou'surprise me' to a frat house bartender. I donk inhim going in for aprised again.I

Stella ran out the front door of the frat house and jumped into the car.

Stella: "Well aren't we all looking beautiful this morning?"

Kate: "Want to go change clothes then get some food?"

Darci: "No time. I need waffles, stat."

Brooke: "I'm not going anywhere like this."

Darci: "Do you want me to vomit in your car?"

Brooke: "*All right*, we're going like this."

They drove down the main road until they spotted a restaurant called Kerby Lane. It happened to be right across from their dorm, but they still decided against changing first, since the situation had become desperate for the girls, who were all made carsick by Brooke's driving. They pulled into the parking lot, went in, and found a booth in the back. The waitress gave them all funny looks, but they didn't even care. They just started listing every item on the menu they saw and sucked down a full glass of water each.

"I discovered a little something while we were driving," Darci said. "I have pictures on my phone. Ready for a slide-show?"

They all turned their full attention to Darci's phone.

Darci: "We have Stella making out with the bartender."

Stella: "Yeah, he was hot."

Kate: "Aw, you guys would be cute together. What's his name?"

Stella: "Bartender."

Darci: "And here we have Kate trying to force-feed Bryan drinks."

Kate: "Yeah, no luck with that. I had to drink them all myself."

Brooke: "Had to?"

Darci: "And here's about seven in a row of Brooke pole dancing in the cage."

Brooke: "What? No, I didn't!" She paused for a moment and looked at a picture as Kate pulled another hand sanitizer out of her purse and handed it to her. "Oh wait, it's coming back to me now. Shit."

Stella: "I have to say, overall, not a bad time at the Omega Chi house. Want to play high-low?"

Brooke: "What's that?"

Stella: "What was the highest part of your night and what was the lowest? Like, my high was clearly Bartender, and my low, I would have to say, was when I leaned on a table someone had just thrown up on." They all ewed simultaneously and leaned away from her. Kate took the sanitizer from Brooke and slid it towards Stella.

Brooke: "Okay, I've got one. Well, my low is obvious because he was still in my room this morning. But my high was when that big group of people saw my awesome dance moves and asked me to teach them how to Dougie when the song came on."

Kate burst out laughing.

Kate: "That's not exactly what happened."

Darci: "Nobody *asked* you, Brooke. You just ran up and started dancing at those people."

Stella: "And what you were doing was not the Dougie."

Brooke: "Yes, it was."

Darci: "Okay, what do you think the Dougie looks like?"

Brooke thought about it for a few seconds, and when she couldn't even picture it, she realized they were probably right.

Kate: "I'll go next. My high was when we were all taking those shots together." She paused so the girls could all 'awww.'

"You know, before we all basically blacked out and embarrassed ourselves. And my low was when my heel broke and I ate shit down the stairs."

Brooke: "Oh my god, that's right! Are you okay?"

Kate: "No, I died. Thanks for asking."

Darci: "Don't worry, you're okay. I checked you for signs of internal bleeding last night."

Kate: "Um, excuse me?"

Darci: "Yeah, see, I was talking to this cute guy last night who's a pre-med major. *My* high in case anyone was wondering. So I'm thinking of making a career-path change. You were my first patient… when you were passed out."

Kate: "Major violation, roomie. Hard limit."

Darci: "That's what I get for saving your life? Being a doctor is a thankless job. I switch back."

Brooke: "To *what*?"

Darci: "It's still my turn! And my low was mistaking some other blond dude for the hot pre-med guy and bringing him back to the dorms. Frat guys all look the same."

Brooke: "Shame. Sounds like you guys had something special."

Darci: "True, we did have a very deep conversation while smoking out of his giant bong. Oh, so I guess technically that was the highest part of my night, if we're going to be literal about it."

Stella: "Well I literally might fall asleep right now, so can we please go find the pool on campus so I can at least get some color while I'm out cold?"

The girls stopped back at the dorms to change into their swim suits, then located the pool and posted up for the day. Within about 30 seconds, they all fell into near comas to sleep off their hangovers.

None of them woke up until they heard Darci's phone going off a few hours later. While they were all still coming to life again, Darci suddenly gasped. "Our fake IDs are ready!" she said, holding her phone in the air.

Brooke rolled over and looked at her phone too. She had a text from Nolan: "Hey, I don't know if you guys have IDs but we're going to this club on 6th called the Jackalope tonight so you and some friends (which must include Stella) should come."

"How convenient," Brooke said aloud.

"What?" Kate asked as she stretched out her arms and yawned. Brooke read the text for them.

"Oh, we're going," Darci said. "We're going to test these babies out."

Chapter 6

After packing up their stuff at the pool, Darci went to pick up the IDs, while Brooke, Stella, and Kate went back to the dorms to start getting ready. The girls all pulled out their cutest dresses, laid them out on Kate's bed, and tried them all on until they were satisfied. Darci brought back the envelope containing their IDs, poured them into her hand, then passed them out.

The guy who made them used the pictures from their actual driver's licenses; he just changed all their information. They started to memorize everything as Darci got ready, and by the time Nolan texted Brooke with a five-minute warning that he would be there to pick them up, they were all set to go.

They got to the parking lot just as Nolan was pulling up. They piled in his lifted Chevy, and Brooke introduced him to Darci and Kate, pointing out in a taunting way that he'd already met Stella. Nolan made small talk, getting to know everyone as he drove. It turned out he was an Omega Chi too and actually lived at the frat house. He'd just decided to go to a few bars instead of the party the night before.

Nolan explained how they were heading to his friend's place to drink before hitting the club, and Brooke and the girls got a little curious and concerned over whether he was someone they'd met at the party already. He assured them, though, that his friend wasn't in the frat and proudly told them how this mystery man was on the football team, as if he was his trophy friend or something.

Brooke realized this was probably the guy he'd mentioned before and instantly felt a little disappointed at the thought of their night being spent with some guy who surely needed to have his ego constantly managed. They drove into the downtown area of Austin toward all the cool restaurants, bars, and clubs, as Nolan explained that his friend had lived in this place since they were freshmen.

"Why wouldn't he live in the dorms as a freshman?" Brooke asked Nolan.

He laughed at the question. "If you had more money than you could spend, would you live in the dorms? Or would you live in a nice condo downtown?"

"Dorms," Brooke said just for the sake of not letting him make his point.

Nolan laughed. "Yeah, right! If your parents gave you a condo as a going-away present, you wouldn't say, 'No, thanks, I'll share a three-by-three box with an under-wear-sniffing weirdo who doesn't shower.'"

"I called ahead to make sure they wouldn't assign you to my room, Nolan."

The rest of the car laughed, including Nolan, but Brooke was annoyed. She thought about the GPS her parents had given her as a going-away present. They were so excited to give it to her, and here's this guy, who probably never even lifted a pencil in school, just tossed a ball around and took his pick of universities, and his parents forked over a piece of real estate like it's nothing. He probably didn't even bother with so much as a "thanks."

They pulled into a gated condo complex, parked, and followed Nolan up the outdoor staircase and into the condo.

"Hey, buddy," Nolan said.

"Hey, come on in," Brooke heard someone call out. She noticed there were already a few people there. Nolan's friend crossed the living room to greet them.

She couldn't help noticing he wasn't terrible-looking. He was tall, probably 6'3", with brown hair and kind of a killer smile. Was this the guy she'd seen outside Java City? She remembered more clearly and realized he was definitely one of those jocks. So he was good-looking, wealthy, and on an undefeated football team? She had him figured out before even needing to meet him. This guy was an asshole.

"Hi, I'm James," he said, holding his hand out to the girls. "Stella," she said, shaking his hand. "Nice to meet you." "I'm Kate. This place is amazing."

"Darci. Great spot. You're so close to the bars."

"Brooke." Instead of shaking his hand, she pulled her hair back and twisted it into a bun. She counted to three in her head, making sure her opinion of him would stick. She wasn't sure how much control she'd have over a first impression, but she wanted no outside influence on what she already thought.

"Grab a seat. I'll get you guys something to drink," James said. Brooke introduced herself to the other people on the couch and took a seat next to Stella.

"What'll it be?" James called from the kitchen.

"Whatever you have is fine," Brooke said nonchalantly. It wasn't that she didn't care what she'd be drinking—she just didn't really know her drinks well enough to call one out with confidence.

"I've got a pretty big selection over here," he said.

Show-off, she thought. *I mean, what college kid doesn't have a huge, downtown condo decked out in Z Gallerie and a fully stocked bar?*

"I may have overdone it a little, but I didn't know what everyone would want," he continued.

Darci went to the kitchen to help, and Brooke and Stella both pulled out their fakes and tried again to memorize their new info.

"Okay, what's your address?" Brooke asked Stella.

"Um, 5230 Dudley Drive… um, some city in Massachusetts?"

"You got none of that correct," Brooke said.

"Damn it. Okay, when's your birthday?" Stella asked Brooke.

"April 8, nineteen eighty… *six*?"

"You really think you can pull off 27?" James interjected as he handed her a drink. The rest of the room laughed, but she shot him a glare to show she didn't appreciate the comment. Whether he was saying she looked young or mocking her math skills, she didn't care. She was starting to get stressed out about messing up, so she didn't need this jerk breaking her concentration and making her more nervous. Besides, he didn't even know her. Why would he think it was okay to make fun of her? She chose to ignore him and turned back to Stella, making sure she planned to do the same, and they continued to go over their IDs.

When it was time to go, they filed out and headed toward James's car. Of course he had a brand-new black Range Rover. The dealership plates were still on. She saw him set the same cup he'd poured in the condo into his cup holder. *Great, he's cocky* and *stupid.*

"Hey, if you're planning to drink and drive us there, I'd rather just take a cab."

He smiled at her in the rearview mirror. "Don't worry, Brooke. I'm All-State." She was surprised he'd even bothered to remember her name.

"What?"

"You're in good hands."

She rolled her eyes. *Who rips off a line from an insurance company commercial?* They only drove about five minutes before he parked. Then he downed his drink in a few short swigs and everyone filed out. *Okay, at least he didn't drink before he drove us.*

They walked up to the club, and Brooke and the girls got in line.

"Nope, this way," James said as he walked past them. Brooke followed the rest of the group to the front of the line, and the bouncer lifted the rope and told them to show their IDs to a woman wearing a black cocktail dress and an earpiece. She was tall and thin, and her hair was slicked back in a perfect ponytail.

Brooke envied her for just a moment. She could never achieve that perfectly polished look with her wild hair and limited makeup skills, and even in four-inch heels, she wasn't 5'10" like this one.

She reached into her clutch and suddenly felt her stomach drop. Her fake ID wasn't in there. She grabbed Stella's arm and asked her if she had grabbed it off the table. Stella gasped, confirming to Brooke that she definitely left it behind. She reached forward and pulled on James's arm.

"What's up?" he asked. When she told him she'd left her ID at his place, she expected him to be annoyed, but he just paused, gave her a self-assured "Hmm" and said, "Come with me."

He pulled Brooke up to where he was then ushered her over to the hostess checking IDs. She resisted, but strength-wise, she really didn't stand a chance.

"Hey, Amber," he said to the perfectly polished woman. "We have a small dilemma. She left her ID. Can we get in without it just this once?"

She looked Brooke up and down like she didn't approve. "Sorry, James. I wish I could, but they got raided down the street last week, and we can't risk it."

He turned to the group who seemed confused by the holdup. "We'll meet you inside," he said, then looked down at Brooke and gestured for her to follow him.

Brooke looked back worriedly as Stella shot her a distressed glance, she then turned to follow James. He flagged down a cab by barely lifting an arm, and when it pulled up to the curb, he opened the door for her.

So rarely seen these days, she couldn't help but think. She climbed in and scooted over as he gave the driver his cross streets. A few minutes later they pulled up to his place. "Where do you think you left it?"

"Coffee table," was all she could get out.

"Don't drive off without me." He hopped out and disappeared. She answered text messages from Darci and Kate, who were inside the club, as he ran up the flight of stairs to his front door. A minute later he reappeared.

"For you, ma'am." Before she was able to grab it from his hand, he pulled it back, just slightly out of her reach. "Can I trust you to hold onto it until we get there?"

She snatched the ID and tucked it safely in her clutch while he told the driver to head back to the club. She told herself to be nice; he'd just done her a favor, so it's the least she could do.

"Thank you. Sorry about this." She looked over at him, and the second they made eye contact, her mind went blank and she felt a wave of heat run through her. "I'm not normally so forgetful. Well, I guess that's not entirely true. I've forgotten plenty of things. Keys, usually, my wallet all the time, sometimes my purse altogether. Oh, but forgetting clothes is the worst. Not like I forget to put them on, I mean, I just always leave them places. Well, not just anywhere, but like people's houses, you know. Not like I go to people's houses and take off my clothes. I mean friends' houses and jackets or scarves. I don't just strip down anywhere I go. I'm definitely not *that* kind of girl. I just meant—"

She paused when she spotted the cab driver looking at her in the rearview mirror. She looked at James to see he was looking at her too with his lips curled in as if to keep from smiling at her over-share.

Oh my god, shut up, Brooke. What is the matter with you?

Being polite was one thing, but what was this crazed rambling that had just occurred? And why would she care if he thought she was forgetful—or thought anything about her, for that matter? She decided to bite her tongue for the remainder of the drive, which turned out to be more difficult than she'd thought. And what a jerk. It was like he was being extra silent just to make her feel worse. The first two drives had proven to be quick five-minute trips, but the silence made this one feel like an eternity. They finally pulled up in front of the club, and she reached into her bag to get her credit card.

"No, no, no. I don't want you juggling cards around." He handed the cab driver cash as she tried to hide that her face had turned red. He stepped out on the side with the curb, and she crawled over to get out on that side as well. He stood by the side of the door and held out his hand to help her out.

What is this, the 1800s? But as she tried to get out independently, she realized she was a little unsteady on her heels, so she accepted the help and put her hand in his. It made her nervous suddenly, and she didn't know why. It certainly wasn't a first for her to hold someone's hand, so it was weird that her heart was racing. She realized it was just because he was basically a stranger to her, that's all.

He closed the cab door behind her, but instead of letting go of her hand like she expected, he tightened his hold and led the way as he navigated through the crowd. They'd been gone less than 15 minutes, but the swarm of people must have tripled in size since they left. They approached the bouncer who let them in the first time, but he told James it was going to be a wait now because they were over capacity.

Brooke looked up at James apologetically. Just because she didn't like the guy didn't mean she wasn't starting to feel a little badly about everything. She had to be ruining his night. If he was bothered by it all, he wasn't showing it though. He just gave her a smile to convey he wasn't the least bit discouraged then nodded his head in the opposite direction. He kept his hold on her hand as they made it through the crowd, heading around the corner in what seemed like completely the wrong way.

She followed closely as they turned down a poorly lit, narrow alley. What was going on? Should she be worried? She was, after all, in a dark alley with whom she'd just determined to be a complete stranger. James glanced back at her. If anything, though, she felt safer than ever before. Like she blindly trusted that this guy she didn't even know would just lead the way and it would all be fine.

She tried to watch the ground, but her eyes got stuck looking at her hand in his. They were out of the crowd, it was just the two of them back here, so why hadn't he let go? As if he could hear her thoughts, he pulled his hand away, and at that same moment her heel caught in a crack and she flung forward, instantly knowing her face was about to meet asphalt.

As suddenly as she'd started going down, she felt James's hand grab her arm, and she popped right back up like it hadn't happened at all.

"You okay there?"

"Yeah," she said, way more high-pitched than she'd intended. She brushed the hair out of her face and straightened up. "I mean, you probably bruised the crap out of my arm," she scolded as she wiggled free and rubbed the spot where his hand was, "and I wouldn't have actually fallen, just so you know, but there's a huge crack right there that someone should really look into fixing because I bet people trip there all the time."

"You know, I bet you're right," he said with a patronizing tone and a smile. "But why don't you come here? There are lots of cracks around, so you just lean right... here." He had one hand on each of her shoulders, and he directed her to a wall in the narrow alley. "Don't move, okay?"

Part of her thought, *Don't tell me what to do*, but she stood still, barely even breathing, as he faced her straight on with little room between them in the alley. When he seemed convinced she was steady, he reached his hand into his pocket and pulled out his phone. He sent a text then tucked it back in his pocket.

She looked down at her Chanel patent leather black pump and saw a huge white scuff. "Oh no!" she said, somewhere between a whisper and a yell. She'd sold two purses to come up with the money to buy them at the Barneys outlet in Camarillo, and now they were ruined. She leaned against the wall, lifting the foot with the scuffed shoe and resting it on her opposite knee so she could assess the damage.

As Brooke was brushing at it, James reached down and took her ankle, sending a shiver up her spine. "Hm, I don't know if the patient will pull through, doctor," he said. She started to lose her balance again, and without thinking, she rested one hand on each of his shoulders to steady herself. He licked his thumb and rubbed at the scuffmark. Within a few seconds, it disappeared. "She's going to be okay!" he said, mocking the gravity of the situation.

I could have done that myself, she thought. "Hm, decent work today, nurse. But you're fired for patient endangerment in the first place. Where the hell are we?"

"*Nurse?*" he said, looking up at her. She hadn't noticed before that his eyes were a light shade of brown. It was difficult to see anything in the dark alley, but the dim light shone on him just enough to reveal how annoyingly handsome he was. His smile was perfect, and his hair was a little bit long, not shaggy, and slightly brushed off to the side. His shoulders were wide, and when he let go of her ankle and stood up straight, she was able to take in how tall he really was. For the first time ever, she had to think about breathing.

Suddenly, a door she hadn't even noticed swung open, and music came blasting out. Nolan poked his head out.

"Where'd you two run off to?" he asked them with a suspicious smile.

James shook his head and smiled at Brooke. "Come on, clumsy. After you."

Within a few seconds, they were reunited with the group. Brooke went with James to the bar so they could at least try to catch up with the rest of them, who were already a few drinks in. They decided a shot was the way to go, and he let her choose what kind it would be. She ordered two shots of tequila and demanded he let her pay to say thank you.

She wanted to pay her debt off now so she wouldn't feel badly about the cab ride later. He agreed, then handed the bartender his card while she was still digging through her clutch. The bartender slid two shots in front of them before she had time to argue, and Brooke clinked her glass against his then lifted it to her lips.

"Wait!" He stopped her. "You have to toast to something."

"Oh, um, okay." She cleared her throat. "To making a trip back to your place when we could have snuck in the back all along." If he wouldn't let her pay off her debt, then she'd at least make it seem like it was his fault for wasting money— not that it was something he had to worry about, though.

He rolled his eyes at her then held up his wrist to show his watch said midnight. "And to you making it through another day. Five minutes of knowing you, and I have a feeling that's no easy task."

Asshole, she thought, even though she couldn't help the smile that started to tug at her lips. They threw back their shots and made their way back to where everyone else was.

She and the girls left him and the rest of the group behind at the table and hit the dance floor. Every once in a while, Brooke would check her ankle and wonder why it almost felt as if James's hand had left some kind of invisible mark on her. She convinced herself that if she decided to glance over at him, then it wouldn't be because she *cared* whether he was watching her; she was just curious. After a few more minutes of debating it back and forth, she rationalized that it was worth a peek, so she quickly peered over to see if he was looking at her. He wasn't. He was talking to a cocktail waitress wearing next to nothing.

Chapter 7

The next morning Brooke's phone rang, waking her up. She glanced around the room. She was in her bed, Sophie was across the room in hers, and Kate, Darci, and Stella were on the floor between them. She let her phone go to voicemail without checking who it was, but when it started ringing again, she answered just to make the noise stop.

"What?" her voice cracked into the phone.

"Hey, did she say anything about me?"

"Nolan, it's 8 in the morning."

"You guys left without even saying 'bye, which is kind of rude, if you ask me. So has she said anything about me?" Brooke exhaled in annoyance, hoping Nolan would get the point. He didn't. "She's the hottest girl I've ever seen," he pleaded.

Brooke looked down at Stella, who was passed out on the floor with her mouth wide open. "I know, bud. She's a beauty."

"Listen, after you guys ditched out, James and I got to talking. He thinks you're interesting."

"Well, I think he's stupid!"

"What?"

"Sorry, that just came out." She tried to recover. "'Interesting' just sounds like an insult after 'hottest girl ever.'"

"Hey, if he just wants hot, he can have it. Trust me, there's no shortage of girls throwing themselves at this guy. I've known him a while, and he's—"

"Just get to your point so I can go back to sleep."

"I want the four of us to grab dinner next week."

"Like a double date?"

"Exactly."

"'Bye, Nolan." She hung up the phone and set it next to her on the bed.

Thinking about James and that cocktail waitress probably going home together last night got Brooke a little heated for some reason. It was just so obnoxious that guys like James could do whatever, and whoever, they wanted. She immediately judged that cocktail waitress, too, for being into a guy like that. She was fully awake now and decided that if she couldn't sleep, no one else should get to.

She grabbed a necklace off her nightstand and dangled it over Stella's face. She watched as Stella's hand started twitching and then weakly swatting the air. Brooke pulled it up for a second then lowered it directly on her forehead. Instead of swatting at her own forehead like Brooke had intended her to, Stella smacked Kate square in the face.

Both sets of eyes fluttered in confusion and looked up to see Brooke with a huge, guilty smile. "Morning, sleeping beauties!"

Darci woke up too, and the girls decided to get up and collect their usual morning-after-a-night-out ensembles, complete with oversized sunglasses, jean shorts, and loose-fitting tank tops, and head out for manicures and pedicures.

They walked over to a nail shop close by and posted up in the giant, comfy chairs. The place was called Funny Nails, but as far as they could tell, there was nothing funny about it. Dozens of plastic cats that moved their eyes and waved their paws simultaneously lined the shelves, and it certainly wasn't helping any of their hangovers.

Darci: "Who called at the crack of dawn, Brooke?"

Brooke: "Stella's lover. He wanted to talk about how much he enjoyed making out with her all night."

Stella: "What! No! No?"

Brooke: "No. But he still wants to jump your bones."

Stella: "Not happening."

Kate: "Why not, Stella? He seems like such a nice guy."

Stella: "Exactly."

Brooke: "Um, yeah, gross, who would want that?"

Stella: "This school is huge, and there are so many people to meet still. I'm not going to couple up with the first dude I run into."

Darci: "I'm with you on that. I have no intention of coupling up, probably ever."

Stella: "Well, it's not forever for me, but definitely not in the beginning of the year at a new school in a new city. So, sorry, Nolan!"

Brooke: "Fine by me. He wants to double with that James character, so I couldn't agree more."

She didn't know why she even mentioned that.

Darci: "What was going on with you two last night? I saw you making the eyes."

Brooke: "I made no eyes."

Stella: "Oh, you made eyes."

Brooke: "I was drunk. I made those same eyes at a burrito an hour later."

Darci: "Mmm hmm."

Stella: "At least admit he's insanely hot."

Brooke: "Drop it. Not interested. He's a total asshole. A well-mannered asshole, but an asshole nonetheless."

Darci: "I'm sorry, I'm confused. What is he?"

Brooke: "An asshole. I'm just saying, you can totally tell he's one of those guys that only goes for really slutty girls."

Darci: "Then you're just his type!"

Brooke rolled up the magazine in her lap and smacked Darci with it.

Brooke: "This conversation is over. Can we go? The cats are making me seasick."

Stella: "Sure, okay. You can be in denial. Let's go."

Darci: "Yeah, I'm ready. Kate?"

They turned to look at Kate, who looked like she had passed out in the chair with her eyes half closed. Brooke snapped her fingers next to Kate's face, and her eyes shot wide open.

Kate: "Yeah, you guys should get married! Wait, what are we talking about? Are we leaving? What'd I miss?"

Brooke stared at Kate then leaned over to whisper to the other girls, "Don't look directly into the cat eyes."

As they exited the elevator back in the dorms, they saw Garrett, Bryan, and Kyle's door open and listened in on their conversation.

"Guys, I'm dead serious," they overheard Garrett say. "You were passed out, and you were passed out."

"What seems to be the problem, boys?" Brooke asked as the girls all walked in, took a seat on Garrett's bed, and invited themselves to judge the situation.

Bryan: "Garrett here has made an additional tally, but he can't prove he's earned it."

Darci: "Mmm hmm, I see, and to what do these tallies refer?"

Garrett: "These guys are just jealous of my game."

Brooke: "No, seriously, Garrett, you've actually hit on all of us at one point, and it's been determined you have no game. So what is this *really* about?"

Kyle: "Garrett keeps a tally of all the girls he's hooked up with." He pointed to the wall next to Garrett's bed with a bunch of pencil markings on it.

They all screamed and jumped up to get off the bed as quickly as possible.

Stella: "Bullshit, Garrett! There are more tallies here than days we've been in school."

Garrett: "Yeah, well I got here a week early, and three-somes count for two."

Kate: "You've never had a threesome."

Garrett: "Shut up, I have too!"

Darci: "Well since it's *Garrett* we're talking about here, assume he counts every body part he's excited to see individually. Divide that number by three."

Brooke: "Three? Please, he'd be excited if a girl showed him her elbows."

Unconsciously, the girls adjusted to cover their elbows.

Kate: "Regardless, this is gross. Get checked, Garrett!"

Brooke: "Yeah, I'm getting checked after sitting there."

The girls turned to walk out.

Garrett: "You probably should after a night with Stan."

Brooke froze in her place then slowly turned to look at him. "What did you say?"

Garrett: "Oh, c'mon, it's a frat. Guys are going to talk about their hookups."

Brooke: "I did *not* hook up with that disgusting creep! Is he telling people that I did? I'm going to kill that lying chunk of grease! You better go back to your stupid frat house and tell every single person in there I wouldn't touch him if I was wearing a Bubble Boy suit!"

Garrett: "Um, okay, sure you didn't."

Bryan: "Super Senior Stan! That dude's on his sixth year of college, at least."

Garrett: "It's brotherhood, Brooke. We don't lie to each other. And he's not the only person we heard it from, anyway. A bunch of Kappa Phis were at the house talking about it too."

Brooke turned a hundred degrees hotter. She knew who the culprit was: Maddie.

Brooke: "Set the record straight. I'm not kidding. They are all fucking liars. And clean your room. It smells like a dead animal in here!"

Brooke stormed out with the girls following behind. She was still fuming mad when they made it back to her room. She pulled out her laptop and decided to look Maddie up like she had suggested. She wanted to know who she was dealing with. Apparently Maddie was from Dallas and had a father in the oil industry. They were loaded beyond belief. Maddie was obviously one of those girls who'd had everything handed to her her whole life and had never heard the word "no" before. Brooke even pulled up a video from an episode of *My Super Sweet 16* on MTV that showed her getting a brand-new white Escalade and throwing a crying fit because she'd said she wanted pink. Maddie was a spoiled brat, and there was nothing that Brooke loathed more.

Brooke walked into her psychology class Monday morning and found Nolan saving her a seat. She had dodged his calls and texts the rest of Sunday, but she wasn't surprised to see him sitting there looking eager and hopeful. There was no breaking this guy down.

"How was the rest of your weekend?" he asked as she set her things down and took her seat.

"It was good. How was yours?"

"Good. So I'm thinking a nice restaurant downtown, then out on Sixth again, or The W and then maybe—"

"Oh shhh, class is starting," she said, cutting him off.

They sat quietly through the lecture, and at the end of class, Professor Bornstein gave them their assignment for the week. They would have to do a five-minute presentation explaining one of the behavioral psychology theories they'd gone over and apply it to a real-life example. Their presentation could fall on either one of the following days their class met this week, meaning Wednesday or Friday, so he reminded them to be prepared for either one.

After her next two classes, Brooke decided to take the long way back to the dorms since the weather was so nice. As she was walking down Guadalupe, she stopped dead in her tracks when she saw a killer dress in a window display. She went into the store, found it on the rack, and searched the dress for a price tag. *Shoot*, she thought, *way too expensive.*

She held the dress up in front of her for one last look. It really was gorgeous. It was black satin with a low-cut, heart-shaped neckline and thin studded waist belt to make it a little edgy. The hemline was shorter than something she'd normally go for, but it was so insanely cute that it could be worth showing a little extra skin. She convinced herself there was no harm in trying it on, but the second she zipped it up, she fell even more in love with it.

Okay, she told herself, *you've gotten your fix. Just take it off and put it back now.* She unzipped herself and put it back on the hanger. *Although!* She remembered she did have that paycheck coming eventually. Sure, it was earmarked for the speeding ticket, but she'd totally be able to come up with more money before it was due.

When Brooke got back to her room, she just had to try on the dress again. She turned and twisted in front of the mirror for ten minutes straight. It was just way too short and low-cut. She decided that taking it back would be the only way to solve her dilemma. As she was hanging it up on the rim of her closet doorframe, Sophie came back from the library.

"Wow, that dress is so cute!" Sophie said. Brooke was surprised she liked it, since she'd only ever seen Sophie in pastel denim and sweaters. But she realized she had never really taken the time to get to know the girl. Brooke was always with her friends and Sophie spent most of her time studying in the library, so their paths didn't cross much even in the same room.

"Thanks," Brooke said. "It actually has to go back, but it's still pretty to look at. How was the library?"

"It was fun." Not a word people typically chose when talking about the library. "This really cute boy sat at my table for like an hour!"

"Oh cool, did you talk to him?"

Sophie looked at her like she was crazy. "No!"

Okay, she was shy, but at least Brooke knew now that she did like boys, and it seemed like she was enjoying that they were talking, so she went on.

"Have you had a boyfriend before?" Brooke asked.

Sophie just laughed shyly and shook her head. "But I kind of want one. I'd really like to start going out and maybe meet someone. My cousin let me have her old driver's license, so I can get into clubs and bars and stuff. I heard there are cool places downtown."

Brooke hadn't been giving Sophie enough credit, she realized. "Well, if you ever want to come out with us, just let me know. We'd love to hang out with you."

Sophie looked like she was on cloud nine. Brooke felt like she was like the little sister she never had, and she sort of liked having someone to look out for.

Wednesday morning, Brooke sat down in her usual seat and saved a spot for Nolan. She pulled her notebook and pen out of her bag just as Nolan shuffled across the aisle and took his seat.

"Hey, you ready for today?" he asked her.

"Yeah," she answered without really giving the question thought. "Wait, what's today?" Nolan stared at her questioningly, waiting for some sign of recognition. And with a sharp, loud gasp, it hit her. "The presentations!"

"You didn't do it?"

"I completely forgot."

"Just wing it then. It won't be too hard."

"No, you don't understand. I hate public speaking—I can't get up there and wing it!"

"Well there's a 50/50 chance that you don't get called on today."

Brooke turned pale and sank in her seat as Professor Bornstein, her favorite teacher who she was about to disappoint, walked in and set his briefcase on his desk.

"Okay, class," he announced. "We're going to get started right away. Let's try to get through as many of these as possible so Friday will be a short day."

"Okay, maybe a 40/60 chance," Nolan said. Brooke elbowed him as if it was his fault.

"We'll start by taking volunteers for those of you who want to get the presentation out of the way first, and when we run out of those, we'll just go alphabetically."

"What's your last name again?" Nolan asked her.

"Aarons," Brooke whined, cursing her great-great-whoever chose the name.

"Oh yeah, you're screwed."

"Show of hands, do we have any volunteers?" Professor Bornstein asked.

To Brooke's surprise, there were actually quite a few of them.

"See? You might be okay."

"Are you going to volunteer?"

"Oh, absolutely not, no."

"Dammit."

One by one, the students who volunteered went up. But as the number of hands dwindled, Brooke's stomach started turning. She was watching the clock, hoping they'd run out of time before they ran out of volunteers, but when Professor Bornstein announced they had time for one more, Brooke realized that wasn't going to be her luck.

"Anyone else? No hands? All right then, we'll go to the roster."

As he crossed the front of the room to get his class list, she felt a bead of sweat form on her forehead, and she gripped the sides of her desk so hard she knew her manicure was shot. He picked up the list, which no doubt started with her name. All she could do was hold her breath and wait for the inevitable humiliation and disappointment that was about to occur.

Nolan looked at Brooke, who looked like she could pass out at any moment. He grabbed the back of her chair and turned to face her.

"Agree to a double date on Friday night, and I'll volunteer."

"What?"

"Okay, let's see here," Professor Bornstein started. "Going once…" Nolan said.

Professor Bornstein pulled his glasses out of his shirt pocket and put them on his face. "Going twice…"

He cleared his throat.

"Going three times…"

"We have Br—"

"Okay! Okay! Do it, and I'll go!"

Nolan slapped his desk in excitement and his hand shot up, "I'll go, Professor!"

"Oh, okay, wonderful. Come on up."

Brooke exhaled so long, it made her light-headed. Forty-eight minutes of terror had finally culminated in a moment of sweet relief. Nolan finished just before class was dismissed, so she grabbed his things with hers and met him outside the door.

"Well played, Mr. Greenwald. Well played."

With a victorious smile on his face, he said, "So how do you feel about sushi?"

Chapter 8

Later that night, the girls all took their spots on their washing machines, each with a mixed drink in their hand. Darci was sipping out of a 7-Eleven Big Gulp cup, Kate had a mug that said "World's Best Mom," Stella had a red plastic cup, and Brooke was clutching a tiny Dixie cup she'd snagged from the cafeteria.

"Since we're all in such good spirits," Brooke started, "Stella, I have a fun surprise for you! You, my friend, are getting a *free* sushi dinner this Friday night. Yay!"

"Oh, Brookey, what did you do?" Stella said, looking worried.

Brooke smiled bigger and then decided to drop the act. "I'm really sorry. I traded a date with you to save my ass. But if you think about it... um... this is what friendship is really about. So you're going on a date with Nolan Greenwald. Pass the shaker!" Brooke refilled Stella's red cup from the martini shaker. "But I'll be there too, and so will that annoying meathead, and it'll be great. We'll get dinner, get some drinks, and get out. I swear!"

Stella picked up her pile of quarters, dropping them one by one in her hand then back to the other. "All right, fine," she finally said, "but I get to raid your closet every day for a week."

"Done. Here's my room key—raid away!" Stella hopped off her machine, snatched Brooke's key, and exited the laundry room.

About fifteen minutes later, Brooke said goodbye to Kate and Darci and brought her pile of clean laundry into her room to present Stella with more options.

"I have another request," Stella said.

"Shoot."

"Can I crash in here tonight? My roommate's got some nasty-looking dude in our room, and I do not plan to miss a night's sleep because they're dropping E and waving glow sticks around again."

Brooke just laughed. "Of course."

"So this James character, do you like him? Seriously, you can tell me."

"I don't even know the guy." Brooke flashed back to the alley and the spark she felt when he touched her ankle. She deliberately replaced it with a picture of him and the cocktail waitress to remind herself that he was still every bit the guy she pegged him for. "He's just got this ladies' man attitude. Nolan even called him a whore."

"A whore?"

"Well, he just alluded to the fact that he's had or can get plenty of girls."

They continued talking about it as they wedged into Brooke's twin bed and pushed and elbowed each other until they finally both found comfort and fell asleep.

The next morning, Brooke and Stella woke up to frantic knocking.

"Brooke, open up!" Kate called from the other side of the door. Brooke hopped out of bed and ran to open it.

"What? What's wrong?" Brooke asked as she opened her door.

"Did you get your laundry last night?"

"Yeah, why?" She heard Stella gasp behind her.

"I forgot mine!"

"Well, Christmas came early to the fifth floor!" Kate said stepping back from the doorway so they could see what she was talking about.

All three girls peered down the hall, and as far as they could see, every door handle was graced with one of Stella's thongs. She screamed so loud that Sophie woke up in a panic, smacked her head on the ceiling, and fell back down on her pillow.

The three of them ran down the hall, grabbing each pair while Stella screamed and Brooke and Kate were cracking up. When they got to the guys' door, they saw it was slightly cracked and could hear them laughing.

"You bastards!" Stella charged the door, knocking them back and swinging at anyone in her reach.

Brooke and Kate tried to restrain her, but they were laughing so hard, it was impossible. Soon enough, everyone was on the floor laughing except Stella, who was proclaiming revenge. "Oh, if it's a war you want, you've got one! After I rewash my underwear that now have your grubby, disgusting fingerprints all over them."

"Oh really. Well apparently we're not the only ones who got our hands on them, considering you weren't in your room this morning," Bryan said to Stella in a taunting way while Garrett and Kyle hollered and whistled.

"I slept in Brooke's room, you idiots."

"Wait," Garrett said, suddenly looking serious, "were you guys being lesbians? You have to tell me."

"Garrett, you're a dumbass," Brooke said as they all got up from the floor.

They left the room and collected the rest of the underwear before getting ready for their classes.

That evening, after her classes, Brooke worked her shift at Java City with Jeff-who-continues-to-be-no-help, and Friday morning in Professor Bornstein's class, she volunteered to do her presentation first so she could knock it out of the park and be done with it. She was back on track to ace his class. Happy with her performance, she returned to her seat to sit next to an equally smug Nolan.

"So flowers or no flowers?"

"No flowers."

"Yeah, that's what I was thinking too. Black shirt or blue?"

"I so don't care."

"Yeah, I think black. We're going to pick you guys up at 8 tonight."

"Okay. Be quiet."

He lowered his whisper. "So make sure you're ready to go, and don't forget a swim suit and something to sleep in."

"Wait, what?" she exclaimed loudly, causing half the class to turn around and face her.

That night, Brooke and Stella got ready together in Brooke's room so they could both pick through her closet.

"How's this?" Stella asked.

"Cute! If you spill on it, I'll kill you. How's this?"

"My grandma dresses more risqué. Show some cleavage."

Stella pulled the dress Brooke was planning to return down from the doorway and held it up. "Wear this. It'll blow his mind."

"Nothing is being blown. And *this* is going back."

"He's buying you dinner. The least you can do is look good."

Brooke was about to launch into a speech about how men's money and women's looks being used as an equal exchange was an archaic notion, but Stella held up her hand to stop her and went on.

"And we both know you were never actually going to return it. You were going to take it to the store, then midway through the return change your mind and bring it right back here to stare at it some more." Her fast friend knew her well, apparently.

"Oh, what the hell!" Brooke yanked the tag and pulled on the amazing, low-cut dress just as her phone started ringing. It was a number she didn't recognize, but she picked up anyway.

"Hello?"

"Hi, is this Ms. Aarons?"

"Yeah, who's this?"

"This is your date for the evening."

The second she realized it was James, her heart rate picked up a little.

"Oh… hi."

"I realize I didn't officially ask you if you wanted to go out with me, so I thought I should call and see if you'd like to?"

"Aren't we kind of already planning on it anyway?"

"Is that a yes, you'd love to go out with me?"

She remembered how cocky he was, but she could tell this time he was kidding. "That's a yes, I'll go."

"Great, I'm two minutes away with Nolan here too, so whenever you ladies are ready, we'll meet you downstairs, okay?"

"Um… okay. 'Bye." She hung up her phone and turned to Stella. "They're almost here." Brooke stared at her phone for a second before dropping it into her bag, then decided to grab a few more things out of the closet and stuffed them in too.

"Let's just get this over with," Stella said. They walked downstairs, and as soon as they exited the building, Brooke saw James standing there next to his car. *Shit*, she thought. He was cuter than she remembered. It was already starting to cloud her judgment.

"So you know how you're borrowing my clothes for a week?" Brooke said to Stella quietly as they were walking toward the car.

"Yeah."

"Since that's happening, I didn't see any point in telling you to grab a bathing suit and pajamas, so I grabbed us both a set of each."

"What!"

"Shh."

"Hey, Stella, you look beautiful," Nolan said as Stella looked at Brooke to convey how much she hated her. "Let me get the door."

"Hi," James said.

"Hi."

"I see you managed to not forget clothes again today."

"Nothing gets past you."

"Well, you did a good job, with the choice you made, is all I'm trying to say. You look great." Brooke glanced at the ground and then up at him again as she thanked him for the compliment. She felt a little overdressed and couldn't tell if it made her look like she was trying too hard—trying at all, for that matter—but she made an effort not to worry about it. It was ridiculous that she would even care. "Now do you have everything you need? Various forms of identification and whatnot?"

"Yes, I do, thank you. Should we go?"

"Yup. I'll get your door."

She looked at the front passenger doorway to the Range Rover. Getting in his car was easy in a looser cocktail dress, but this one was skintight. As if he could read her mind, he held out his hand. She just stared at it a moment, debating whether or not she wanted to take it, then put her hand in his and steadied herself into the front seat. She felt the spark again.

"Buckle up," he said before he closed her door, walked around the front, and climbed in on the driver's side.

"So we were thinking we'd take you to this sushi place downtown called Maiko and we could go to a club called Kingdom afterward. How does that sound?" Brooke agreed that it sounded okay, and then he proceeded. "There's also a pool in my complex if anyone is interested. But if after the club you guys want to get a cab back, I can pay for it so you don't feel stuck."

He was actually sort of considerate. She debated for a moment if the only reason he made the offer was because he planned to slip a roofie in her drink and knew he wouldn't be paying for that ride. She decided that was unlikely enough that she could go ahead and rule it out.

When they walked into the restaurant, Brooke's concerns about being overdressed vanished. It wasn't the typical Sushi Hut by campus that had already given her and each of her friends a round of food poisoning. This place was swanky and much more upscale than she had imagined. The lighting was dim from the white lanterns that hung from the ceiling, and every dish she saw go by looked more elaborate than the one before it.

The four of them sat down as the waiter came up to the table. James asked if everyone liked sake then listened as the waiter listed a few sake choices and appetizers for the table. As soon as the sake was poured, everyone lifted their glasses, and Brooke suddenly remembered James's thing about always toasting to something. Sure enough, he asked who wanted to make a toast.

Nolan went first, dedicating his to Stella looking beautiful, and James finished it with "and to my good buddy Nolan, who is just a fool in love."

Brooke had never had sake before. The idea of warm alcohol sounded awful, but it wasn't bad at all, actually, and she eventually had a weird happy-drunk going on. At least she attributed the happy part to the sake. She was already having a surprisingly good time. James did appear to have a good side. He made a good date even if they were both only there for Nolan. There was no harm in giving him at least a little credit for that.

After a few more rounds and toasts, Brooke decided to chime in with one of her own. Unfortunately, when she said, "I'll volunteer!" Nolan started in on his whole story about how the date even came to be. James looked at Brooke with his glass still raised.

"You didn't want to go out with me?" James asked. The way he said it made her want to hug the guy and tell him it wasn't true.

Instead Brooke lifted her glass higher and said, "To not basing *everything* on a first impression." She clinked her glass against his and they both drank, but their eyes remained locked.

He set his glass down and leaned in closer, resting his crossed arms in the middle of the table. "I bet I can change your mind about me."

She wasn't sure if it was just the sake sinking in, but everything around her started to fade away until he was all she could focus on. She leaned in to mirror the way he was sitting. "Maybe my mind's already set," she said. "I'm a lot more stubborn than you'd imagine."

"Well, it looks like you've just met your match then. Stubborn is my middle name."

"Really? You look more like a Judith."

"Good guess. That's what I go by when I dress in drag and host bingo on Tuesdays. Aside from *that*, the only thing you should probably know about me is that my stubbornness has won awards on a national level. You may be out of your league, kid."

"Oh, so you're a one-upper?"

"I don't think I can be categorized any which way." She laughed to herself knowing she'd categorized him as an asshole the second they met, and she was trying her hardest to keep him there. He had to be pretty secure with himself if she jumped on an opportunity to emasculate him and he ran with it. None of their banter was even making sense anymore, and they couldn't stop smiling and laughing at things that weren't even funny.

When the bill came, James and Nolan split it without even letting Brooke and Stella pretend to argue. They left the restaurant and stepped into the warm night air. The club was a short distance away, so they decided to walk the few blocks and enjoy the scene. Music poured out of every bar and restaurant they passed, tons of people filled the streets, and the weather was perfect.

"So what'd you think?" James asked Brooke. "Of the restaurant or your toasts?"

"The restaurant, but I'll take any constructive criticism if you're offering it."

"Delicious, great choice, and I wasn't particularly impressed by anything you said. But don't feel bad; it could have just been poor delivery."

"Still playing hardball, huh?"

"I have this theory you're going to wind up slipping a roofie in my drink anyway, so what does it matter?"

"Oh, no theory. I did that already back at the restaurant. It should hit you in about three, two, and…"

"Wow, nothing's cuter than flirting about date rape drugs."

"You're flirting with me?" He smiled coyly.

She blushed instantly and looked at the ground to hide it.

"My mother may have passed down some paranoia."

He cocked his head back as if her statement had solved all the mysteries. "So that's what happened to you?" he joked.

She went to push him away playfully, but instead managed to launch herself in the opposite direction, while he didn't even budge. She regained her composure and kept walking like nothing had happened, but it didn't stop him from laughing. She shot him a glare as she tried to keep from smiling. "I'm sure no one has ever told you this before, but you're kind of obnoxious," she said.

He corrected her. "It's pronounced charming. Now, I know I already asked, but you're a little unpredictable. Do you have your ID?"

"Check," she said with a nod.

"Then right this way." They stepped up to the front of the line outside Kingdom and the bouncer let them in ahead of everyone who had been waiting. It was a pretty small place, but the music was great. They took a seat at a table reserved for them, and a cocktail waitress walked up to their table with a bottle of Grey Goose and an ice bucket wearing fishnets and a corset with what could only be considered underwear.

"Hi, James," she said as she pulled the bottle out of the ice.

"Hello." The way he said it was upbeat and friendly but without recognition. She clearly knew his name, though. He'd probably slept with her and forgotten all about it. Brooke stiffened a little and leaned away so their shoulders weren't touching anymore.

"What'll it be?" the waitress asked James.

He turned to look at Brooke and studied her. "I'm guessing you're a cranberry vodka."

"Wrong," she said. He tapped his finger against his bottom lip. The cocktail waitress was still standing there waiting to hear what they wanted her to mix. When she wasn't getting an answer, she turned to Nolan and Stella to take their orders.

"Vodka soda?" James guessed.

"Nope."

"Ah, you're one of those skinny girls who only drink vodka waters with one lemon slice."

"God no, gross." She decided to end the game before it got any flirtier. "Tequila pineapple." She tried to sound confident in her order, even though she'd only had the drink once before.

"Unpredictable again."

"And I'm guessing your favorite kind of cocktail is a waitress." She didn't mean to say that; it just came out. She tried to recover. "I just, I saw you chatting with one the other night and assumed…" That wasn't helping. It just made her sound jealous. Why didn't her brain work when she was around him?

"Oh, right, that one. What were we talking about?" he asked himself aloud, then paused to try to remember. "Whiskey! We were talking about whiskey. I ordered a glass, and then she said she'd be right back with it. Unfortunately, I saw her doing the same thing with some other guys. And some girls, too. I don't think it's going to work out with us."

Brooke felt like such an idiot, but it didn't stop her from glancing at the cocktail waitress pouring drinks right in front of them. "And I'm guessing she knows my name because she has it written down along with our table number. Plus, I've actually been here before, and my name hasn't changed since the last time so…"

"Okay, okay, you made your point. No need to be a smart-ass about it," Brooke said, turning it back on him. All he did was smile, though.

"We can go up to the bar if you don't want to wait."

They stood up and started walking through the crowd. Brooke heard someone calling her name and turned to see who it was.

"Brooke, hey! It's Sophie!" Sophie said, pointing to herself, as if Brooke wouldn't recognize her outside of their room.

"Oh hey, I didn't know you'd be here."

"This place is so cool! I was in line right when the doors opened to make sure I'd get in."

"Nice. Sophie, this is my friend James. James, this is my roommate, Sophie."

"Hi, nice to meet you," James said to Sophie.

Sophie juggled her clutch and drink around so she could shake his hand. "I'm running to the bathroom," Sophie said to Brooke. "Want to come with me?"

"Oh, I'm okay. We're just running to the bar and—"

"No, no, no," James interjected, "girls can't go alone. It breaks your code, and what about the buddy system? You never know which creeps are walking around with a pocket full of roofies."

"Again with the date rape drugs," she said, shaking her head at him.

"You ladies go," he said. "I'll meet you back here with the drinks. It's crowded up there anyway. Sophie, do you want anything?"

"I'm okay!" She walked into the bathroom and let the door close behind her.

Brooke turned to follow. She put her hand on the door handle to open it but then she heard James say, "Hey."

"Hey what?"

"You called me your friend."

"Yeah, so?"

"So you're warming up to me already."

Brooke paused for a few moments then pulled the door open but didn't go in. It swung outward toward the bar, and Brooke put her foot in front of it to hold it in place. She thought she heard some commotion behind her, but the second she looked up and caught James's eyes, it was like no one was around again.

The music was loud, so he leaned down closer to her face to hear her.

"I thought it was rude to say my fellow wingman forced to hang out with me so his BFF can try his best to get it on with mine."

"Forced?"

He really was painfully handsome. When she felt her knees starting to go weak, though, she pushed that thought out of her head immediately.

"We're not friends. I hardly know you."

"All right. But you should know, I'm a really good friend to have. I save my friends a seat in class, I can change a tire, and in special cases, I will even go to the bar and get a friend a tequila pineapple."

"Well I can't say I've seen you make good on any of that," Brooke said, smiling.

"Then I'll be right back." He turned and walked toward the bar as she took in a breath and let it out slowly.

After he disappeared into the crowd, Brooke noticed a group of guys whistling and hollering, so she looked behind her to see what all the fuss was about. Just as she turned, Sophie came running out of the bathroom yelling, "Shut up, shut up, shut up!"

They kept cheering for her as she made her way through the crowd.

"Sophie? Sophie!" *What was that about?* Brooke thought. She decided to go inside the bathroom anyway and fix herself up. She realized once she was inside that it was a one-person bathroom, no stalls—just a sink and toilet in the corner. "Ohhhhhh," Brooke said aloud as the whistling suddenly made sense. She had just held the door wide open to the club so everyone could see Sophie with her underwear around her ankles. How could she be so oblivious that she didn't even realize Sophie was sitting there screaming for her to close the door? Brooke made a mental note to apologize for that one as she locked the door and shook it to make sure it stayed locked.

Brooke looked at herself in the mirror. Her mind wandered back to James, and her stomach flipped like she was on a roller coaster. She brushed her hair out then pulled it up in a stylish-looking bun. Then put it back down. Then put it back up. *Stop it, Brooke. Get it together. You are not some dumb girl who falls for cheap tricks. He is not the first guy to buy you a drink, and you are not losing control of yourself because this guy knows how to turn on the charm. By not putting out tonight, you'll never see him again anyway, so just go find Stella, stick the rest of the night out, and go home.*

She opened the door and saw James standing there, drinks in hand as promised. Despite her best efforts, a smile formed and the pep talk she had just given herself was already fading. She walked up to James and accepted the drink with a curtsy. *What the fuck? Did I just curtsy?*

He gave her a funny look then held up his drink. "To officially becoming friends now." Their glasses clinked, and they both took a swig of their drinks.

"Let's go back to the table," she said. He turned around to lead the way.

The club was packed, and they had to cross the dance floor to get back to the table. James held out his hand to help lead her through, but she pretended she didn't see it. After that curtsy, she couldn't trust herself to do anything that would make her any more absentminded around him, especially touching.

She emerged from the crowd about five seconds after James did to see him staring with his jaw dropped. She followed his eye line and saw he was staring at Stella and

Nolan. Making out. Not just making out—Stella had him by the collar of his shirt with one leg over his lap, and he had one hand in her hair and the other on her butt.

To Brooke's surprise, she burst out laughing and looked up at James to watch his face go from worried to surprised to laughing with her in just a few seconds.

"How long were we gone?" she asked.

He looked at the table. "Half-a-bottle-of-vodka long." She couldn't stop laughing from shock, and when she finally got it together, she surprised herself again. "Do you want to dance?" For whatever reason, she just decided to loosen up. Seeing Stella all over Nolan reminded her that tonight was about having fun, nothing more. There was no point to all her self-righteousness. It wasn't like having a good time with James was going to turn her into some lovesick groupie.

Brooke and James stayed out on the dance floor until they were sweaty and disheveled, but she couldn't have cared less that she was a mess. This was the most fun she'd had since arriving in Texas, and that was saying something. They collected Stella and Nolan, stepped outside into the humid night air, and hailed a cab. James's place was a five-minute drive, and they all decided jumping in the pool was the best idea anyone had ever thought of.

While Brooke and Stella changed in the guest room, James and Nolan made drinks in the kitchen. Brooke finished changing and walked out into the living room. Nolan, who probably should have cut himself off, passed Brooke, and a few seconds later she heard Stella screaming, "Get out!"

James and Brooke looked at each other, he handed her a cup, and they waited for the yelling to subside. "Okay, well, we'll meet you guys outside," he eventually called down the hall.

They were both drunk, so none of their yelling was making any sense, which became all too clear when, as they were closing the front door, they heard Nolan yell, "But I'm in love with you!"

She and James looked at each other again, laughed, and walked out to the pool. They both dove completely under and swam around for a little while before getting out and lying on two lounge chairs.

"I still can't get over how warm it stays here at night," Brooke said.

"I know. It's already getting cold back in New York. But I am a little bummed I'm missing out on fall in the city." So that's where he was from. "So how'd you end up at UT?" he asked.

"The psychology department here is great."

"I bet the parents love that career path."

"Hey!" She laughed, "Yeah they're hoping it's a phase and throw in their 'better' ideas whenever an opportunity presents itself."

"So that's what you want to be when you grow up? A psychologist?"

"Yeah, I do."

"How come?"

"Because I didn't feel like being an astronaut or ballerina. What do you want to be when you grow up?"

"An architect."

"Okay, that's actually really cool. When did you realize that's what you wanted to do?"

"I didn't. Family business."

"Ah, the family business. Have you always lived in New York City?"

"Born and raised Upper East-sider."

"So you probably took the end of *Gossip Girl* pretty hard."

"I didn't get out of bed for a week. Gossip Girl was a guy! It made me question everything." She knew they were joking around in that moment, but she couldn't help wondering what his life back home must be like. It was so far from her own that all she could do was think of what she'd seen in movies and on TV. Suddenly she felt a little intimidated.

"So you grew up there with Nolan?" she asked, confused about his Southern accent now.

"He's actually from Dallas, but we went to the same high school in Connecticut. My parents wanted me to go to this private school because of their football program. We've known each other since we were 13."

"Oh, 13. I bet he's got some great photos of you in your awkward stage."

"Naw, I didn't have one of those. I've always been this good-looking. You and Stella just meet here?"

"Yeah, I came here knowing no one."

"Fearless."

"No, I just had motivation to get out of town."

"OK. Which town?"

"You've probably never heard of it. Camarillo, California?"

"I know it. That's north of Malibu, right? My family has a place there, and I always saw the signs."

He has place in Malibu? His vacation house was probably ten times the size and price of the house she grew up in. She wondered how many of these places he had around the country—around the world for that matter. "OK, so how many guesses do I get?" he asked, pulling her out of her own thoughts.

"Guesses?" She laughed, figuring it out. "Oh, um, three."

He thought for a few seconds then said, "You were the high school dork who got a makeover over summer and decided to change your name and start a new life."

"Please. Prom queen two years running." She put down one of the three fingers she was holding up.

"Okay. You were the bitchiest prom queen there ever was and the town rose up against you and forced you into exile."

"I'm a sweetheart. Who wouldn't want to keep me?" She put down a second finger to leave one remaining.

"You killed a man."

"I killed the last man who called me bitchy, but that's not why."

"You're smart enough to not kill me in front of witnesses."

"What witnesses?"

"You're kidding me. You really haven't noticed the two people having sex in the Jacuzzi?" Brooke leaned up from her lounge chair and peered at the hot tub behind her. She gasped, turned around, and sank low in her chair, covering her mouth to muffle her laughter. "I don't even think they live here," he said, starting to laugh too. "So tell me," he finally said.

"I love where I grew up. Camarillo is beautiful and you can't ask for more than to grow up near the coast in California. There are plenty of great schools around there, but I just wanted something different for myself."

"Different than what?"

"I don't know. Small town life, I guess."

"Sure, that makes sense. You want to avoid the small-town-America life, so you leave LA for Texas," he joked.

"Camarillo can't even be compared to Los Angeles. It's completely small-town there. Just the kind that's easy to never leave, you know? It's home and I love it, but every once in a while, it felt like I was suffocating. I just didn't want to settle down, look back, and think I didn't do enough with my life."

"Okay, so why not UCLA or USC?"

"Because I've watched a hundred people go off to start their lives and end up right back where they started when things got tough. I figured the farther I went, the harder it'd be for that to happen to me. What's your story? How'd you wind up here?"

"My parents both went here. It was always the plan for me to play ball here then join the family business."

"So you're living the dream, then?"

He just gave a small smile. "Depends who you ask. It's not bad. Aside from the long list of people telling me what to do with my life. That's why I've got to stay away from girls. Your kind just loves to be the boss, and if I let that happen, I wouldn't get a say in anything, would I?"

She smiled and shook her head at him. "Nice generalization."

"So you think Stella and Nolan are almost here?" he said, changing the subject.

Brooke laughed knowing full well they had not embarked on the 30 second walk. "Fighting or, you know, *not* fighting?" she said with a wink. "What do you think?"

"I'm going to go with passed out." He looked at his watch. "It's 4:30 in the morning."

"Really?" Brooke was genuinely shocked.

"Yeah, we should get to bed."

"We should get to beds," Brooke corrected.

"See? Bossing me around already."

They walked back to his apartment, headed up the steps, and swung the door open. Brooke was not prepared for the devastation before them. There were spilled cups, a broken bottle, and—here's the kicker—Nolan standing in the corner peeing on the floor with his head against the wall. Brooke stared in disbelief as he finished, turned around, looked at them with completely blank eyes, and face-planted on the couch with his arms at his sides.

She was frozen in the doorway. If it were her place, then she would absolutely freak out, lose her mind, start screaming, and not stop until everything was back to the way she'd left it. She looked up at James. This was it. He was finally going to show his true colors and be the jerk she knew he was doing a great job of hiding.

She watched as he walked over to the kitchen, reached into a cupboard, and pulled out a bottle of carpet cleaner, a broom, a dustpan, and a roll of paper towels, then walked over to where Nolan was lying and set everything on the coffee table in front of him.

He nodded at Brooke. "He'll know what to do."

She was stunned—absolutely stunned. He wasn't even mad. She watched as he walked down the hall and disappeared for a moment. She heard the squeak of a door opening then closing. As he walked back, he whispered, "So you have two options. Stella is sleeping face down in the guest room in the shape of an X. The girl's got some long limbs, but I'm sure you can find a way around. Or, and I say this respectfully, I have a bed that comfortably fits two and you are welcome to share with me."

Her head took no time deciding that's where she wanted to be. But that wasn't a good idea. She'd have to decline. "Sure, um, I don't want to wake Stella up." *Hey, I didn't approve that answer*, she thought. He held out his arm to direct her then turned down the hall to where his room was.

Brooke picked up the bag with her pajamas from the living room floor and followed his path to the bedroom.

"Okay, over there is the bathroom, over here is the bed, and right there is a window, in case you'd like to jump out now and end it all. It might not be high enough to cause anything but a broken leg or two, but I can promise it'll get you out of some forced double dates for a while."

Brooke was about to protest. It felt like a million years ago that thoughts of not wanting to be around him had been in her mind. Instead, when she opened her mouth she said, "Um, the bathroom is this way?" *Dumb question.*

She turned around, went inside, and closed the door. After kneeling down and opening her bag, she pulled out shorts, but where was her top? She fished around frantically. *No, no. Where is it? Stella must have grabbed both tops by accident.*

She opened the door. "Hey, um, I'm having a little issue in here."

"You sure you need to tell me about it?"

"No, it's not… oh, shut up. Do you have a shirt I can borrow? I think Stella grabbed both of ours." He walked to his dresser and pulled out a blue shirt with a logo and handed it to her. She unfolded it and stared. "The beavers? You went to an expensive private school, and the best mascot they could get was a beaver? You *paid* for a beaver?"

"Whoa, that's a whole different question." Brooke shook her head at him then went back inside the bathroom. "But I'm actually a big fan of beavers," he called as she closed the door. She laughed quietly so he wouldn't know his bad joke got a response.

She'd forgotten how he could make her feel nervous, but now that it was just the two of them in his room, it was creeping back in. She pulled the shirt over her head. It was huge. It went down to the middle of her thighs, and the sleeves nearly covered her elbows. She opened the bathroom door and stepped out.

"It fits!" he joked. She was about to rebut, but when she looked up and saw him standing there in just black briefs, her throat closed up. She looked at the bed, and he must have seen her.

"Okay, I know what you're thinking, and here's how we're going to solve it." He picked up a long body pillow and laid it down the center of the bed. "This is so you don't try anything."

She swallowed hard then tried to sound cool. "I'll keep my hands to myself if you do," she said, allowing herself to be flirtatious.

"Easy. You look like a hobbit in that shirt."

The shutdown made her laugh, and she relaxed a little. She crawled in on her side and put her back against the center divide. He turned out the light and crawled in on the other side.

"I have to tell you something," Brooke said.

"Afraid of the dark?"

"No! Well, I don't love it, but who does?"

"I do," he said playfully.

Oh, now he flirts back, she thought. "Okay great, but that's not it. I think it's only fair I should warn you: sometimes I kick in my sleep."

"If you kick me, I'll kick you back."

"That's mature! I was giving you fair warning so you'll know it's an accident. Your kicking would then be intentional and therefore not on an even scale. An unconscious kick gets forgiven, but an intentional one warrants payback."

"Can you cite a source for that one?"

"Um, I had to read Sophie's bible pretty closely, but it's in there. It's a clause under the eye-for-an-eye section. Sounds simple but it gets complicated."

"That just reminded me." He cleared his throat, and Brooke rolled on her other side to see what he was doing. "Dear Lord," he started in the most ridiculous Texas accent. "Thank you for the food and the alcoholic beverages, and please protect me from the devil I just allowed into my bed. Protect me from the bodily harm I may endure tonight as a result of my kindness and generosity toward strangers." He opened one eye to peek at her. When he saw she was fighting back a smile, he continued. "And help this demon to stop being such a stubborn ass and realize what a sweet, innocent boy I am, and…"

"Amen!" Brooke interrupted. "You already said 'ass' to God, and you're going to lie to the man too?"

He rolled on his side to face her straight on. The truth was, everything she had thought about him was changing. She wasn't so sure he was the spoiled playboy she'd pegged him for anymore. She held his gaze for another few seconds before forcing her eyes to break away. Light was starting to come through the window behind him. She looked at him one more time before he closed his eyes, and then she did the same. Maybe she'd been wrong.

Chapter 9

In what felt like a blink, the room was bright and there was a banging on the door. Stella was calling her name. Brooke jumped up as quickly and as delicately as she could and ran to open the door.

"It's time to go, it's time to go, it's time to go!" Stella said in a panic. "I called Kate already. She and Darci are a few minutes away. So hurry, let's go." Stella was in pajamas, with Brooke's borrowed dress dangling in the hand holding open the door and her other arm waving in circles telling Brooke to hurry up.

Brooke glanced behind her at James. He was a hard sleeper. She put on her pumps, grabbed her bag, and looked back at the bed. "Oh shit!" she whispered. There was a perfectly round drool spot exactly where her face had been. She tiptoed in her heels back to the bed and slid a pillow directly over it.

She made her way back to the door quietly, but as she started to pull it closed, the hinges made a horrible creaking noise. She watched as James's eyes started to open and caught her glance. Stella saw Nolan on the couch starting to stir at the sound too and realized she couldn't risk staying another second. She grabbed Brooke's arm and pulled it, causing her to slam the bedroom door. She pulled her all the way through the living room and out the front door before letting go.

Once they were safely outside and in the parking lot, they looked at each other and cracked up. Stella was in pajama shorts, heels, and a tank top with makeup so smudged she looked like a raccoon. Brooke was in heels and a shirt so huge it made it look like she wasn't wearing shorts underneath, and once again, the humidity had gotten the best of her hair. It was huge and matted, and when it air-dried after the pool, it had formed a a life of its own. A few seconds later, they heard howling and turned to see Darci and Kate driving toward them. Brooke and Stella jumped over the sides of Kate's white convertible, and Stella yelled, "Drive!"

Darci turned around from the front seat. "So, ladies, how much did you make last night?"

Stella: "I need a Bloody Mary."

Brooke: "I need sunglasses."

Stella: "I need Advil."

Brooke: "*You* need to explain yourself."

Kate: "Well I need a bagel and I'm driving. We're going to our spot, and then we'll take you both home and hose you off."

At the restaurant they were greeted with the usual stares as they were seated. Brooke and Stella looked across the table at Kate and Darci, who were only slightly less disheveled than themselves.

Brooke: "So what did *you guys* do last night?" she said tauntingly.

Darci: "Golf Pros and Tennis Hoes party at the Omega Chi house. I have a vague memory of dancing in the cage."

Brooke: "Ah, yes. I know that cage well."

Kate: "Someone should really take some Lysol to that thing. I got sucked into a game of strip pool."

Brooke: "That's surprising."

Stella: "Yeah, you play pool?"

Kate: "Obviously not. How is it you can start playing literally anything over there and the next thing you know the word *strip* is in front of it?"

Brooke: "Because it's a frat house."

Darci: "How was your little double date?"

Brooke: "I drooled in his bed."

Stella: "I've peed in a guy's bed and he still called. He thought he did it."

Darci: "I left a tampon in a guy's nightstand drawer once."

Stella: "What the fuck?"

Darci: "Yeah, he didn't call."

Brooke: "How do you live with yourself?"

Darci: "Hey, I was totally mortified when it all came back to me the next day. But then I remembered what a huge douche he was."

Brooke: "Well, that makes it okay then."

Darci: "And now I laugh every time I imagine what his face must have looked like when he opened the drawer."

They all paused for a moment to picture that reaction.

Kate: "Well why did you sleep with him if he was such a douche?"

Darci: "Because he was hot."

Brooke: "Fair enough. It's actually amazing anyone could find *us* attractive, but look—6 o'clock."

They all looked different directions at first but then caught sight of a guy walking up to their table. He was about their age, so they assumed he went to UT.

"Hey, ladies, I couldn't help but notice you from across the restaurant." *Typical opener*, Brooke thought. "I've seen you here before and, forgive me if this is forward, but I was wondering"— the girls all just exchanged smirks—"if y'all knew where I could score some blow?" All at once, their faces changed.

Kate: "Oh my god, he thinks we're on drugs."

She instantly covered her face and looked down at the table in embarrassment.

Brooke: "What the hell, dude?"

Darci: "Fuck you, man!"

Stella: "Thatla: , man! d, asswad."

"Oh, I'm sorry!" he said putting his hands up like a shield.

"I just thought… It just seemed like… You guys kind of look… I'm sorry!"

Brooke: "Get out of here, loser. We don't look *that* bad!"

He ran backward away from the table and out the front door. They all calmed down and sank back in their seats.

Kate finally looked up. "Guys, do you think we should start, maybe, like, putting on real clothes when we come here?"

Stella wasn't fazed. "That just reminded me, I'm totally out of weed. Do you guys know anyone out here?"

"Oh, totally," Darci said. "He's a Facebook friend. I'll get you his number."

Kate looked at Brooke, who just smiled and shrugged at the irony.

Darci suddenly looked confused by something on her phone. "What's up with this picture of your roommate on the toilet?"

"Oh my god," Brooke said, remembering the incident. "I have a major apology to make."

"Can it wait until after the pool? I need to detox," Kate said.

They made a quick stop by Kate and Darci's room, since Stella and Brooke already had swim suits with them, then walked over to the pool in the hot sun. It was one of those days where they knew sunburns would be instant. They found four lounge chairs and laid their towels down, and as they were loading up on sunscreen, Kate pointed out Kyle, Bryan, and Garrett, who were all passed out on the other side of the pool. Stella held out her hand with a mischievous look. "Hand me the sunscreen." Brooke passed it to her and watched as Stella walked to where the guys were lying. The rest of the girls jumped up and followed to see what she was doing.

If there was one thing they'd learned, it was that partying the night before made it near impossible to wake up from those afternoon recovery naps. The boys were all lying face down and completely out cold.

Stella took the sunscreen bottle and leaned over Kyle. She carefully squeezed it just enough to get a straight line to form, and letter by letter spelled out "I <3 BOYS" on his back. Moving on to Garrett, she wrote "TEENY WEENY" and finished off with Bryan, writing "PENIS" with a giant heart around it. They all shuffled away quietly and ran back to their lounge chairs.

"So Stella already confessed to an accidental make-out sesh with Nolan. Do you have anything to share with the class, Miss Aarons?" Darci coaxed.

Kate weighed in. "Yeah, you know, the fact that you haven't already started heartlessly mocking this guy's flaws for our entertainment is speaking volumes right now."

"Oh no, he's flawed," Brooke said. "Loads of flaws!"

"Let's hear it then," Darci said.

"So... okay... well... there's... I mean, he's... It's totally annoying how he... um..."

Kate propped herself up and pulled her sunglasses off her face. "Oh my god. You like him!"

"No, I don't like him—like, *like* him like him. I like him. He's likable. I don't dislike him, but *like* him like him? No, I don't like him like that."

Now Darci was sitting up too. "Did you just have a stroke?"

She felt her face flush.

"It's too hot out here. I'm going in the pool!"

"Woooo, thinking about James makes you hot!" Darci teased.

"Fine, you go cool yourself off. We'll get the story from Stella," Kate said.

"The only thing she knows after last night is if Nolan wears boxers or briefs."

"Hey, what did I do to you?" Stella called after her.

Brooke lowered herself into the water and dunked completely under. She had a sinking feeling her friends might be right. But with all the alcohol out of her system and clarity finally coming back to her, she was starting to remember all the bad things she'd thought about him before last night. Every time she remembered dancing with him or lying next to him by the pool, though, she felt the excitement of being with him and it was like none of the negatives could hold weight against it. She didn't know what to make of him, and as a future psychologist, it was extremely frustrating.

She got out of the pool and threw herself onto her lounge chair. "Yeah, I have a fucking crush. How do I make it stop?" The girls laughed, and Brooke told them everything about their night.

Two hours passed before they finished gushing over each little detail. Just as they were wrapping up and feeling like they'd had enough sun for one day, they noticed stirring from across the pool—the guys were waking up. One by one they all deliriously jumped into the pool and starting roaring over their sunburned backs.

Stella rubbed her hands together. "Excellent." They watched the guys get out and collect their things. The girls quietly grabbed their bags and followed at a distance so the guys wouldn't notice.

"Nice, fellas!" a girl yelled, then turned to giggle with her friends. The guys smiled and waved to the group, looking around to make sure they were talking to them.

"Love the pride!" another girl yelled.

Brooke, Stella, Kate, and Darci could hardly hold in their laughter as they followed them toward the exit.

A group of guys started laughing. "Yo, dudes, you got punked," one of them yelled. The guys looked totally confused, and the girls were loving it. They exited through the gate and started walking down the path toward the dorms. The girls continued to follow, sticking close to the bushes.

Two girls on bicycles came up from behind them, and one yelled, "Hey, boys—where's the parade?" The guys finally stopped and tried to figure out what was going on.

"Dude, your back!" Kyle exclaimed when Garrett turned around.

"Dude, *your* back!" Bryan yelled when he saw Kyle's.

"Aw, what the fuck, man?" The girls couldn't hold it together anymore, so they ran out from the bushes with their water bottles in hand, and as the guys turned to see them, they were sprayed with water from all angles.

"Payback, suckers!" Stella yelled.

"Oh, you're dead!" The guys wrestled the bottles away and sprayed them back.

"Retreat! Retreat!" Stella yelled, and all the girls sprinted back toward the dorms as fast as they could.

They landed safely inside Brooke's dorm room and all piled on the floor laughing.

"Hey, guys!" Brooke looked up and saw Sophie sitting at her desk.

"Oh, Sophie, hey! Listen, I am so, so sorry about that bathroom door situation at the club. I can't even begin to tell you how bad I feel. I was just, I wasn't paying attention to anything that was happening around me last night." The girls looked at each other, and Stella gave them a see-I-told-you-so nod.

"Oh, I understand," Sophie said. "It happens. I actually got a whole bunch of Facebook friend requests after."

"Um… that's really cool, Sophie, but honestly I still feel horrible."

"Actually, I should thank you. This guy who said he was in the club last night messaged me and asked me out! He said he's really into girls who wear full-bottom underwear, so he wants to go to the movies on Wednesday night."

"Soph, that's great, but you should probably be careful of guys who say… *anything* like that."

"No, it's okay. I checked out his profile. He has a *ton* of Facebook friends. Plus I keep pepper spray in my backpack, and I intend to let him know I'm packing."

"Okay, well I still feel really badly, so just tell me what I can do to make it up to you."

"Borrow her clothes," Kate offered.

"Yeah, my closet is yours for a week, two weeks, whatever!"

"A week," Stella said. She looked at Brooke. "I only got a week."

"You also dry-humped in a bar, so you're welcome. As long as you want, Sophie."

"Thanks, Brooke. That's so cool of you."

"Okay, shower time for me." Brooke picked herself up off the ground, as the girls left the room, and then Brooke hopped in the shower. When she got out, she pulled on some shorts and a T-shirt and wrapped her hair in a towel. She pulled her phone out of her clutch from last night to put it on the charger and noticed she had two new text messages.

The first was from Nolan. "Hey did Stella say anything about last night yet?"

And the other was from James. It was a photo. She opened

it up to see it was one of his legs with bruises all over it. "You wouldn't know anything about this, right?" she read. She laughed then debated for a moment how to respond.

"Wow those make you look so tough. Must have been quite a fight you were in" she responded.

"Oh yeah, just wait until the boys in the locker room find out the other guy was a tiny chick." Before she could defend her average stature he sent another photo. "How about this? Does this ring any bells?" She opened up the photo to see the exact round drool spot she ran out on and gasped. She should have been mortified, but how could she be when he was so easily having a sense of humor about it.

"Hmmm," she wrote back, "I'd love to take credit, but I think that wet spot might have been Nolan. When I was on my way out, I heard him say something about me stealing his side of the bed last night and needing to mark that territory too. Very strange."

James: "That does make sense. Can I thank you for solving the mystery over dinner sometime this week?"

The excitement ran through her again but she managed to contain it. She did had to redeem herself, though, after the drooling incident. That's the only reason she was agreeing to go. Plus it would be a free meal, so why not kill two birds with one stone, right?

Brooke: "Mystery-solving plus bruise-giving plus the door-slam-wake-up-call you failed to mention might actually add up to a little more than dinner. I'd argue a movie might have to follow…"

James: "A negotiator? All right, if you're calling the shots, then I'll go ahead and let you decide the day and movie. Would you also like to pay?"

Brooke: "Let's not get ahead of ourselves. I'll explain my reasoning over dinner at a location of YOUR choice, but would you mind if we went Wednesday?"

James: "Wednesday is fine with me, but can I get a hint as to what this reasoning might be?"

Brooke: "Secret mission spy stuff."

James: "I had a feeling you might be crazy. OK, that's cool with me. As long as we're clear on one thing: previews are my favorite part of the movie, so no talking. Pick you up at 6 p.m.?"

Brooke: "I'll see you then!"

She sent one more text, to Nolan. "I'll put in a good word, buddy."

Chapter 10

"Okay, cough it up," James said while they were sitting at a restaurant called Manuel's. "Who are we stalking tonight, and what did he do to you?"

"No, it's not like that," Brooke said. "You met Sophie. She's sweet, right? But also somewhat inexperienced in the dating world, and she's going on a date tonight, and I just want to make sure she's safe. I get the sense she's a little more trusting than she should be. Plus it's kind of my fault she's going out with this creeper, so I feel responsible."

"So you know the guy she's going out with?"

"No."

"But you consider him to be an untrustworthy creeper we need to follow?"

"Yeah."

"Your mom really did mess you up, huh?" She punched him in the arm, again, hurting herself more than him. "Well, I think it's very admirable that you're looking out for your roommate, but what, may I ask, makes you the expert on guys who are the ones to watch out for? Or do you just hate all men?"

He was twisting her words. "No, I do not hate all men. And I don't claim to be the expert, but *some* guys may seem really sweet and sort of charming at first, they may even be reasonably good-looking, but they're just reeling girls in to right where they want 'em."

"That sounds so dangerous," he said, pretending to be captivated.

"I know. And sweet girls like Sophie would never see it coming."

"But if I may, for the sake of argument, say you keep thinking every guy is a villain, then your *friend* might not get to know a really great guy even if he's sitting right across the table from her?"

She rolled her eyes. "Oh, right because you're the shining example of a perfect gentleman." She said it sarcastically but then racked her brain to find something to base it on.

"No. But I'm not the bad guy, either."

He flashed her a smile, and all the jitters came rushing back. She pulled her lips in as hard as possible to try to hold back a smile. She wanted so badly not to like him, and yet all she wanted to do was scoot closer. Still fighting the smile, she said very matter-of-factly, "That's exactly something the bad guy would say."

He laughed. "You've got it all figured out, kid."

"Kid? Is that what you think I am? Don't tell me I have to Google you, too. Hate to disappoint you, old man, but I'm no longer a minor as of six months ago, so if that puts me out of your target range, then we can just get the bill."

"Thanks for looking out. The age isn't ideal, but thanks to your maturity level, you still seem far from legal."

She kicked him under the table, but he just laughed.

"You're welcome to get me something good to make up for that comment when my next birthday rolls around."

"I don't know," he said. "Six months is pretty far away. I doubt we'll still be hanging out then."

She shook her head smiling and took a sip of her margarita. Then she glanced at her watch and was once again shocked at how fast time flew. "Oh my god, we've been here for two hours! We have to get to the theater or you'll miss the previews." He paid the bill, and they grabbed their things and hurried to the theater. He'd already bought their tickets online, so they bypassed the line and went straight to the theater where the movie was playing. The lights were already down so he reached back to take her hand as he led her up the stairs.

"How are we going to find Sophie and the future feature of *To Catch a Predator*?" James asked.

Brooke had completely forgotten why she had wanted to go to the movies in the first place. With her hand in his, she couldn't think of anything to worry about. "You know, maybe you're right. Maybe he'll turn out to be an okay guy." As soon as she heard herself, she decided it was best to let go. She was clearly better off not touching him.

She followed closely behind as they turned and carefully maneuvered down an aisle in the dark. Just as they were nearing two empty seats, her platform shoe caught on some-one's foot and suddenly nothing was about to stop her from landing on some stranger's lap or a certain-to-be sticky floor. She threw her weight to avoid the lap option, reached down for the closest thing to stabilize herself with, and found her hand on the head of a person just below her.

It happened to be a girl who had just lifted a bottle of Dr. Pepper to her mouth, and as Brooke wiggled the brown head of hair back and forth to find her own balance, whoever it was doused herself in soda. Brooke regained her balance, stood up straight again, and shuffled as quickly as possible away from the scene of the crime. She reached the empty seat, sank down next to James, and tried to forget that she basically just gave some random girl an aggressive noogie.

"Did you just fall?"

"Me? No. That was… that wasn't me."

She hated what a klutz she was around him. It reminded her how nervous he could make her, and those jitters didn't settle once the movie started like she'd hoped. She could barely pay attention. All she could think about was where to put her hands— in her lap, on the arm rest, on the other arm rest—and whether to cross her legs toward him or away from him or put them up on the seat.

When the movie was over, she and James filed out of the theater with the rest of the crowd.

"Brooke, hi!"

Brooke turned to see Sophie, who had already exited the theater. "Hey, Sophie! I totally forgot you were seeing this," she lied. They walked toward each other. "You remember James, right?" When they got close, Brooke noticed Sophie was wearing one of her shirts and there was a huge stain on it. "Oh my god, Sophie, my shirt. There's a huge stain! Is that soda?"

"Oh, um, actually it was y—. Never mind. Sorry."

Brooke paused for a second and remembered how James had handled Nolan trashing his condo. "Don't worry about it, actually. I'm sure it'll come out." She looked the guy standing next to Sophie up and down. He was short and skinny with dark brown hair parted down the middle.

"Hi, I'm Sophie's roommate."

"Hi, I'm Kevin."

"Kevin what?" she said, shortly.

"M-Mitchell."

"Okay, well, I'm going to be heading to our place right now, where I'll be waiting for Sophie, and expecting to see her within the hour, so…"

"Um, yeah, yeah for sure."

"I'm such a pain of a roommate. I always keep track of exactly where she is. Half an hour goes by without us talking and I'm ready to file a missing person report."

"Yeah, no, that's good," Kevin said, shifting his weight back and forth.

"And my dad's a cop."

"I thought you said he worked at a newspaper," Sophie said.

"Nope. No, I said he was *in* the newspaper. Because he's caught so many rapists. You'll get her home safely then, right Kevin Mitchell? See you soon, Sophie." She gave Kevin another glance. "I'll be up and waiting."

As they walked away, James leaned down so she could hear him. "What do you bet that poor guy just wet his pants a little?"

"What do you bet if we go on *MegansLaw.com* there's a red dot over his dorm? I'm just looking out. I'm a good friend."

"*I'm* a good friend. You're a dad with a shotgun."

She couldn't help but laugh since it was exactly what she'd just acted like.

"So," James said, "I know you said you need to get home, but do you have time for one more stop?" It could have been 3 a.m. and she would have had time for one more stop.

They walked for a few blocks, talking and enjoying the warm night air. James came to a halt under a yellow neon sign. She read it to herself. *Midnight Cowboy Modeling, Oriental Massage?* "What are we doing here?"

"You'll see," he said as he ran his finger down a list of interesting names then pushed a button next to one. *Are we at someone's apartment? What is this place? Does he actually know someone named Harry Johnson?*

A few seconds later, a man opened the door a crack and asked for the name on the reservation.

"James Cartwright."

The man stepped back and held the door open so they

could enter. It was so dark, Brooke's eyes had to adjust, but she heard a hostess tell them to follow her. Suddenly, she realized they were at a speakeasy. She'd heard of them but had never been to one before. She stayed closely behind James, and when he reached back, she took his hand instinctively. When her eyes adjusted, she looked around to see they were in a very dark, small, but really cool-looking bar.

With historic-looking crown molding, the smell of oak, and the waiters' outfits, she felt like they were back in the 1920s. The music was quiet, but the place had such a cool vibe that Brooke instantly loved it. The hostess stopped at a table that had curtains draped on either side and held out her hand to show them it was theirs. They sat down, and she placed two menus in front of them. "How did you know this was here?" Brooke asked.

"Stick with me, baby," he said. "I know people." She laughed and looked down to hide that the term of endearment made her blush. He was still as cocky as ever, but now she found his confidence made him even more attractive.

The drinks on the menu all had crazy names: Smoke + Mirrors, Carmine Swizzle, The Alamagoozlum. When the waiter came over, Brooke couldn't even look up when she ordered the Lovebird. She was quick to proclaim that she was only ordering the drink because it had tequila in it. James ordered a drink called the Joe Buck, and then they talked about the movie and took a couple guesses at whether Kevin Mitchell ran into hiding after Brooke's threat, before their drinks arrived. James took one sip then put on a serious face and went into interview mode.

"Favorite color?" he asked.

"Green."

"Favorite food?"

"Trail mix."

"That's not a food."

"Really? And all this time I've been eating it."

"Moving on. Favorite sport?"

"Uh, next question."

"Okay. Biggest fear?"

"Oh, we're getting deep now? Okay, fine, I'll play, but no judgment. And we have to close these." She nodded at the curtains. "This is getting too personal."

"Fine by me," he said as he reached over and pulled the curtains closed.

She took a deep breath and paused for a moment. "I have two."

"They are?"

"Storms drains and clowns."

"Come again?"

"Storm drains and clowns," she repeated more slowly. "I guess I'm not so much afraid of storm drains as I just hate them."

"I'm going to have to get the backstory on that one."

She cleared her throat. "It was Halloween 2001. I was out trick-or-treating all night and we were just leaving the last house to head home and count up our goods. I was so excited about all my candy that I started running and I tripped."

"No, not you!" he interjected.

She raised her eyebrows. "Do you want to hear the story?" He clasped his hands in his lap to show he was ready to listen again. "I tripped, and my entire bag spilled down a storm drain. My mom tried to comfort me, but she kept laughing because when I tripped, I ripped my costume, and to her, it was hilarious. She made my sister share her bag, but she would only give me the Dum Dums from the cheap houses. Nobody likes the Dum Dums; they're gone in like three licks."

"This is the saddest story I've ever heard. On many levels."

"I know!" She chose to ignore that he was making fun of her. "And then I saw the movie *It* and became less concerned about what goes down storm drains and more afraid of what comes up and grabs your ankle as you walk by."

"For those of us who haven't seen the movie, that would be…"

"Clowns."

"Ah, I see. Have you ever had a run-in with an evil clown?"

"Unfortunately, yes."

"I'll need the story on that, as well. Does it involve you falling down?"

"Unfortunately, yes again. This time with a concussion."

"I can't wait."

"When I was in second grade, my mom was trying to become head of this city beautification committee in our town. They handled flower-planting in public places, which doesn't sound exciting, but the position was highly sought after by many. The woman who currently held the position had a son my age who was in my class, so my mom decided to take advantage of that and talked her into getting us kids together. The woman decided on this place back home, called Ice Cream Mountain." James started to say something, but she cut him off first. "Don't mock the name—it was amazing. Not that I would know actually since I couldn't—never mind. Anyway, as we were walking toward the car a group of punk teenagers suddenly came running through the parking lot wearing scary clown masks and yelling. It was some kind of prank, but I guess I just panicked. I dropped everything and started screaming and sprinting through the parking lot. I came to a few seconds later after getting hit by a car."

"You got hit by a car?" he exclaimed.

"Okay, technically I hit the car, since it was parked and no one was inside, but I was trying to graze right over that. When I came to, I looked up and saw my mom staring at me like *what just happened*, and the woman seemed kind of judgmental about it."

"I stand corrected. *This* is the saddest story I've ever heard."

"That stupid boy told my whole class I was possessed and, needless to say, my poor mom didn't even get asked back for the committee."

She started laughed just watching him laugh. She couldn't believe she was telling him all these embarrassing stories, but he was so easy to talk to; everything just sort of spilled out.

"So what's your biggest fear?" she asked.

"Well, I was going to go with failure or disappointment, but yours were so humiliating that I want to try and make you feel better."

"Thanks," she said sarcastically.

"Truth?" he said. "I hate cats. I'm sort of afraid of cats."

"Like, wild cats?"

"Domestic. Lions and cheetahs don't attack the back of your neck when you're just sitting on the couch trying to watch some TV. And their eyes, they just stare at you, watching and waiting to make their move."

"I have just the spot for you, if you're ever in need of a pedicure," Brooke said. "A little place that has plastic cats everywhere. They just watch you and wave one paw back and forth. It's called Funny Nails, if you ever want to go."

"That's not funny. Why would they have those? Why would you go there? Why would they call it Funny Nails?"

Brooke pulled the candle on the table toward her and leaned over it. "Legend has it, after they close at night, the cats come alive and roam the city of Austin, just waving one paw back and forth as they watch you sleep, waiting for your neck to be just exposed enough to pounce."

Brooke couldn't hold in her laughter anymore. The thought of this tough guy being afraid of a house cat was hilarious.

She finally stopped laughing when his eyes met hers as she took the last sip of her drink. Was he going to kiss her? She suddenly got overwhelmingly nervous but at the same time wanted him to so badly. She couldn't breathe. She couldn't think. This was it.

"You ready to go?" he said. "It's already midnight."

"No. I mean, yeah! Yeah, let's… I should get back. Class tomorrow. And you know, midterms are coming up so—" She got up after him and followed him out.

They walked out into the warm, night air. The city lights barely brightened the night sky, and it was almost completely quiet outside. As they walked back toward the car, Brooke second-guessed everything in her head. *Did I say too much? Is my hair out of control?*

It was the clown thing, wasn't it? No, it was the cats—that was weird. And nobody looks good with candle lighting under their face—that's just scary.

He opened the car door for her and held out his hand to help her in. She took his hand and stepped up on the ledge of the car, then felt his hand close in around hers. She turned around to see what was up, and he stepped in closer. The step put her just about at his eye level, and his other hand moved to her waist. She put her hand on his shoulder to balance, and he pulled her in. She wrapped both arms around his neck as he kissed her.

Chapter 11

After Brooke's last class on Friday, she checked her phone to see if she had any messages. As she had hoped, there was a new text from James.

"I'm sure you have plans to go out tonight while I have to sit at home because of the game tomorrow, but can I talk you into going somewhere with me when you get out of class?"

Talk me into? Brooke thought. *That would be unnecessary.* She typed, "Where are we going?" and hit send.

He wrote back, "Where's the fun in telling you? Pick you up in 30." That gave Brooke just enough time to sprint back to the dorms, brush her teeth, put on just enough makeup to look like she wasn't wearing any, tousle her hair to look effortlessly perfect, spritz herself with perfume, and run back downstairs.

She timed it perfectly. He pulled up, and she hopped in the car. "Hey, great timing. I just got here from campus. I just put my books upstairs and came right back down. That's all."

She saw him glance at her with a smirk, "Yeah, I bet." He clearly knew that wasn't the case but chose not to call her on it.

"So where are we going?"

"You'll see."

She glanced down at his iPhone sitting in his cup holder, still open to the page of recent calls. She recognized her series of digits unnamed. "Hey, you don't have my number saved?"

"Yeah, you know, my phonebook is getting pretty full," he said with a smile. "I don't know if I can squeeze you in. I mean, maybe under, like, Brooke number four?"

She decided to play along. "I'm really not a number four kind of girl. If space is limited, why don't you take out one of the contacts less important than me? Do you really need your mom in there?"

"All right, I'll put you in under 'Mom.' Don't be surprised when you get texts asking for money."

"And don't let your friends think it's weird when Mom gets drunk and sends flirty texts in the middle of the night."

"If you only knew my mom."

Brooke laughed out loud at his joke. It did bug her for some reason that he hadn't bothered to save her in his phone, but she tried not to dwell on it.

They drove for about forty minutes chatting the whole way about absolutely nothing and still not having a beat of silence between them. She hadn't figured out yet how she could be all nerves with him and still want to be around him and tell him everything. It was a weird combination she wasn't quite able to explain. "Did we just pass a sign that said Georgetown city limits? Where are we going?"

James just smiled as he pulled off the highway. He drove a little farther, then slowed the car and turned into a parking lot of what seemed to be just a normal shopping center. There was a market, a dry cleaner's, and a Starbucks. Where was he going with this?

He parked the car, jumped out, and walked around to her side by the time she'd opened her door. He put his arm over her shoulder when she crawled out and used his hand to cover her eyes. "What are you doing?" she asked.

"Just walk."

"Do you *want* me to trip?" she said as he led her through the parking lot.

"I've got you," he reassured her. "But you might be right. I don't want you taking us both down. I've got to play tomorrow." She elbowed him in the stomach for the comment, and he took his hand down from over her eyes. She shook her head and blinked to adjust her vision. "You think you're the only one with an Ice Cream Mountain?" She looked directly in front of her. There it was.

She looped her arm through his and playfully squeezed his arm. "Did you have to cover my eyes?"

"I'm into theatrics." She couldn't believe the guy. "Now don't worry; I already made a phone call and had the parking lot checked. No circus folk here." She couldn't wipe the smile off her face if someone paid her to. As they headed inside, a nagging voice in the back of her head told her not to do it, not to get any ice cream, but the blissfully happy part of her brain shut it up.

The walked and talked with their ice creams in hand until the sun began to go down. As much as Brooke didn't want their little excursion to end, they eventually headed to the car and started driving back toward Austin. After twenty minutes, she'd broken into a complete sweat and sank lower and lower in her seat, turning and twisting but unable to find comfort in any position. James kept glancing over at her, but she'd just smile and keep talking. Every time the noise would start up, she'd talk really loudly to try to cover it, hoping it'd be enough.

When there was no hiding it anymore, she nervously said, "I guess I'm still hungry," hoping it would explain the horrible noise coming from her stomach.

He looked at her questionably and said, "Do you want to stop and grab something to eat?"

"No!" she screamed, "No, no, no, I'm good. Um, I'm on a diet. Ice cream is okay, but anything else is, um, I can't have it, so no, don't stop!" He started slowing at a signal, and she almost had a panic attack. "Go, go, go, it's still yellow!"

"It's definitely red. You sure you're okay?"

"What? Yeah, I'm great," she said, wiping sweat from her forehead. "It was just yellow."

They finally pulled back up to the dorms, and she thanked him again before jumping out of the car and sprinting for her room. She spent the rest of the night curled up in a ball on the floor next to the bathroom. There was no way he could have known she was severly lactose intolerant. *Still worth it*, she thought as she lay on the floor hugging her knees in agony. *Totally worth it.*

Saturday was a big game against TCU, and the girls decided to attend their first football game of the season. They all dressed in their orange school shirts and jean shorts, and Brooke got so into the school spirit that she even tied an orange ribbon in her ponytail. It definitely wasn't her usual style, but she sort of didn't hate it either. They mixed a few drinks in water bottles before heading to the tailgate. They found Kyle, Bryan, Garrett, and a bunch of other people in the parking lot posted up at Bryan's truck and started drinking with them. Brooke hadn't had the opportunity to fill the girls in on her last two dates with James yet, so the second they were set with drinks, she spilled everything.

Stella: "Wait, you told him what?!"

Kate: "I can't believe you told him about your weird clowns phobia."

Brooke: "What? It's not that weird. I can't be the only one who has a problem with them."

Stella: "Maybe the only one who would admit to it."

Darci: "Hey, I actually think clowns are kind of a turn-on."

Brooke: "I don't even want to touch that issue."

Darci: "Though, I am surprised he actually kissed you after that confession. But then the ice cream? He has to think you mentally capped off at the age of seven."

Brooke: "That would explain why I hang out with you guys."

She heard Garrett's voice from behind her suddenly. "Yeah, Brooke, I gotta tell you, that's pretty embarrassing." She turned to see him with Bryan and Kyle refilling their red cups at the keg.

"Garrett, your face is embarrassing," she said, considering for a moment that she may have the maturity of a seven-year-old after all. Getting excited over ice cream probably didn't exactly scream sexy. She made a mental note to come up with a plan to make up for that.

Garrett: "You guys know Omega Chi is throwing a huge Halloween party, right? You want to go?"

Brooke: "Sure, why not."

Garrett: "Cool, we'll add you to a list."

Stella: "We don't need to be on a list. It's a frat house."

Darci: "You guys let anything with boobs in."

Garrett: "Fine, you two are good. Kate and Brooke, we'll add you to the list."

Brooke: "Screw you!"

Kate: "Hey!"

Garrett looked at his phone, "Hey, it's almost kick-off. Let's get in there." They all went into the stadium together and walked around trying to find the student section. They heard cheering, so Darci hopped up on a bench to look over the wall. She was already so drunk that Brooke was surprised she could even get up there without falling.

"Hey, I see seats!" Darci yelled, and they all looked in her direction just in time to see her legs go straight up and over the wall. Brooke heard a shriek from the other side, and they ran around the side to see Darci giving two thumbs-up.

"I'm okay!" she yelled. "Found the student section." She struggled to get up, and Brooke saw Sophie underneath her.

"I broke her fall," Sophie said weakly. That poor girl was just always in the wrong place at the wrong time. Brooke helped Sophie up, and then they all filed in and turned to face to game. Brooke didn't take her eyes off the field for a second.

"Damn, Brooke, you're really into it," Kyle said. "I thought you hated football."

"No way, who told you that?" Something happened on the field, and she started clapping her hands and yelled, "Yeah, get 'em! Woo!"

"No, that was bad for us," Kyle said. She noticed the other side cheering.

"Dammit. Well, I don't get it, but I don't hate it either." She ignored everyone making glances and smirks at each other.

After the game, they went to a popular sports bar on Guadalupe Street called The Local Pub and Patio to celebrate the victory. Brooke looked down at her phone to see she had a new text message from James.

"You gave me your bad luck!"

"What are you talking about? You guys won!"

"Doc says I got a concussion."

"No way! I saw that last hit you took. That guy wasn't exactly the minivan I took on, but nonetheless pretty sizable."

"What are you doing?"

"Just at Local. Come!"

"No can do. I've got to lie low tonight and try to keep from falling asleep. Want to keep an injured man company? I have movies…"

"Oh sure, I can be your nurse. Be right over."

Brooke looked around, trying to find her friends. When she couldn't spot them easily, she decided to send a mass text letting them know where she'd gone. She hopped in a cab, got to James's place, and smiled when he opened the door with a big, pathetic frown. She laughed and reached up to kissed him.

"So what are my movie choices?" She knelt down to see the DVD selection and gasped. "You have SORRY! I love this game."

"Of course I have SORRY! Best game ever," he replied, only half kidding. "My mom sent it in a package a year ago, but I haven't exactly seen an opportunity for board games come up yet."

"Until now. Movies will just put you to sleep, and we can't have that." She set it up, and he sat at the table across from her.

"You remember the rules?" he asked.

"Duh," she said.

"Good, because I don't tolerate cheating in this house."

"I've never cheated in my life. Can you say the same?"

"Actually I can."

In that moment, they weren't talking about the game. They each took a few turns, and then Brooke heard her phone going off in her purse. She pulled her phone out to see Stella had replied to the mass text, "You left?"

Brooke typed back, "Yeah, I'm at James's place."

Kate: "Whatcha doooooing?"

Brooke: "Playing SORRY!"

Stella: "The board game?"

Darci: "I'm SORRY, you're doing what?"

Brooke: "Yes, the board game."

Kate: "Fun!"

Darci: "Oh my god, does he think he's going to get community service hours for hanging out with you?"

Brooke: "Bite me!"

Darci: "At least tell me you took that ribbon off your head."

Brooke: "Shit…"

Stella: "Take the ribbon off!"

Kate: "Don't listen. It looks cute."

Darci: "Cute on a clown-fearing, ice cream-eating, board game-playing seven-year-old!"

Brooke: "I don't want cute! And Darci, I'm about to smack you!"

Stella: "JUST TAKE IT OFF!"

"Your move," James said.

"What? Oh." She thought for a second, then tucked her phone back in her purse. "Um, can I suggest a rule change?"

"I'll consider it. Go ahead."

"Every time you pull a SORRY! card, the other person has to take something off." His face suddenly lit up like it was Christmas.

"*Strip* SORRY?"

"Are you in?"

"Oh, I'm in!"

Brooke pulled a card first. It was a two.

Then he pulled a card. "Well, look here. SORRY!" he said with a huge smile. "No, I'm not. Any regrets about your rule change?"

Brooke teased like she was going to take off her shirt, then her hand continued up until she found the end of her ribbon. She pulled as it untied, and she set it in the middle of the board. "Nope."

"That doesn't count!"

"It's something."

They pulled a few more cards until she flipped over a SORRY! card.

"You know what to do," she said to him with a smile. He took off his shirt and threw it into the living room.

Another few passed before he pulled the next SORRY! card, and she followed suit, throwing her shirt next to his, revealing an orange bra, the same color as her shirt.

They continued to take turns back and forth. The longer they went before the next card, the more the tension built. She was so unbelievably attracted to him, it was taking all her strength to just stay in her chair. He pulled a card, and she knew instantly what it was by the way his eyes widened and a smile formed on his face before he turned the card toward her.

She stood up, slid her jean shorts off, and walked over to the pile in the living room. She dropped them on their shirts and kept walking.

"Hey, where are you going? The game's not over!"

"I want to play something else." And with that, she turned and walked into his bedroom, mentally high-fiving herself for turning things around. Within seconds, he was standing in the doorway.

Chapter 12

The next morning, Brooke woke up to see she was alone in James's room with a blanket laid on top of her. She stood up and walked out into the living room, where she picked up her shorts and put them on. As she pulled her shirt over her head, she heard him say, "G'morning."

"Oh, hi." He was sitting in the kitchen reading a text-book.

"You know, you're not a very good up-all-nighter buddy. You're not supposed to sleep."

She gave a nervous laugh. "Do you have any coffee?"

"Yeah, it's right there." He pointed to a pot on the counter.

"Thanks." She didn't really know what to say. She hadn't considered that he might be one of those guys who could lose interest once the chase was over. "So, you think you could give me a ride back to the dorms? I should probably do some studying too."

"Come here," he said. As she walked over, he looked up at her to kiss him, so she did.

"Hm, I had a feeling," he mused.

"A feeling that what?"

"That you might just throw me away after you got what you wanted. And while I'm feeling very sensitive and a little used right now, I was hoping you might at least want to grab some breakfast with me, before I write this all down in my diary."

She tried to keep from smiling. "I don't know. Breakfast, then you're going to want to meet my parents, and the next thing I know, we're at IKEA debating if the dog should be allowed on the couch. But I guess a girl's got to eat…"

"Yes you do," he said, standing up to slip his shoes on. "We're going to get you a big glass of milk, maybe a bowl of yogurt, order some extra butter for the table and everything. That's okay, right?"

Her eyes widened when she figured out what he was doing, and she felt her face turning red. But when she saw how hard he was fighting back laughter, she couldn't help but bury her face in her hands and start laughing too. She realized her moment of having the upper hand was short-lived and now over, but she didn't care. She shook her head, refusing to comment, then walked with him toward the front door wondering why was it so impossible for her to be cool around him for more than a second.

They drove over to a restaurant called Stubb's and parked the car. Brooke could hear the music before they even opened the door. She thought it was kind of loud for a breakfast place, but when she opened the door, she couldn't even believe her eyes. There was an entire band and a man singing, and everyone clapping their hands to the music.

"What," James said, "you've never been to a gospel brunch before?"

Brooke just shook her head with wide eyes. "Welcome to the South!"

A hostess showed them to their table, and the next thing Brooke knew, she was clapping her hands with the rest of the crowd. They spent half their time eating and the other half out of their seats dancing around like fools.

By the time they'd finished, she knew she was head-over-heels hooked.

She couldn't get enough of him. When she wasn't with him, she was thinking about him. Every time her phone made a noise, she ran to read his texts like they were would disappear if she wasn't quick enough. Text conversations would go back and forth until they could speak on the phone or meet up and would start up again the second they parted.

During midterms, she convinced him to study in the library with her, but only minutes in, she realized it was the worst possible idea. She couldn't even come close to focusing next to him. She must have read the same line in her textbook thirty times and still didn't register what it said. His leg would intentionally graze hers, and then she'd do it back. She'd brush her arm against his, and he'd nudge her. Once he put his hand on her leg, it was all over. Self-control no longer existed. Suddenly she remembered something Sophie had told her in passing—something about a place people snuck off to in the library.

She looked around then wrote on her notebook, "6th floor, NW corner," then tilted it toward him for a few seconds. She closed her notebook, slipped it in her bag, picked up her stuff, and glanced back at him as she walked away from the table.

The entire section was dark, and there wasn't a single person in sight. She started wandering through the aisles when she realized she had no idea which direction northwest was. But then she turned another corner and found James looking for her.

After midterms were over, the girls turned all of their focus to Halloween. They realized they were all fanatical when it came to the holiday, so they wanted to go all out with their costumes for the Omega Chi party. They went to a Hustler Hollywood store where they knew there'd be a Halloween section and ended up spending two hours there. Some of it was spent trying on costumes, but the rest of the time they mostly ran around, hitting each other with whips and laughing at things they couldn't figure out. Eventually, they all walked out with their costumes in bags, with the exception of Darci, who opted to spend her money on a few adult toys instead.

The following night they got ready together in Kate and Darci's room surrounded by their usual chaos of loud music, makeup, and wires stretched in every direction.

Kate decided to go as a sexy nurse in a white minidress with a red cross on it and a matching hat. Stella was a sexy ladybug in a two-piece red and black costume with antennas on springs that wiggled around. Brooke was a sexy NASCAR driver with a red, black, and white long-sleeved, checkered shorts jumpsuit that zipped up the front and aviator sunglasses. And Darci was a...

"Darci, what *are* you?" Brooke asked as she tried to figure out the strips of black leather that covered only the essentials.

"I don't know. But if this piece of tape goes, it all goes."

Once again the frat house blew them away with the decorations: cobwebs, skeletons, strobe lights, the works. They didn't see Kyle, Bryan, or Garrett at the house—not that they could recognize anybody—but there was no shortage of Jell-O shooters, beer bongs, and even an ice sculpture they could take shots off of.

They stood at the edge of the courtyard, taking it all in and knowing they were looking good, when suddenly they all got hit with a cold shower of beer from above. They looked up to see Maddie and three other Kappa Phis standing directly above them on the second-story balcony, each holding an empty red plastic cup dripping with beer

"Whoops!" Maddie called down with her horrible, annoying laugh.

The girls took a second to wipe their faces and shake their hands off before Darci yelled up to them. "Awesome," she taunted, "now we smell like beer. You just made the guys here want us *more*." She licked her fingers as Brooke wrung out her hair, Stella wiped the eyeliner out from under her eyes, and Kate squeezed the beer from her dress.

"By the way, wrong costume, guys!" Brooke called up. "The Average Joes and White Trash Hoes is *next* month!"

Maddie and her friends had no comebacks, so they just walked away pretending they'd had the last laugh.

"Bathroom?" Kate said. They all agreed and filed into the tiny frat house bathroom. It was disgusting. The toilet had a layer of green film covering every inch of it, there was no form of paper or tissue anywhere, and it smelled horrible. Darci pulled out an emergency roll of tape from her clutch, and the girls started taping her back up. In a mess of arms and elbows, they took turns trying to rinse out their hair. They smiled big and snapped photos on Darci's phone to document the moment, emerging with desperation when they couldn't take being in the bathroom anymore.

They all agreed the Kappa Phis' attempt was weak but still totally worthy of retaliation. As they were walking back down the hallway, Brooke paused in front of Maddie's Omega Chi Sweetheart picture hanging on the wall. "Darci, get a photo of this too," Brooke said. She did, and then they all went into the pool table room and took a Longhorn shot together, limiting themselves to just one of those.

As the night wore on, Brooke did her best to dodge Stan, but when there was an inevitable run-in, she didn't even let it get to her. She still hated him for telling people she'd slept with him, but she was too happy these days to let anyone get to her.

"So are you coming up to my room later, or are we going back to yours again?" he said loudly after finally cornering her.

"She's not interested, Stan," Stella jumped in. "She's taken." He looked around seeing who could hear, then stepped in closer to Brooke and spoke more quietly.

"Yeah, I know who you're talking about, and that's a joke. Give it a week, sweetie. I guarantee it'll be done and you'll come crawling back to me."

"Stan," Brooke said calmly, "if I wanted to get herpes, I'd prefer to make out with that frat house toilet. It's cleaner." He was too stupid to be offended by the comment.

"Whatever, babe." His voice returned to an obnoxious volume. "I know you can't wait to get back in the sack with me." She decided to let it go and walk away. She turned around and saw Nolan in the doorway.

"Hey, Brooke. Hi, Stella."

"Um, I'm going to go get a drink," Stella said as she hurriedly headed off to the bar.

"What was all that about?" Nolan nodded his head toward Stan.

"Nothing at all." She just waved her hand like it would clear the air, not even wanting to validate it with an answer. "Hey, did you know Maddie back in Dallas?" she asked, trying to change the subject. Clearly the girl was more ruthless than Brooke had anticipated, so it was worth finding out a little more.

He laughed. "Oh yeah, she's a real piece of work. Pretended like she didn't recognize me here until she saw me hanging with James. Next thing you know, she wants to be best friends. She's been into him since our freshman year."

The news caught Brooke off guard. *Had they dated? Was it just a one-sided crush? Did Maddie know she was with James?* She had more questions for Nolan but a few of his frat brothers called him away before she could collect her thoughts. Stella rejoined her.

"Where'd Darci go?" Stella asked.

"She probably found a guy and is back at the dorms," Brooke said.

"Yeah, good point. I only gave that costume until midnight anyway," Stella said.

"A true Cinderella story. What a fantasy."

"Speaking of fantasies," Stella said, looking toward a handsome guy in a pirate costume, "Polly wanna cracker."

"Is that a white joke?"

"I didn't intend for it to be."

"Just go get him."

Brooke realized Kate was already gone too. Clearly no one was following the check-in-before-leaving rule. She decided to head back to the dorms. It was pretty late anyway.

When Brooke opened the door to her room, it was pitch black, somehow darker than usual. She frantically felt around for the light switch as she carefully stepped farther in. She finally found it, feeling relieved, but right as she flipped the light on, two monstrous clowns jumped out from either side of her roared. She screamed at the top of her lungs and threw everything she was holding. She continued screaming as she ran out the door, into a wall, and then all the way down the hallway.

Busting into Darci's room, she heard Darci yell, "Oh shit!" and suddenly with a loud thud, another clown flew out at her from above and dropped at her feet. She screamed again and ran backward for the door. She was halfway out when she heard, "What the fuck, Darci? Brooke, Brooke, chill out. It's me. It's Garrett!"

Brooke suddenly heard familiar laughter coming from the hallway. She leaned against a wall and slid to the floor to catch her breath as Bryan and Kyle came into the room laughing hysterically, taking off their wigs. Then she looked behind her, saw Garrett, and looked up to see Darci in her bunk bed with her sheet pulled up to her chin and some white paint smeared on her face.

"Hey, there you are, man," Bryan said to Garrett. "You missed it."

"You idiots! I hate you!" Brooke yelled. "Hate, hate, hate you! And Darci, I am so disappointed. Garrett? Really?"

"Oh no, I know," Darci said. "I'm just as disappointed in myself."

"Hey!" Garrett said, rubbing the elbow he'd landed on to make her feel guilty.

"Don't act surprised," Darci said.

"Whatever. Welcome to the tally wall." Garrett held up a hand to high-five Brooke, but she just looked at him with disgust until he put it down.

"Your Bozo nose is bleeding," Brooke said looking even more repulsed by him.

"Darci!" he yelled up towards her with a whiney voice.

"Put your head back," she said, "or tip it forward. I know these things. I used to date a doctor. Well, a pre-med major. Actually, I didn't get his name."

"Oh my god, just go bleed somewhere else, Garrett! Bryan, go fix your stupid roommate. Kyle, you too, out! I hate all of you!" Brooke yelled as she stomped her foot. " I hope you sleep well tonight, boys because after this, you'll never see your payback coming!"

Bryan leaned his hands on his knees as if he needed to hold himself up. "I don't even care. That was so worth it." They kept laughing as they walked out the door, while Garrett followed with one hand holding his nose and the other stretched out to guide him.

Brooke was still catching her breath as she got up off the

floor. "I'm too hyped up to go to sleep. Want to go back to the frat house and find Kate and Stella?"

"Nah, I just had Garrett in my bed. I'm hoping if I fall asleep fast enough, I'll just think it was just a bad dream."

"Fair enough."

Brooke walked back to her dorm room and collected her things that were now strewn around the room. She picked up her phone and saw a new text from James.

"How was your night?"

She typed, "Good. Until I fell victim to a calculated clown ambush," and hit send.

"Sounds terrible. What was your costume again?"

"NASCAR driver. I'm getting into this whole Southern thing after all."

"Having trouble picturing. Can I get a visual?"

She turned her phone around, snapped a picture, and sent it to him. He wrote back.

"Hop in a cab. Meet me at my place."

"I actually haven't had anything to drink in a few hours, so I can drive. Plus any alcohol I would have left was just scared out of me."

"You wet your pants?"

"No! Shut up! See you in 20."

James's coach had called an early meeting for the Sunday morning following Halloween, most likely in an effort to prevent his whole team from getting trashed. Brooke kissed him goodbye, and they both got into their cars and drove off.

Brooke picked up her phone and called Darci.

"Hey! I thought I'd wake you up from that nightmare you were having." It took Darci a minute to figure out what was going on.

"Ohhh thank god, it was just a dream."

"No it wasn't. You got yourself immortalized on Garrett's wall. I'm coming to get you. Is Kate back?"

"Nope!"

"We really need to come up with a better system before one of you gets lost." Brooke automatically ruled herself out since clearly she was the responsible one. "Let's pick up her and Stella from Omega Chi and grab breakfast. I'm starving."

"Okay, I'm getting up."

Brooke pulled up to their building and was surprised to see Kate walking out with Darci. They hopped in the car and Darci said, "Look who I caught sneaking out of the boys' room."

"Oh no, not you too, Kate!"

"Please. When Darci told me what she did, I threw up in the hall. You texted Stella, right?"

"Yeah, she said she'd be right out." As they slowly turned the corner onto frat row, Brooke took notice of something happening in one of the back windows of the Omega Chi house. "What the…"

Kate saw it too. "Is that…?"

"Stella!" Darci yelled.

Just as Stella spotted them, she lost her balance and fell out of the window and into the bushes. She got up, ran quickly and crookedly toward the car, and threw herself over the side.

"Drive!" she yelled.

They looked back toward the window to see Nolan's head pop up.

"Stella!" he yelled. "Stellaaaaaaa!"

Kate and Darci turned to her and started hollering at Stella as Brooke turned onto the main road.

"What happened to the pirate?" Brooke asked.

"He had a wench," she answered bitterly.

"So the next best thing, huh?"

"My Humps" by The Black Eyed Peas came on the radio, and they all sang at the tops of their lungs, completely embracing the spectacle they must have been in their messed-up costumes. Brooke couldn't stop thinking about how happy she was in that moment. She loved her friends and their messy lives, and she couldn't help but think how lucky she was to have met James.

They sat down at their usual booth at Kerby Lane.

Brooke: "Okay, so Stella, let me catch you up. Darci was caught red-handed last night in bed with Garrett, and Kate was caught this morning sneaking out of the culprit's room, which, as you know, he shares with two others. So the question remains… who done it? Or *her*, in this case. Place your bets."

The girls all set their clutches on the table and opened them up.

Darci: "I've got one matchbook and the phone number of a guy named David, on Kyle."

Stella: "I've got a coupon card to Le Girls Gentlemen's Club—two more punches and you get a free lap dance— and I say Garrett doubled-timed."

Brooke: "I've got… whoa, where did I get a joint?"

Stella: "Yeah, that happened to me last week. It's good stuff."

Brooke: "Well I've got a joint and two pieces of Trident on Bryan. I've seen the way he stares at her."

Stella: "So, Kate, go ahead."

Kate: "Bryan."

Kate smiled bashfully as they all hollered, and Brooke pulled the pile of loot to her side of the table, tossing the joint to Stella.

Kate: "Judge if you want, but he's actually very sweet."

Brooke: "Kate's got a boyfriend, Kate's got a boyfriend."

Kate: "No! Kate doesn't have a boyfriend, but you do, Brooke."

Stella: "Seriously. You're at James's like every single night these days."

Darci: "And you go on actual dates, which is weird."

Kate: "And when you're not with him, you're on the phone or texting. You are one step away from meshing your faces together in one of those what- would-your-baby-look-like?" sites.

Brooke: "Already did. Practically identical to one of the Jolie-Pitt kids."

Darci: "The black one or the Asian one?"

Kate: "Aw, I want to see. I bet it's Shiloh. He's the cutest."

Brooke: "Um, Shiloh is a girl, and oh my god, Kate, I'm kidding."

Darci: "I've got to say, I did not peg you for the relation-shipper."

Brooke: "I know, me neither. It's weird, but I'm just so stupidly happy right now, I don't even know what to do with myself."

Kate: "You are so in love."

Brooke: "I am not."

Kate: "You are, though. It's obvious. Try to talk about him without smiling."

Brooke couldn't even think of a sentence without smiling.

Stella: "Well, you need to lock that up if you want him, because he's a catch."

Chapter 13

The next morning Brooke walked into class, sat next to Nolan, and pulled out her notebook.

"Good morning, class," Professor Bornstein started. "Today we'll be focusing on theories by a psychologist named Robert Sternberg." He picked up a piece of chalk and walked over to the board. "We'll start with his development of," he read along as he wrote, "the Triangular Theory of Love." Brooke winced at the lame name as he drew a giant triangle, taking notes as he described the theory's three main elements.

"*Intimacy*," Professor Bornstein explained, "is the feelings of closeness and bonding two people have. There is a connection between them. They enjoy each other's company, they spend a great deal of time talking to each other, often sharing things that are personal, stories they don't tend to share freely. *Passion* is feelings of limerence, which is an overwhelming romantic and sexual attraction to another person. When they're together, they want to engage in, well, you understand that one. And *commitment* is the decision to remain with one another. They agree to certain rules and behaviors, and there is a shared understanding that they are in a relationship with each other. In Sternberg's opinion, all of these three elements together add up to his definition of love."

Brooke was still thinking about the lecture as she walked out of class. Love was certainly a strong word. There was no way she could be in love with James. Things were pretty great, though. All the elements did seem to be there too. Granted they hadn't exactly made a binding contract or anything about what they were, but everything else seemed crystal clear. It was confirmed even further when she checked her phone and saw a text from James.

"Hey, you. I just realized I have a favorite spot in this city and I haven't shown you yet. Wanna see it?"

She just smiled to herself and typed back. "Was that a rhetorical question? Of course I want to see it! Tonight?"

"Yeah pick you up at 6:30?"

"Sounds good!"

After her next class, Brooke stopped by Java City to pick up her paycheck. When she walked in, she saw a familiar face behind the counter. "Kyle, you work here?"

"Yeah, I do. I didn't know you did until I saw your check today."

"Speaking of which, hand that sucker over." He passed her the envelope.

"Have you recovered from the clown attack?"

"No, and I never will," she said, tucking the envelope in her purse. Then she leaned forward on the counter as an idea began to form in her head.

"It was all Bryan's idea, I swear," Kyle blurted out.

"I don't care. I blame you all equally. But you can help make it up to me." He suddenly looked worried. "What can you tell me about sneaking into the frat house after hours on weeknights?"

He gulped. She had him cornered.

Brooke's stomach flipped when she saw James leaning against his car. She wondered how this gorgeous, perfect guy could actually be waiting for her. He opened the door for her, and they pulled onto Guadalupe. When they reached Fifth Street, he parked the car and hopped out. The sun was just going down, and the buildings were already lit up. She followed him until he came to a stop. He positioned her to stand directly in front of him then pointed at the tallest building straight ahead. "What does that look like to you?"

She'd seen the building plenty of times; it was impossible to miss downtown. She stared at it for a few seconds until she saw a shape form. "An owl?" Brooke said, kind of confused.

"Yup."

"That's cool," she said, trying to figure out why he had a thing for owls.

"It's the Frost Bank Tower. It's only a couple of years old, but there's a funny story behind it. See, the head architect who designed it applied to UT, but he got rejected. He ended up going to a different school, and after he graduated and became successful, he was asked to design this building in downtown Austin. He designed it to resemble an owl, with one side facing Longhorn Stadium." He pointed directly behind him so she could see what he was talking about, "because an owl was the mascot of the school he went to after UT denied him. It's kind of a 'fuck you' to UT, but I think it's cool. My dad brought me here when it first opened."

Brooke knew nothing about architecture. She had no clue what went into designing a building or how long it took to build, or what made a building good or bad. She wasn't particularly impressed by the owl or understood the architect's motives. But she knew one thing for certain; she loved that moment.

When she turned back to face James, she knew she looked smitten. She wanted to fight it but she just couldn't anymore. Since they had met, she had been trying to stay in control, to stay ahead of it, but her defenses all came crashing down in that moment and she couldn't help but give up and give in.

Wednesday night, after the girls finished their laundry, they all went to Brooke's room to compile everything they needed for their mission. Darci texted the photo she'd taken of Maddie's portrait to Brooke, who then uploaded it into an app called Fat Booth. They were nearly in tears as Maddie's cheeks and chin inflated to make her look like she'd instantly gained 200 pounds. She emailed the photo to herself and set the size to the biggest her printer would allow. While it printed out on an 8 1⁄2 x 11-inch sheet of photo paper, the girls changed into all-black outfits so they wouldn't be easily spotted.

They drove over in Brooke's Jeep at 3 a.m., parked half a block away, and, as quietly as they could, hopped over the back wall. They found the sliding glass door, which Kyle had left unlocked for them, and quietly snuck in. They pulled Maddie's photo off the brick wall, opened the back, and replaced the picture.

Stella pulled out a bottle of superglue and squeezed out half the tube to seal it back up and the rest to stick it back onto the brick wall. Then they quickly snuck back out and ran for the car, trying to hold in their laughter.

The next day Brooke was dreading her shift at Java City. Why should she be there when she could be with James? She pulled out her phone and typed, "Are you free tonight?" and sent it to him.

He replied a few minutes later with "No plans."

She typed, "Dinner?" and hit send.

"Love to." he replied. Brooke smiled to herself and before she could reply he sent, "I have a restaurant in mind. I'll pick you up at 7."

She typed a new text to Kyle and hit send. It read, "Please, please, please, please, please, will you take my shift tonight?"

They exchanged a few more texts back and forth until she finally got him to agree, again reminding him of all the intense therapy she'd be paying for thanks to his prank.

Brooke paced the sidewalk outside the dorms, excited and nervous as usual, until James pulled up. They drove to a restaurant downtown, chatting about how their days went. James looked so handsome, she couldn't resist reaching over to put her hand in his.

"Almost forgot. Here," he said pulling his hand away and reaching behind the seat. "I thought you might want this. You left your hair ribbon thing at my place."

"Oh," she said, thinking about how she'd forgotten about it completely. "Thanks. You didn't have to bring that. It's not exactly a crucial item." She twirled it in her hands a few times before setting it in the cup holder.

"Well, at least you'll have it back in case you need it while we're crushing Ole Miss next week." She laughed at his confidence and told herself it was considerate of him to remember such a silly little thing.

The food and atmosphere at the downtown steakhouse were amazing. The wait staff was so attentive, everything felt classy and upscale, and with a display of steaks grilling right in from of them, she definitely felt like she was in Texas. Brooke was having such a great time, so she ordered a second glass of wine.

"So my parents are coming to visit this weekend," James said. She inched forward in her seat a little to be closer to him. "And I bet they'd love to meet the amazing girl you've been gushing about," she said flirtatiously.

"Hah, well actually it's a good thing you texted me today,

because I probably won't be able to see you this weekend. I'll be with them."

"Oh, right. That makes sense." Why would she think he'd introduce her to the parents? This wasn't high school where it couldn't be avoided. For no reason she could rationalize, she decided to see if he'd say more about it though.

"Not big on introducing your parents to the ladies, huh?"

"Not really, I guess."

"Do you have some traumatic story that stems from?"

"Can't say that I do."

Now she was getting curious. "They've never met any past girlfriends or anything?"

He glanced around the restaurant in a way that revealed he was obviously uncomfortable with the direction the conversation was turning. "Well, I've never had any for them to meet." That surprised her. They weren't even official, and he was already acting like the perfect boyfriend. "I just don't really plan to get serious with anyone for a couple years. Not until I'm ready to settle down and really be in a relationship and start thinking about marriage and everything, and that's a long way off. It's college. We're just having fun. I just don't see the point in making yourself only available to one person until later on in life, you know?"

Brooke went silent. No, she didn't know. The way he said it was so matter-of-factly, and yet this wasn't just any piece of information—it mattered. Her face had to show how stunned she was. What was he talking about? He wasn't going to be with only one person for years? What did that mean? She wanted to be with him. Didn't he want to be with her? Wasn't this the order of things? You meet someone, you fall for each other, and then you're just together, right? *Unless,* her mind started swirling and she felt a little light-headed, *was it all one-sided?* She started retracing everything in a new light and realized what a complete fool she had been making of herself. She'd been throwing herself at him, parading around like they were this happy couple, when she was really just one in a rotation. He wasn't giving her back her stuff; he was getting it out of his place. How many girls was he with? How many girls had he brought to this restaurant? How many girls had he shown that stupid owl building?

She had been such an idiot. He'd been giving her hints all along, and she completely looked over them. Hell, it was in practically their first conversation when they were lying by the pool. She racked her brain to remember what he'd said about not wanting a girlfriend to be one more person telling him what to do. She had just blindly overlooked that like a love-drunk moron. Everything had been on his terms—his car, his apartment. He'd never seen her dorm room or hung out on her side of town. Why would he have to when she was at his beck and call?

She realized he'd been saying her name.

"Brooke?" She looked up at him. "Are you okay?"

"Fine." The word was nearly impossible to get out.

"You look kind of pale." He pushed her water toward her, but instead she reached for her wine. She emptied the glass in three gulps and set it down so hard she was surprised it didn't break. "I'm fine. I just need some air," she said. "This place is stuffy. Are we done here?"

"Yeah, um, you want to go?" He passed the waiter his card when he walked by, then they waited in silence for him to bring it back. He signed the bill, stood up, and went around to help pull her chair out.

"I've got it," she said sharply. They walked out of the restaurant, and she made sure to get to the car before him so he wouldn't be able to open her door for her. The drive was silent with the exception of some small talk he tried to make. She wasn't listening. She was a million miles away, replaying every moment she'd ever spent with him. When he started to make a left toward his place, she snapped out of it. "No! Um, can you take me home?" He didn't say anything, but he obliged. They pulled up to the dorms, and she unbuckled.

"Wait," he said before she could get out. "I wasn't trying to hurt you; that's just how I am. I don't want a girlfriend right now." She suddenly started feeling the wine. She didn't trust herself to speak, not that she knew what to say anyway. She leaned against the car door as if she had to be as far away from him as possible.

"I still want us to be friends," he said. "I really like hanging out with you."

"I just… I don't… I'm… I need…" What she needed was to get out of there. She reached behind her and swiftly pulled on the door handle, forgetting she was leaning on the door. The door swung wide open, and she fell out of the car and onto the ground with a painful thud.

Welcome back, low self-esteem, she thought. *Haven't seen you since junior high. I'm not getting up. Maybe if I just lie here, he'll run me over when he leaves.*

No such luck. He was around the car in a second asking her if she was okay helping to pull her up.

"I'm fine!" she yelled, and he let go. Her head filled with images of him talking to cocktail waitresses or being surrounded by a bunch of football groupies. Every single insecurity she'd ever had about herself hit at once, and she hated him for it.

"This doesn't change anything, Brooke."

"No, it changes everything!" she yelled. The wine was in full swing now. "I don't want to be one on a list. I don't want to constantly be thinking you're with someone else." She couldn't believe how jealous she was. This was a new side of herself she'd never seen before.

"Who says I'm with anyone else?"

"You could be! Any time you want, and I want to reserve the right to be pissed off when that happens, because it will—we both know it will—if we're 'friends' or whatever. I don't want to just shrug my shoulders like an idiot and say, 'Yep, saw that coming,' and just carry on without you. Or worse, stick around and pretend it doesn't bug me!"

"I don't know what to tell you, Brooke. I like spending time with you, but I don't want to be anyone's boyfriend."

Anyone? She was just an "anyone." She took a few breaths, not knowing what to she was going to say next. What was she going to do, beg him to like her more? She felt light-headed again. "Then I can't do this anymore," she said quietly. "Whatever *this* is, I don't want it. I don't want to see you anymore."

"You're blowing this out of proportion." She couldn't tell if she was or wasn't, but to her it felt like the appropriate response, the only response. "So you just want nothing to do with me now?" he asked.

Inside her heart was pounding, and every conscious thought she had screamed, *No, don't let this be the end*. But instead she just looked down, then back up at him, saying nothing.

"Fine. If that's what you're choosing." He walked back to his car, leaving her standing in the street. She brushed the asphalt off her hands and untangled her purse strap. That was it. She turned around and started walking toward the dorms. *Hold it together*, she told herself. She walked into the building, took the elevator to the fifth floor, and made a right toward Darci and Kate's room.

She opened the door and, just as she'd hoped, Stella was in there too watching TV. They took one look at Brooke, and she fell apart. She collapsed on the floor and let tears start streaming down her face. She told herself it was only the wine making her cry this hard, but she knew it wasn't.

"Brooke, what happened?" Kate asked, panicked and confused.

"Should we call 9-1-1?" Darci yelled, already reaching for her phone. "Do you need medical attention? How many fingers am I holding up? I don't know how to react when people cry." Brooke shook her head and pushed Darci's hand back down, but it took a while to even catch her breath enough to answer.

"Tell us what happened," Stella begged.

Brooke: "I don't know." She took another sharp breath. "But it's over."

Kate: "You and James?"

Stella: "What? Back up, how did it get to that?"

Brooke: "I don't even remember, but he just gave me a cop-out line saying he doesn't do the whole girlfriend thing."

Saying it out loud was embarrassing. It sounded like nothing and she knew she looked ridiculous for crying, but to her it was devastating.

Darci: "Ugh, sleazy."

Brooke: "But he's not, though."

Stella: "If he says that, he is."

Brooke: "No, if he says that, it's code for *I'm* not it. I'm not what he wants."

Kate: "You said it yourself before; he's an asshole."

Brooke: "No, he's not."

Stella: "Yes, he is!"

Brooke: "Fine, but he was *my* asshole."

The girls all exchanged looks of disgust but Brooke didn't notice.

Brooke: "I thought he was, anyway. God, I'm an idiot. I've been running around like I'm in love, and suddenly it's like *psych*—it all meant nothing, you fool."

Darci: "Well one, no one says 'psych' anymore, and two, why does it have to be over? Being in a relationship isn't everything."

Brooke: "I know. But I just can't do the casual thing. Not with him. I want all in or I want nothing to do with him. Finding out he was with someone else would hurt so much more than just nipping it in the bud now. Why did I ever try to convince myself he was anything but what I thought he was?"

Stella: "Because you really liked him."

Brooke: you rea

Kate: "Cookie?" Kate held out a tray of Oreos. Brooke said no, then took one anyway.

Brooke: "What are you watching?"

Darci: "*Sex and the City*."

Stella: "Oh my god, he's Mr. Big! Fear of commitment. He's totally Mr. Big."

Kate and Darci agreed enthusiastically, like identifying him as a fictional character would solve everything.

Kate: "Carrie winds up with Mr. Big in the end, Brooke."

Brooke: "When she's like fifty!" Brooke screamed with Oreo in her mouth before collapsing back onto the floor. "Can we have a sleepover tonight?"

"Of course," Kate said just as her phone started going off. She tried to hide the smile that formed on her face when she read the text.

"Who is that?" Brooke asked, hoping it would be someone with an amazing party or great piece of gossip that would distract her from her own mess.

Stella answered for Kate. "It's Bryan. They've been texting all night." Despite the small disappointment that she'd have to go on thinking about things, Brooke was happy for Kate. But when she realized she'd never get another text from James, she lost her breath all over again.

Chapter 14

The next morning, Brooke woke up earlier than usual and went back to her room. She looked in the mirror to see her eyes were still swollen. If possible, she felt worse than the night before. Why was this hurting so bad? She had a boyfriend in high school for two years, and when they broke up, it didn't even faze her. She'd known this guy what, two months? And she felt like her entire universe had collapsed.

On her way to class, she remembered Nolan would be in there. *Oh crap, I don't want to be around him.* Too late. Nolan called her name and caught up with her, and they walked into class together without speaking. They took their seats and sat there silently for a few minutes. She unconsciously glanced at him then snapped her head back toward the front of the room when he noticed.

"Just ask," he said.

"I'm not going to ask," she said.

"Just do it. I know you're dying to."

"Nope."

"Fine then, don't ask."

She took a deep breath, already hating herself. "Did he say anything about me?"

"Yes, I heard about last night."

"So you do gossip like girls."

"You're done with the guy?"

"I'd argue it was the other way around, but the end result is the same."

"I can't believe you actually tried to *boyfriend* him." She snapped to look at him so fast it hurt her neck. "I mean, I could have told you that that was never going to happen."

So this was just common knowledge? Everyone knew but her?

"Well, why didn't you, then?" she said louder.

"I'm sorry. I just thought you knew better."

"No, you little shithole, I didn't *know better*! Who would know better? Why would I just assume a person lacks normal human emotions? I mean, if someone has some kind of love-re-pellant disease, they should be forced to wear a sign or tell some-one upfront, right? It's like… it's like *forgetting* to mention you have herpes, Nolan! Then just running around town fuckin' up lives! What kind of person does something like that?"

Nolan sat there stunned for a second, taking in the entire class staring, then cleared his throat. "First off, I do not have herpes," he announced loudly. "Second, there is zero correla-tion between a failed crush and warts on your junk for life. I don't even know how you got there. And third, you just dropped the L-bomb."

She retraced her words for a few seconds. "Okay, I did, but that's not what I meant."

"Well, you said it."

"Well, screw you. It's not what I meant, okay?"

"You're kind of scary to be around today."

"I know, sorry. I'm fine, though. I don't care."

"Yeah, it shows," he said, picking up his books and moving one desk over.

Professor Bornstein walked in, and Brooke let out a frus-trated sigh at Nolan but turned her attention to the front of the room.

He began his lecture talking about Walter Cannon Bradford's theory on the behavioral manifestations of the fight-or-flight response. She tried to take notes as he explained how the prehistoric behavior patterns still exist today when humans are put in stressful situations. Some respond with aggression, which can be interpreted as *fight*, and others respond with physical or social withdrawal, which can be interpreted as *flight*.

She did her best to put a few things down on paper, but nothing was getting through to her. She remained in a daze the rest of the class, gave up on taking notes, and just sat there obsessing over all the ways she looked like a fool.

After class she lay on her bed and stared at her phone wishing it would ring. She so badly wanted to talk to James. Maybe she misunderstood what he was saying. Maybe she was too quick to cut things off? But then she remembered her number wasn't even saved in his phone. He knew the whole time she wasn't even worth keeping around, and there she was imagining the speeches at their wedding reception.

It made her so angry, but it still didn't take away the feeling of wanting to talk to him. She convinced herself the only way to handle this was to make not contacting him just another one of her personal challenges. She knew if she thought of it that way, she could do it. She was still staring at his name in her phone when she decided to do herself a favor. She clicked on his name and phone number and hit delete. He was erased from her phone for good. If only her memory worked the same way.

Brooke spent the rest of the night just moping around, barely having the energy to get out of bed. She convinced the girls she was just tired from the week so they should go out without her, and the next day she gave the same excuse to get out of going to the game. She didn't have the energy to fight. She just wanted to withdraw.

Pathetically, all she could think about on Saturday was how James's parents were in town, what they'd be doing, and how she wasn't a second thought to him while he was all she could think about.

Her door suddenly burst open, and the girls marched in.

Darci: "Get up, Brooke!"

Stella: "We're going out."

Kate: "You're putting on a dress and some makeup, and we're getting out of here."

Brooke: "I can't, you guys. I'm tired."

Darci: "Bullshit."

Kate: "Up, up, up!" she said, clapping her hands.

They grabbed her arms and pulled her out of bed.

Brooke: "I don't feel good."

Darci: "That's why I brought this." Darci pulled her flask and four shot glasses, one of which was a double, out of her bag. She poured vodka into all four of them and handed Brooke the double.

"Of course," Brooke said. The girls threw their shots back, and Brooke followed reluctantly, coughing like she might die.

"Oh please. Now get in the shower. You smell like depression," Darci said without a trace of sympathy. "Stella's picking out a dress for you. Kate's on hair and makeup, and I've got our agenda. Austin City Limits is going on, and the place is crawling with hundreds of guys to hook up with and never have to see again."

"Oh good. Contracting mono will make me feel better," Brooke said.

I also hacked your Facebook and changed your profile picture to the happiest one I could find. It's standard procedure when I guy dumps you. Every girl does it.

Brooke reached over and tapped on the space bar of her laptop to see her Facebook page light up the screen. The image that was now her profile picture was blurry and cropped tight around her face. At least six other people had been in the original photo but now it was just her with her mouth wide and her eyes practically rolling back in her head. She looked bat-shit crazy.

"Hey, did you see James's parents at the game?" she said, changing the subject.

Darci looked at her as if the question was a personal insult then poured another shot and held it out. Brooke looked at her questioningly.

"In case going out doesn't fix everything, we're also making an effort to speak your psycho-babble-language," Darci said.

Stella cleared her throat, "We're going to be borrowing a page out of our good friend the psychologist Mr. Pablov's book."

Brooke: "It's Pavlov. What are you talking about?"

Stella: "We'll be performing a little psychology experiment called classical conditioning."

Brooke: "So you're going to ring a bell and make me drool like a dog?"

Kate: "Um, sort of, but no."

Stella: "We're going to train you to not think about James."

Darci: "Every time you say his name, you have to take a shot of vodka as punishment. Eventually your brain will learn to shut the fuck up about him."

Brooke: "Can't you just spray me with a water bottle?"

Darci: "No."

Brooke: "Can I at least have tequila?"

Darci: "No."

An hour later, Brooke blacked out.

Chapter 15

Brooke was awoken by birds chirping and opened her eyes enough to see it was light out. She didn't understand how it could be morning, but another observation had her more puzzled. Why was she *outside*? She looked down, and as her eyes focused, she saw a giant "W" under her face—with a puddle of drool. Where was she? She heard distant voices that seemed to be getting closer.

She leaned up to see she was lying on a welcome mat. There was a man's voice she didn't recognize, then a woman's, then… *Oh shit!* She popped onto her hands and knees. She was lying on James's doorstep.

How the hell did she get there? She ran down the steps as quietly as possible, barely keeping her balance, and ran to the parking lot, pulling her phone out of her purse—53 missed calls. That had to be some kind of record. She called Stella. *Pick up, pick up, pick up*, she thought.

"Brooke!"

"Oh my god, come get me! I'm at James's. Hurry, please!"

"Okay, we're coming!"

Brooke walked to the entrance of the complex so she could jump right in and get out of there as fast as possible. She paced back and forth for what felt like forever, staring at the entrance, then the apartments, then the entrance, then the apartments again. Just as she was looking in that direction, she saw a black Range Rover turn the corner. It was James's car, most likely with his parents in the car too.

She needed cover. On her left, she saw a cactus and wondered for a second if hiding behind it would work like it did in cartoons. She ruled it out immediately, spotted some bushes on the right, and debated whether she could make it there in time. In full panic mode, she ran and flung herself into the bushes and crouched as low as she could. She didn't know if it was in her imagination, but it felt like an eternity before the car exited and turned onto the main road. She stayed there a few more minutes until she finally saw the girls pull in. She jumped in the car, buckled up, and didn't say a word. They all stared silently at Brooke as Kate picked a twig out of her hair.

"I need pancakes," Brooke said. "Right now."

"So," Brooke said calmly after swallowing her first bite of pancake and setting her fork down gently on their usual table at Kerby Lane, "who would like to tell me what the fuck went down last night?"

The girls looked at each other and started to explain.

Kate: "Well, it all started off innocently enough."

Stella: "But by the time we got to the bar, you'd already had about six shots."

Darci: "You seemed fine and like you were having fun. You were dancing with everyone. Literally *everyone*."

Kate: "But then you kind of took a turn after shot number eleven."

Brooke: "I was still saying his name after ten shots?"

Stella: "No, these ones were your choice."

Kate: "You also might want to check your bank statements. You bought shots for a lot of people."

Brooke: "Um, I'm broke, so why would I buy shots for people? Oh my god, I'm so screwed. I was supposed to pay for that ticket. Ugh, at least I'm a nice drunk."

Stella: "Yeah. For a while."

Darci: "Then you flashed a guy and asked him for a hickey because you said you were trying to make some guy jealous."

Brooke gasped and clasped her hand over her neck. She pulled out her compact from her purse and screamed when she saw it was true.

Brooke: "No! I was slutty drunk?"

Stella: "Totally."

Brooke: "Tell me that's the worst of it."

Kate: "It's not."

Darci: "Then came angry drunk."

Brooke: "Oh no."

Stella: "Oh yes. You yelled at a guy who I guess didn't want to buy you a drink because he thought you'd had enough and…"

Darci: "And you went Kanye on his ass."

Brooke: "I-stole-his-thank-you-speech moment?"

Stella: "No. Eh em, and I quote, 'There's a thousand you's; there's only one of me.'"

Brooke: "Oh god. I rapped at him?"

Darci: "You did. Throwing up hand moves and all. I have a video on my phone, actually. It's amazing."

Brooke: "Well, misdirected as that was, at least I haven't lost sight of my value."

Stella: "And then you tried to punch his friend in the face because he called you crazy."

Brooke: "Oh shit."

Kate: "You missed and hit Sophie."

Brooke: "Sophie was there?"

Stella: "We called for backup."

Brooke: "And I punched her?"

Darci: "She's totally okay, though! At this point you were only a danger to yourself."

Brooke: "Tell me the story is over soon."

Kate: "And then we lost you."

Brooke: "How do you *lose* me? I am a human being!"

Stella: "Well the guys you were bitching out were actually pretty cute, so Darci and I started talking to them, you know, just to make sure they weren't mad at you or anything, and Kate took Sophie to the bathroom to make sure her face was okay, and…"

Kate: "We do know that you made a phone call at 12:48 a.m."

Brooke: "Please tell me it wasn't to James."

Darci: "Shot! Oh. Sorry, it's a habit now."

Brooke glared at her.

Stella: "No, you called Kyle."

Brooke: "Why would I call Kyle?"

Darci: "Because you wanted a ride and you knew you weren't going to get one from us. The guys came and picked you up, but we didn't know."

Brooke: "So they dropped me off on James's doorstep and drove off?"

Stella: "No, they didn't actually get out of the car. They just watched you walk up the stairs… which took thirteen whole minutes."

Brooke: "Thirteen minutes? It's like ten steps."

Darci: "They have it on video. I saw some of it. It's also pretty hilarious."

Brooke: "Nobody helped me? Not one of them got out of the car and thought to help me? What gentlemen. I could have died."

Stella: "Well you made it to the top eventually, so they left."

Kate: "We looked for you until the club closed, so we

figured you must have hopped in a cab and gone back to the dorms."

Darci: "When we saw you weren't in your room, we ran all through the building and finally ran into the guys who told us where you were."

Stella: "And while we were very disappointed in you for going there, we figured you'd at least be safe inside James's place."

Brooke: "Nope, never made it inside."

Kate: "What?"

Brooke: "I slept on a doormat."

Stella: "Wait, so he never even knew you were there?"

Kate: "That's great! You totally lucked out."

Brooke: "Yes, last night was a big success for me. Oh my god, I have officially gone off the deep end."

Darci: "Yeah, in my professional opinion as a psychologist, you might actually be crazy."

Brooke: "No! You have no professional opinion because you are not a professional anything. You are an undeclared clown-fucker who is forever banned from experimenting with my brain!"

Darci: "Ouch. Someone woke up on the wrong side of the door this morning." Darci elbowed Kate to get her to laugh, but Kate just shook her head.

Brooke's phone buzzed, and she looked down to see a text from some 212 area code she didn't recognize. Clearly she'd given her number out too. She deleted the text without reading it and rested her head on the table with a thud.

They went back to the dorms after breakfast, but as Brooke was walking back to her room to sleep off her hangover, she passed the guys' room and heard them laughing. Remembering they'd left her to fend for herself on the staircase of death, she kicked open the door and saw them watching a video on Garrett's phone.

"I'm sorry, Brooke," Bryan said. "I just can't get enough of this." They were watching the video of her trying to get up the stairs again. Suddenly all the anger she had for James, for them, for their stupid, rumor-spreading frat brother, and for every single person in the world who had ever wronged her just came bursting out. She started screaming at them for being such assholes, telling them what real gentlemen were like, and listing every grievance she had with the male gender.

She went on and on and *on*. Kyle tried to interject a few times, which only made her yell louder, so they sat back and waited for her to finish. She finally stopped to catch her breath, and Kyle raised his hand. She pointed to him and said, "What?"

"It's just that," he hesitated, "one of your boobs popped out of your shirt a few minutes ago, and we've all been staring at it ever since." She looked down. Yup, there was it was. The last piece of her dignity. She straightened her shirt out, took a deep breath, and turned to leave. Behind her, she heard Bryan say, "You got that on video right?"

"Oh yeah," Garrett confirmed as he got up, grabbed a pencil, and made another tally on his wall.

Brooke walked into her room, took her wallet out of her purse, pulled out a $5 bill, crossed the room, and dropped it in the curse-word jar. Then she picked up her pillow, put it over her face, and screamed every last penny of it out.

Chapter 16

November continued on. The weather began to change, but Brooke still couldn't shake the dark cloud over her head. She hated that she still wanted to talk to James and that it physically hurt not being able to. No matter which way she rationalized it; she was never really with him, she'd only known him for a short time, it was so easy for him to forget about her, it didn't help. He hadn't called or texted once after their conversation. Meanwhile, nothing could make her stop caring. What happened to that confident person she used to be? This wasn't her at all.

The semester was wrapping up quickly, and it was time to start studying for finals. She went to the library, but just thinking about that time she and James studied together emotionally punched her in the stomach. She tried studying in her dorm room, but her mind just kept wandering back to him. When she walked out of a building on campus and saw the football stadium, it was another punch in the stomach. When she looked downtown and saw the Frost Bank Tower, it was another one. Anytime she saw a tall guy with dark hair, her heart stopped until she realized it wasn't him. He was everywhere, and nowhere—it was unbearable.

There was no explaining how badly she wished she could just reverse the clock and undo that entire night the last time she saw him. If that conversation had never happened, would it have made a difference? Would she still be as happy as she was a few weeks ago?

So many times she wanted to pick up the phone, but she never did, and she was glad for the extra security of no longer having his number. She was too stubborn to cave, and she figured she'd made it this far, so it had to start getting easier soon. Right?

Brooke managed to make it through finals and continued to act like nothing was wrong. The girls all decided they would stay a week after school let out before heading back to their hometowns for the holidays so they could hang out without the worry of homework and classes. They mostly just vegged out, caught up on movies, and hung out at the Omega Chi house.

She and the other girls loved hearing people talk about Maddie's reaction to seeing her picture. Maddie, apparently, had a full-blown meltdown, screaming and destroying everything in her path with the exception of the picture, which, thanks to the superglue, had remained in place. They had also slipped a dozen clear plastic sheets under the frame, so even when Maddie tried to cover the image with permanent marker, as she did several times, she always returned to find it in perfect condition. She never figured it out.

Brooke had also become a master at dodging Stan, whom she hated even more for having been right about her and James ending within the week. Still, she and the girls always had a good time when they were hanging out with the Omega Chi guys, and they even brought Sophie along with them to the house for the first time. She was still really shy, so Brooke thought it was sweet when Kyle took her under his wing and introduced her around.

Brooke picked up a shift at Java City on Tuesday to make some extra cash after depleting her bank account that one awful night. She was disappointed to see Jeff was working that shift too. Luckily most of the student body had already left for winter break, so it was pretty quiet. Jeff mostly just sat on the counter, looking disheveled with his shaggy blond hair and his mouth hanging open.

Brooke sighed in annoyance and looked out the window, wishing the shift could be over already. Just as she glanced in that direction, her heart suddenly stopped. James and three of his football buddies were right outside the window. Without thinking, she dove under the counter, knocking down a stack of cups, a box of Splenda packets, and a rack full of clean funnels. She tucked herself as far into a nook as possible and stayed there for at least three minutes. All she could do was cross her fingers and hope he wouldn't come in for a coffee. She looked up to see Jeff was staring at her. "Are they gone?" she finally asked meekly.

"Uh, I guess," Jeff said.

She crawled back out and started picking up the Splenda packets off the floor. "I bet you're wondering what that was all about," she said. He shook his head, but she ignored it and went into the entire story about James, giving Jeff a play-by-play of everything that had happened between them, everywhere they'd gone, every conversation they'd had, every feeling she'd ever felt during those times, and so on. An hour and a half passed before Kyle came in and she stopped for air.

"Hey, what are you doing here?" she asked.

"Just picking up my paycheck. How's it going here?"

"Not horrible, actually. Turns out I haven't given Jeff here enough credit. He's actually a really great listener."

They both turned to look at him. Jeff was still sitting on the counter with his mouth hanging open.

"Um, Brooke," Kyle said, "that guy is stoned out of his mind. There's a good chance he hasn't registered a word you've said."

"No, that's not true." Brooke said. Not that she'd know for sure. She was pretty oblivious when it came to people being on drugs.

"Jeff, have you heard anything Brooke here has said?" Jeff slowly moved his hand to his temple in the shape of a gun and pretended to shoot himself in the head. "Oh, guess you're right. He did hear you."

"Screw you, Jeff," Brooke said bitterly. "I thought we were friends."

She finished out the rest of her shift without saying a word, then walked back to her dorm room. She logged onto her computer to check her emails and noticed a new one from Professor Bornstein.

Brooke,

I'm concerned. Your work all semester has been exceptional. You scored the highest grade in the class on the midterm, but I just graded your final exam. It didn't reflect your performance in the class at all. You earned a 64%. I don't allow retakes, but I hope you'll come to my office hours Thursday to talk. I just don't want to see you throw away a class that you should have easily earned an A in.

Best,

Professor Bornstein

A 64%? How was that possible? She loved his class and really did know the material well. Her head had been in such a fog that she wasn't surprised it wasn't her best work, but still, a 64% was shocking. On Thursday, she decided to go into his office and plead her case for an A. Once she got there, though, her mind went blank and she didn't know how to explain herself. She just sat there saying she was sorry and that she didn't know what went wrong.

"Brooke, is something going on in your life? It usually

takes something heavy to cause such a drastic change in a student."

"No. I don't know what happened. I guess I just didn't know the material as well as I thought."

"Mmm hmm. Explain Pavlov's main theories to me." Brooke explained the theories they'd covered in class without missing a detail.

"And how about Sternberg's?" She did it again, perfectly.

"And Maslow's?" Again, Brooke didn't miss a beat.

"All right, how about Plato?" *Plato*, Brooke thought. *We didn't go over any of Plato's theories. He wasn't even a psychologist. He was a philosopher, wasn't he? Was I really that out of it?*

"Okay, that was a trick question. You didn't learn anything Plato taught in my class. But not all the learning a college student does is in a classroom." She looked at him, trying to figure out his angle. He leaned back in his chair and said, "You know, he has a quote I've found relevant at least once in my life." Brooke had no idea where he was going with this.

"Okay. What is it?"

"In the words of one of the greatest minds, 'Love is a serious mental disease.'" Brooke looked down at her lap and laughed. She was going to argue that didn't apply here, but she remembered she wasn't a very good liar.

"Well, no offense to everything we learned in your class, Professor, but that's the first theory I think I'm one hundred percent on board with."

"Why don't we do this," he said. "Give me a written summary of those first three psychologists' theories, and I'll work with some numbers and see if we can't save that A of yours." She could have hugged the guy, but instead she just thanked him over and over again and left his office to work on the assignment, nearly in tears over catching the break.

Brooke and the girls had booked their flights home around the same time so they could stay together as long as possible. They said their goodbyes in the airport as if they'd never see each other again. A month was forever in college time. Promises of constant texts and lengthy phone calls were made and they laughed about a few of their favorite memories from the semester before finally parting ways. They'd only known each other a few months, but they'd already become one another's family away from home.

Brooke's flight landed, and suddenly she desperately wanted to see her parents. She got off the plane and was thrilled when she spotted them waiting for her at the baggage carousel.

"There she is!" her mom called. It felt like forever since she'd seen her mom and dad. She ran up to them and hugged them both, not letting go for longer than she ever had before.

"Woah, we've missed you too, kid," her dad said.

"Why don't you call more? You need to start calling more," her mom begged.

"Easy Mom, I've been home for three seconds." She smiled and hugged her again. "I've missed you guys."

As they pulled up to the house, Brooke thought it looked even better than the last time she saw it. Her and her siblings' handprints were still in the sidewalk in front of their house, and the dent was still in the garage from the time she was fifteen and her dad was trying to teach her to drive. It felt so good to be home.

She walked in the door and was so happy to see Sarah and Josh in the living room waiting for her. They both ran up to her and gave her a hug.

"So what classes did you take this semester? Have you decided which field you want to focus on?" Sarah asked.

"Do you get drunk all the time? Are your friends hot?" Josh interrupted.

She ignored her brother and looked at her sister. "I'll tell you everything. Where's Mr. Perfect?" Brooke really liked Sarah's boyfriend. He and Sarah were always fun together, and he meshed right in with the family seamlessly. Sarah looked over at her parents and back to Brooke. "He's working. Let's go get ready for dinner, and you can fill me in on everything Mom and Dad can't hear."

They went upstairs. Brooke's room was exactly how she'd left it, as far as she could tell, but somehow it felt entirely different. What had changed? Brooke unzipped her bag and started hanging things up in her closet while she told Sarah all about her friends, the parties, and finally about how Mr. Bornstein let her save her grade.

"Why did you bomb the final?"

"No reason. What's new with you? How do you like your new job?"

"Work is great. To be honest, I was a little unsure about taking a job here in Camarillo, but I really love the company, and Dan's happy here too."

"Speak of the devil, how is Dan? What's going on with him?"

"Oh, you know, he's probably freaking out about life right now."

"Why do you say that?"

"Because he just put *this* on my finger." Sarah held out her left hand to display a gorgeous diamond ring.

"Oh my god! Sarah, oh my god, you're engaged?! *Oh my god*, that sucker is huge! She jumped on the bed and hugged her sister so hard, Sarah choked and begged her to let go.

"When did this happen, and why didn't you call me the second he proposed!"

"It just happened a few days ago and because I wanted to tell you in person."

"Sarah, I am so happy for you! I have so many questions! Have you already set a date?"

"Yes, May 23."

"This May? Sarah, that's less than six months away!"

"I know, and there is so much to do. I'm already panicking."

"Well then it's perfect timing for me to come home. Can we please go dress shopping while I'm here?"

"Um, obviously. Want to go this weekend?"

"Obviously."

"You need to cough up the college life stories first, though. I've waited 18 years for us to get to this point."

Brooke rolled her eyes and smiled. "Well, for starters, they don't hand out beer in class like you said, so way to set a girl up for disappointment."

Sarah paused for a moment. "Wait, seriously Brooke, I was still in high school when I told you that. Why would you believe me?"

"Um, maybe because you're my big sister and up until this moment I believed everything you ever said to me to be true."

"Then I massively screwed you over in life. Massively. Okay, um, I never actually went on a date with Jonathan Taylor Thomas. Grandma didn't take you out of her will because you accidentally gave her that bloody nose, and you're not adopted. Anything else you'd like to know?"

"Are we really part Native American?"

"I got that one from Mom, but let's face it—she's a liar too."

"Fair enough. Will holding in a sneeze cause brain damage?"

"No. Your 'dainty sneeze' phase just annoyed me."

"It was junior high and all the cool girls were doing it!" she defended. "Oh, is mayonnaise really made of cow puss?"

"I actually said that? That's disgusting. But yeah, it probably is."

"Did you steal my blue and red silk dress?"

"Yes."

"I knew it! Can I have it back?"

"No, I lost it. But I am feeling good about getting that off my chest."

"This is the most honest conversation we're had yet."

"I know. Anything else you're curious about?"

Brooke thought for a moment, debating if she wanted to ask. "Can a guy change?"

"You remember how Dan used to dress, right?"

Brooked laughed. "Not just the clothes, though."

"I don't know," Sarah said. "Everyone grows up in college. Some people change, but some just get more set in their ways. Before I started dating Dan, I fell for some guy who was everything I thought I wanted, except a total ladies' man. I thought I could change him, but I ran into him in LA last month at a bar. He had bottle service at a table and a bunch of girls all over him, just like he did when we were at UCLA. I like to think he has a long list of STDs now."

"Oh, that reminds me. If a guys gets more that three STDs, does it become illegal for him to have sex?"

"I'm starting to think that you shouldn't have been let into college. No, men are free to be as disgusting as they want to be. However, I did pass that one on to Josh to keep him out of trouble."

"Nice," Brooke said as she debating asking one more question. "So, are you going to be happy living here, with Dan?" She couldn't tell if the question was out of line. "I mean you knew him all those years before you two even dated. And then you came back here and… how are you so sure?"

Sarah smiled. "He was living on the other side of the

country and I was off at school. We both could have met thousands of other people, but we both wound up here by chance one day and, I don't know, we just knew. I can't explain it, but it's just right. And we could live anywhere together. But wanting to raise a family in the same place we grew up isn't a failure, you know. We turned out all right, didn't we?"

"You're a pathological liar and I drink like a fish these days, but yeah sure."

"Eh, let's just blame it on Mom."

They laughed and talked for a few more minutes before they finally went downstairs and left for dinner. At the restaurant they talked about the wedding and Brooke's friends and classes, and everyone caught her up on what she'd missed while she was away. When her mom asked if she'd met anyone special, Brooke said no, but the question somehow came with one of those emotional stomach punches she'd become so accustomed to.

Brooke decided to take care of a few things while she was home. She made a dentist appointment, just a routine cleaning, so she borrowed her mom's car and drove over to the office.

"Hi, I'm here to see Dr. Roberts," she said as she walked into the office.

"Is that Brooke Aarons?" Dr. Roberts came down the hallway to the waiting room.

"Hey, Dr. Roberts,"

"How are you Brooke? It's been so long."

"Oh yeah, I know, I missed my six-month check up… twice."

"Come on back. Let's see how much damage you've done."

Dr. Roberts was probably in his early thirties, with dark

brown hair and thick dark eyebrows, and since she'd seen him last, he'd gotten a set of veneers that were just slightly too big, giving him sort of a horsey look. Nonetheless a handsome man. She laid down on the chair and opened her mouth. He started looking around with the mirror, pulling her cheeks in one direction then the next.

"Well," he finally said, "you've got a cavity. I see it all the time from college students. You've got to remember to brush before you pass out." He found his own joke to be funny. "Listen, my next appointment just had to cancel, so I can take care of it now if you'd like."

The idea of getting a cavity filled sounded horrible, but she knew that if she left she wouldn't want to find time to come back. "Sure, let's just get it over with."

"That's the spirit."

As he was shooting Novocain in her gums, he made small talk. "You know, I used to live out in Austin. Great city." He pinched her cheek and wiggled it around to test if she could still feel anything.

"Have you ever been to that shopping center called Jefferson Square?"

"Mmm *mmm*," Brooke said to convey yes.

He pulled out the drill and began working. "There's this little restaurant in there, maybe you've heard of it. Russell's Bistro?"

"*Mmm* mmm," she mumbled, conveying no.

"It's amazing. They've got a great brunch. Do you like brunch?"

"Mmm *mmm*," she replied to convey yes.

"They just opened up a place out here, and it's not exactly the same, but it's pretty dang close. I don't know how long you're in town, but would you like to grab brunch with me there sometime? Or maybe dinner at an entirely different restaurant." He chuckled nervously.

Brooke was silent and confused. Did Dr. Roberts just ask her out? Did he just ask her out while he was working in her mouth? She didn't even know the man's first name. She finally said, "*Mmm* mmm," to convey no.

"Great!" He said, misinterpreting. "You're all finished. Spit." He held out a dish for her to spit into, but instead she just kind of drooled onto her paper towel bib. "Come with me." She thought she was following him to the front desk to check out, but then he opened a door on his right and turned inside. Brooke just stood in the doorway.

"Come in, come in. Brooke I'd like you to meet my father."

She didn't budge from the doorway, She just stood there and gave an awkward wave. Her face was beyond the point of numb, and she could tell her mouth was swelling up more by the second.

As Dr. Roberts was writing a note onto a Post-it, Brooke felt something hit her shoe and realized she was still drooling. She tried to make herself stop, but she couldn't feel anything in her face at all, so it was a wasted effort. She just continued to stand there silently and drip while she waited for him to finish writing and for his dad to stop looking at her.

As Dr. Roberts walked up to hand her the Post-it, he grabbed a tissue and wiped her chin for her. "Whoopsy-daisy." Brooke just stood there with an eyebrow raised, taking in all the humiliation, then turned and headed straight for the exit without looking back. "Okay, uh, so just go ahead and, my number is right there, and no food or drink for at least three hours." *What the hell just happened?*

She drove home, parked, and walked in through the garage. Her mom was standing in the kitchen. "Whoa, where's the rest of the Chipettes?" She cracked herself up, but Brooke put her hands on her hips to show she wasn't amused. "What? That was a good one."

"Uh, gueh whah," Brooke slurred through her swollen, numb mouth.

"Guess what? Oh, what?"

"Dr. Woberths juth towally hit on me!"

"What?"

"Yeah, thaths weally weird, wight?"

"Well, you know, honey, I heard he recently called off his engagement, and you know, he and his father are doing really well. They're opening another office and…"

"Thewiously, Ma? I been going to him thinth I was thir-een!"

"Well, obviously he doesn't see you as a kid anymore."

"Thath's disthurbing. He'th like twelve yearth ol'er than me, at leasth."

"Well, I'm just saying, he's a nice man, and he *is* a den-tist."

"Ugh, I feel gwoth,"

"You feel a growth?"

"NO! I feel gwoth!"

"Oh, gross! Hey, at least you know you've got a date to your sister's wedding!" her mom said. "Honestly, honey, I'm concerned. Have you really not met anyone? Are you being nice? Is there anyone you think is cute? Has anyone asked you out? Have you been covering your drinks when you're at parties? It only takes a second for someone to drop some-thing in your cup, you know."

Brooke loved her mom, but she just couldn't hear it. She exhaled dramatically and went upstairs to take a nap and wait for the swelling to subside and the humiliation of the last hour to fade.

Later that evening when she was feeling better, she went downstairs and found her dad sitting in his office.

"Hey, Dad," she said.

"Hey, Brookey."

"What are you doing?"

"Just working, what else?"

"Okay, I won't bug you."

"Not another step. Get in here. What's going on with you?"

Brooke took a seat and rested her forehead on his desk. "Nothing."

"You know, I know my kids pretty well, better than you think I do, and when you think no one is looking, you have that same face your sister wore around for a month after oh-what's-his-name broke up with her. Is it … boy troubles?"

"Not exactly."

"Oh. Was it a girl?"

"Daaaad."

"You know college can be an experimental time—"

"Okay! I'll cough it up if you promise to never try to take a conversation down the experimental road again."

"Deal."

"Yes, there was a guy that I was somewhat interested in, I guess, but we had a difference of opinion and neither of us would budge, so it's done."

"Well, no surprise you wouldn't budge. You're the most stubborn kid I've ever met in my life. But let me tell you a little something about guys. Guys are idiots, all of them. Complete fools. Dumbasses and an embarrassment to mankind. But, there is nothing they won't do when they're in love with someone. I mean nothing. They'll do the craziest, most idiotic crap you could think of. I almost dropped out of school and moved to New Mexico once for a girl I met on a summer vacation when I was your age. And that's the least of the crazy shit I pulled." He patted her on the hand. "He's not the guy for you, kid. If he was, nothing would stop him from doing everything in his power to be with you. I know that probably doesn't make you feel any better about this situation, but I promise you, the right one will come along one day, and he'll do everything he can to make you the happiest girl in the world. And if he doesn't, I'll kill him and make it look like an accident. Fair?"

"Works for me. Thanks, Dad."

To Brooke's surprise, their conversation really helped clear her head. For the first time in weeks, she started to feel happy again, hopeful even. She couldn't believe how much time she had wasted on that one guy. It was a huge world out there, and Brooke had plans to see it all. She reminded herself she didn't need, nor want, some guy to be the source of her happiness. It was as if someone suddenly turned the lights back on. She realized she'd exaggerated everything about James and the way she'd felt about him. It was a relief to finally come back to reality and feel like herself again.

Chapter 17

For the rest of winter break, Brooke and Sarah picked out flowers, tablecloths, and other things for the wedding together and gushed over every detail of it, including the perfect wedding dress. Their mom cried as she pinned the veil in Sarah's hair, and they all made predictions about Dan's reaction.

Christmas and New Year's came and went, and before Brooke knew it, it was time to start thinking about school and her life back at UT again. She couldn't wait to get back to her friends. She even sort of missed Kyle, Bryan, and Garrett, as annoying as they were. She said goodbye to her family and a few hours later touched down in Austin. In less than an hour, all the girls were reunited and filling each other in on what they did over the break. They had planned to go find their classrooms again, like they had the Sunday before first semester but were having too much fun catching up, so they decided to grab some drinks at Local instead.

After their second round, Brooke glanced around the bar and realized how many good-looking guys were there. It was so refreshing. *Oh my god, I'm cured*, she thought. *I'm actually cured*. The girls all mingled and got to know a few of the guys at the bar. Brooke flirted heavily with one of the guys and got his number before they left. It felt so good to have a fresh start.

When they were walking back toward the dorms, they saw Kyle, Bryan, and Garrett walking in ahead of them. Darci was about to call after him but Brooke came to a halt and put her hands up to stop her. "Wait," she said, "hang back for a second. I have a little something planned for these guys." She opened her purse enough for them to see what was inside, and a few minutes later they were up in Brooke's room preparing to attack.

They walked down the hall toward the guys' room, each except Brooke with a water balloon in their hand, and then crouched next to the door. Stella and Darci each held one side of the slingshot Brooke had stolen from her little brother, and Kate held the ammo, ready to reload.

Brooke loaded the first balloon and, sitting with one foot on each side of the doorframe, leaned back far enough to do damage but not too far that she could be seen from the peephole. Darci knocked, and the second Garrett opened the door, Darci kicked the door in, Brooke let go of the slingshot, and the balloon burst onto the stomach. He fell to the ground like he'd been shot, and Kate handed her the next one as Kyle and Bryan both jumped up yelling. She hit Kyle then reloaded and hit Bryan before they could get to Garrett, pulling him back far enough to slam the door. The girls could hear them cursing from the other side of the door, but they couldn't stop laughing. Order was officially restored to Brooke's life, and nothing was going to throw her off balance again.

School was back in session that Monday, and so far, Brooke was happy with all the class choices she'd made. Aside from a few more general ed courses, she had Psych 130: Mental Disorders and Treatments on Mondays with Professor Bornstein again and Psych 140: Personality Assessment on Tuesdays. On Wednesday morning, she headed to Psych 201:

Human Sexuality bright and early at 9 a.m. in Seay Hall. She already knew the building, but room 112 seemed to be a mystery.

Why isn't it here? You can't jump from 111 to 113 without a 112, Brooke thought. She walked up and down the halls, getting more and more nervous as the clock ticked on and hitting a full-blown panic when her watch said 9. The halls emptied, and she was nearly breaking into a sweat. It has to be there somewhere. She frantically checked her schedule again, thinking there must be some mistake. Feeling almost dizzy with stress, she did a 180 next to the staircase to head down a hallway she'd already checked, when she heard a voice behind her.

"You lost, little girl?"

The words traveled all the way up her spine and paralyzed her. She didn't need to turn around to see who the voice belonged to, but she did. He stood up from a step and walked toward her. It wasn't another illusion this time. It was James. The closer he got, the dryer her throat became. The hallway had gone completely silent as the last door closed, and she didn't trust her voice to answer his question. She didn't trust it enough to say anything at all.

"You're looking for a room number, yes?" James asked, nodding like he already knew. He came to a stop only inches away from her, and she knew he had to be able to hear her heart pounding. She began to nod unconsciously, matching his pace, then shook her head abruptly.

"No!" She nearly shouted, breaking her silence.

"No?"

"No. I'm not lost." It took all her strength to keep her feet planted. She felt like her knees could collapse from under her, and she gripped her books until her fingers turned white, hoping it would hide that her hands were shaking. She couldn't tell if she wanted to hit him or hug him, but she held herself back from either with every ounce of restraint in her body. "I'm just running a little late." Her tone turned sour unintentionally. "Which clearly you don't care about since every class in this building is in session and you're just sitting there like you're too cool for school. Which is also kind of literal in this case, since we're at school. And you're just there and sitting... and acting too cool... for school." *Nice one, Brooke. Really nice.*

James stood there with an eyebrow raised until he finally decided to let her remark go. "Yeah, I guess I'm going to be a little late today," he finally said as his expression changed into a playful smile she recognized. "But it was just so damn entertaining watching you race back and forth, *not* being lost, I couldn't look away. Kind of like a train wreck, you know?"

She was mentally scolding him for that comment but working too hard to keep some composure to let any of it be verbalized. "Fine, you solve the riddle. Where's room 112?"

"Right this way." He stepped back and held his arm out to direct her. "My stuff's already inside."

No! He's in my class? This can't be happening, she thought. *And of all subjects, Human Sexuality? What have I done to deserve this?* He led her to where he had set his stuff.

"I actually had enough time to spot you in the hall, go in, scope out the best seats, and save two on the off chance this was the room you were looking for. The rest of the classes at this hour are all upper-division or labs."

She considered asking why he even knew that but ruled against talking at that moment. She followed closely behind as he led the way into the classroom. The professor was already talking, so they settled into the two empty seats quietly.

Brooke was having a hard enough time reminding herself to breathe, so she became almost dizzy again when he leaned in to whisper something. "You were just trying to be late on purpose, right? Silly of me to ever think you don't know what you're doing." He got closer and lowered his voice. "Even if it looks like you're diving into a bunch of shrubbery."

She gasped so loudly the whole class turned to look at her. He knew about that?

That night the girls all got together to do laundry and discuss all their new courses.

Darci: "So any cute boys in your classes?"

Stella: "Actually, I got a few in my auto mechanics class."

Brooke: "Why are you taking auto mechanics?"

Stella: "Because I was told cute boys would be in it."

Kate: "I actually have a class with Bryan, so that's pretty cool."

Darci: "What about you, Brooke?"

She was about to tell them about James being in her class, but then she remembered these girls practically having to drag her out of bed and force-feed her out of depression. She didn't want to worry them. At least she convinced herself that's why she didn't tell them.

Brooke: "No, I didn't notice any."

The following Wednesday, she sat next to James again. She was thankful the class was only once a week, but did it have to be for three hours? Her whole body was so stiff she felt like she couldn't breathe normally, and she knew she'd have to go over the material again, because not a single word the professor said was registering.

It was still cold outside, so Brooke wore a scarf and a thick knit headband that covered her ears. She looked over at James at one point to see he was looking at her curiously. She turned back to the front of the classroom, but when she noticed him doing it again, she looked at him and whispered, "*What?*" before looking away again.

She held her breath when he leaned in closer, and then he said quietly, "I don't want to worry you, but something happened to the top of your hat." The breath she was holding burst out in a laugh, disrupting the class yet again. It wasn't even funny, but she couldn't hold it in. She nearly had tears streaming down her face from trying to stop herself. It was then that she knew she was in trouble.

As the course continued, Brooke realized why he had been so hard for her to get over. Everything with James was fun and somehow exciting. The otherwise boring class had become her favorite part of the week. More times than she could count, he would say things that made her laugh out loud or break into a sweat trying to hold it in. Why shouldn't she be able to maintain a friendship with him? That's all it would be, of course, since she knew now not to get too close. As long as they were in a huge lecture hall, she was fine. As long as they didn't touch, she'd be okay, and as long as they were never going to be in close quarters together, she'd be able to get through this class and make it out in one piece.

The professor dismissed class for the day, and Brooke began her hurried routine to make an exit as quickly as possible. She grabbed her purse and jacket, but when she reached for her books, James had already stacked them on his. She hesitated for a moment, then took the opportunity to pull her jacket on as they walked out the door. She straightened herself out when they made it outside then turned to collect her things from him.

"About the midterm coming up," James said. "I was thinking, maybe we could study for it together." Brooke froze, unable to answer right away. As if he knew exactly what she was thinking, he continued. "We could meet in a safe, public setting, like the library, and you wouldn't have to be stuck with me for more than an hour or two." He was mocking her. It was clear he could see her hesitance to be around him.

"No," Brooke said bluntly. She realized if she wanted to keep the fact that she had a class with him secret, they definitely couldn't been seen together in the library. The girls were certain to be in the library around midterms. "Not there."

"Okay, well I could come to your dorm room. You know, I've never actually been there," he said with a smile.

"Definitely not there." She said it bluntly in hopes of hiding the effect that his smile had on her.

"Well, what about my place?"

She had to get out of this. She needed to plainly tell him she wanted to study on her own, or she was too busy, *anything*. "Okay," she said. "Let's go there." He seemed surprised. But not nearly as surprised as she was.

The following Tuesday, Brooke parked her car in the parking lot outside his apartment, but she didn't get out of the car right away. *Why am I here? Am I crazy? Maybe I'm not actually crazy. I'm just trying to redeem myself from looking crazy, since he saw me in the bushes and all. This is all just so that I can remind him that I'm totally sane. Or at least prove that I can be. But not because I care what he thinks, just for my own peace of mind. Just don't do anything stupid. And don't fall for anything stupid. You can't go down this road again. Spend two hours max then leave.*

She finally got out of her car, walked up the stairs, and knocked on the door. Why was her heart pounding? She'd been here plenty of times. Trying to convince herself of that didn't make a difference. She could tell she was nervous. Would he be able to?

She practiced her opening line in her head as she knocked on the door. *Hey, how's it going? Hey, how's it going. Hey, how's …*

He opened the door.

"Going how's… it?"

"What?" he asked.

"Hey!" She forced the most laid-back look she could come up with on the spot to try and recover.

"Um hey, come on in." She followed his lead then set her stuff on the kitchen table. "I made some steak if you want some."

Every other college kid is eating Top Ramon and he made filet mignon? It was somewhat impressive but she was too nervous to be hungry. "No. No, thank you. Let's just work on this." The nerves had crept into her voice, but she tried to hide it with some authority. "So the test is going to be on everything we've covered in the last three weeks. It's nine sections, but it shouldn't take us long. I already made flash-cards, so I was thinking we could go over each section really quickly then quiz each other."

"Sounds fun."

"We're not here to have fun." She didn't mean to sound so harsh—it just came out that way. *Stop being so awkward, and stop being a bitch. Be cool*, she told herself.

"I mean, we'll just go over this shit until we got it down then we're cool, cool to go, man." *Still a white girl, Brooke. What are you doing? Just try being nice.*

"So it starts on page 90?" he asked.

"Yes! Good job!" He just stared at her, trying to figure out whether she was being sarcastic.

Give up. Just give up.

She didn't know how to be alone with the guy anymore. Sitting across the table from him in a quiet apartment was so much more difficult than she'd imagined. She didn't know how she was supposed to act around him when they were alone now, and it seemed the longer they sat there, the more attractive he became. She couldn't focus. It was impossible to read him, and it was killing her that she had no idea what he thought about her anymore.

Was he still attracted to her? Did he only see her as a friend now? Or a psychopath? Maybe he absolutely hated that she turned out to be in his class and he was just trying to make the best of it. Or worse, he was being nice to her because he felt badly for the poor little nutcase who lost her shit and fell out of his car. What was even crazier was that thinking that he didn't want her was only making her want him more. She kept adjusting the way she was sitting to try to look sexy, then mentally scolding herself for doing so. She decided that she didn't even want him; she just wanted him to want her. That's what it was. Wasn't it?

She realized she couldn't handle being there much longer. She suggested they move on to the flashcards. She pulled the stack out of her bag, divided it in two, and handed him half. They began quizzing each other back and forth a few times, but it didn't take long before it was clear to her that this was much, much worse. Every time he flipped a card, she flashed back to their game of SORRY! and wished they were there again. It didn't help that every question and answer came with that playful smile of his that always made her weak.

He flipped to the next card. "Okay," he said, holding up the card to read it. "What is the purpose of *pheromones*?"

"Um, pheromones…" She knew the answer but struggled to get the words out. "Pheromones send a signal to the hypothalamus to…" she could feel her throat going dry and the back of her neck getting hot, "to illicit emotions such as attraction… arousal… sexual desire… and—can I get some water?"

She pushed her chair back abruptly and stood up. She pulled cupboard after cupboard open, desperately looking for a cup, wondering why she couldn't remember where they were. As she reached up to another cupboard, he was suddenly at her side.

"Here, it's this one," he said reaching up to the cupboard next to her, putting his hand on the small of her back. The moment he touched her, she felt a wave of heat course through her. She turned to look up and met his eyes. He leaned down, but she didn't move. She couldn't move. She shouldn't. But she wanted him, and he was right there wanting her. Had this been what she was wishing would happen all along? All reason slipped away as she gave in and wrapped her arm around his neck. He dropped the flashcards on the floor and lifted her onto the countertop. She had lost control entirely.

Chapter 18

Brooke lay there on the floor next to James and the pile of scattered flashcards. The already quiet apartment suddenly felt painfully silent. Brooke couldn't think of a single thing to say. As if she didn't know how to act around him before, this just took that to a whole other level.

"Well, I think it's safe to say I have a better understanding of human sexuality," James announced. "Thanks."

Thanks? As in thanks for the favor, you can go now? She suddenly felt stupid. What had she done?

"Um… you're welcome." She slid her shirt over to cover herself, then stood up and went around the corner to put it on. "We should be good for the test, so I'm going to go."

Her only thought was that she had to get out of there as fast as possible. She reminded herself that this was the guy who didn't want anyone clinging on to him. He didn't want some chick hanging around, trying to spend the night or get breakfast in the morning. He didn't want a girlfriend. She continued to list all the things he didn't want to herself as she packed up her things as quickly as possible and hurried to her car. But what did *she* want? Dumb question. She pushed it out of her head when she remembered it had never mattered anyway.

Brooke got out of the elevator on the fifth floor of the

dorms with her mind still preoccupied. She nearly had a heart attack when she heard Stella call her name behind her in the hallway.

"Jesus, you scared the crap out of me!"

"Sorry!" she said, clearly surprised by Brooke's reaction. "I thought you said you'd be in the library."

"What? I was!" Brooke instinctively moved her hands to smooth down her hair, which, no doubt, was a mess.

"Weird, I was there too," Stella said. "I didn't see you. And my phone died so I couldn't text."

"Oh, yeah, um, I sat somewhere new. There was this guy next to my usual spot and he had one of those nose-whistling things going on so I eventually just got up and moved."

"Uh, nose-whistlers are the worst. Like, what is that? Go to a doctor." Stella said, fully believing her story. Brooke felt horrible about lying, especially after everything her friends did for her last semester—well, what they tried to do, anyway. She couldn't decide what to feel more guilty about as she carried on a short conversation in autopilot then walked back to her room alone.

Sophie was already asleep, so Brooke changed in the dark and slipped into bed. She tossed and turned the whole night.

Brooke didn't need to wait for her alarm clock to wake her up. She was already wide-eyed and counting down to when the obnoxious tone would start blaring next to her head. When it finally did, her stomach dropped. It was time to face the music.

Never before had she been more nervous than how she felt walking into the lecture hall. She stared at the patches of empty seats scattered throughout the room. Should she sit somewhere different? Should she run while she still had a chance? No. She couldn't dodge him for the rest of the semester, so why even try now?

She sat down in her regular spot, pulled out her note cards, and stared at them without registering the words. She just needed to look busy and calm. She saw James approaching out of the corner of her eye, but she didn't look up. He took a seat next to her, and she could feel his eyes on her. She flipped to another card, stared at it, flipped it over, and stared some more. Finally, she couldn't stop herself from looking over at him. He flashed her a knowing smile then pulled out a note card she must have left behind, flipping it over and over again, clearly making fun of what she was doing. She exhaled like she hadn't breathed out in days then hid a smile by digging through her bag for a pencil.

The professor handed out the scantron sheets and questions, and they began the test. Occasionally, they bumped elbows on purpose.

Brooke finished her test first and got up from her seat, gathered her things, and walked toward the front of the room to hand it to the professor before heading out the door. She debated whether she should wait for James, since they usually walked out together, but before she had time to determine that wasn't a good idea, he was behind her.

"You finished fast," she said as he caught up to her.

"I hate it when girls tell me that," he said, clearly hoping for a laugh. "Um, right." He changed his answer. "Sort of took my best guess on the last few, but yeah. I was trying to keep up with you."

She nodded her head calmly as she channeled all of her nervous energy into squeezing her books into her chest. "Well, I'm going to head back to the dorms since I have a break."

"I'll give you a ride," he offered, already turning in the direction of his car.

"Sure. O-okay," she said cautiously, mentally prepping

herself on the way, the same way she'd just done for the test. *Don't bring up last night. Don't act like you're interested in him. Don't seem like you want to see him again outside of class.* She thanked him as he opened the passenger door and she crawled in. *Let him bring everything up… if he wants to. But don't press the issue if he doesn't. You're not the one who needs an explanation, or to define anything. Be cool and casual. Maybe it was a one-time thing. Maybe he wants to start seeing me again. Maybe he was just as confused as I am.* She ruled that one out instantly. As if this guy ever did anything without control of the situation.

By the time her mind began to quiet down, she realized they were already just around the corner from her dorm. She glanced over toward James, who looked perfectly at peace and relaxed. *Say something!* she told herself. *The ride's almost over, and then what?*

"So you have one more midterm this week?" It was all she could come up with as he pulled in front of her building.

"Yeah, tomorrow. You?"

"Today was my last."

That was it? That's all they could come up with to talk about?

He pulled over in front of her building and turned to look at her. All they could hear for a few moments was the sound of the car running. "Cool," he said. "Well, if I don't see you this weekend, I'll see you in class next week."

She sat there frozen for a second. *Seriously, that's it?* She snapped into gear and collected her things as quickly as possible. "Yup. Sounds good," she said as she hopped out of the car, closed the door, and turned toward her building in one swift move.

As she put one foot in front of the other and forced herself not to turn around, she couldn't help analyzing his words. He obviously didn't want to see her this weekend. He would have asked if she had plans; he would have mentioned what he was doing. He only brought up seeing her this weekend in case it was unavoidable. She was furious at herself for letting him get under her skin. He didn't care if another week went by before he saw her again, so she didn't care either. She wouldn't care. Okay, she'd work on the whole not-caring thing.

By the end of the week, Brooke had finally gotten a reasonable grasp on the situation. James was an idiot. Not hearing from him the last few days just proved what she already knew; that stupid idiot was never worth her time. She needed to have a fun weekend with the girls, and a run-in with him would ruin it. She'd have to deal with that moron on Wednesday but not a second sooner. She was over him. He was so obnoxious, it was a shame she had to be in the same room as him once a week, so even the thought of voluntarily spending time with him was ridiculous. Plus, if she wanted to meet a guy, which she didn't, she could easily meet a guy ten times better than him anyway. So what the hell, tonight, she would.

The self-given pep talk played in her head as she spent over an hour perfecting her hair and makeup, even pausing to watch a YouTube tutorial on how to do smoky eyes, before finding the skimpiest top in her closet. Her phone buzzed on the bathroom sink, and she walked unsteadily over in her high, red stilettos to check it.

"Holy balls! Are you ready yet?" Darci had texted. "Be there in 2!" Brooke replied.

"Hours or minutes?"

"Seconds!"

"Good. We already called a cab."

Brooke grabbed her purse, flipped the lights, and hurried down the hall to Darci and Kate's room.

She opened the door and saw her three friends all dressed like they'd just come from class.

"Um, what the hell, you guys? You said we were going downtown!"

"Yeah, we are, to a dive bar, though," Stella answered.

"We're just going to Lavaca Street Bar. It's super laid-back," Darci elaborated. "Didn't you see my text telling you that's where we were going?"

"Well yeah, but I thought you just meant a bar on Lavaca Street. Meaning downtown, meaning I'm in heels and I curled my hair!"

"You look pretty!" Kate chimed in. "We're all just so tired from midterms this week, we just couldn't get all dressed up."

"Fine," Brooke sighed, "but I'm changing."

She turned to walk back out when Darci's phone started ringing.

"Too late," she said, "Our cab's here!"

She answered the phone and started telling the driver they were on their way down and where to wait.

"Here," Kate said as she pulled a plain black T-shirt off a hanger and tossed it to Brooke.

She thanked her with a dramatic sigh and pulled it over her head as they filed into the hallway. She used her hands to brush her hair back into a ponytail on the elevator ride down. With the combined disappointment of wasting so much effort getting ready, thinking she wouldn't be able to find any guys to show up James, and realizing she was about to look like one of those girls who tries way too hard at a dive bar, she decided a strong drink would be the first order of business.

The cab arrived at the bar, and the four of them flashed their fake IDs at the bouncer on their way inside. Kate and Stella went to check out all the games the place had—miniature basketball, darts, and shuffleboard among them—while Darci and Brooke headed straight to the bar.

They squeezed their way through the crowd and planted themselves against the wooden countertop but eventually grew impatient as the bartender continued to pass by them time after time. Every time she'd walk past, everyone standing in their same section would start trying to get her attention, to no avail.

"Hey, want to make a bet?"

Brooke looked over to see a handsome guy standing next to her with a good-looking friend by his side. She lightly elbowed Darci to get her attention.

"Depends," Brooke answered. "What's the bet?"

"I bet we can get her to get our drinks before you."

"Interesting," Brooke said, glancing back at Darci. "And the terms?"

"If we lose, we'll buy your drinks."

"And if you win?"

"Then we'll challenge you to a game of shuffleboard, and you'll accept."

"I'll need to consult my counsel." Brooke turned to face Darci. "Interested or not interested?"

Darci raised her eyebrows as if she even needed to answer, and Brooke turned back around.

She held out her hand, "You have a deal."

He took her hand and shook it. Their hands lingered a moment longer than she expected.

"I'm Conner, by the way," he said as their handshake rolled into a new purpose.

"Brooke. This is Darci."

"Hi," Conner said, letting go to introduce himself to her. "And this is my buddy, Mike."

"Okay, enough of this friendly business. We have a bet to win," Brooke said.

After a few more failed attempts at getting the bartender's attention, the bartender finally stopped in their section. Unfortunately, she pointed to Conner instead of her.

"What'll it be?"

Conner gave Brooke a boastful smile. "Two Guinness."

"And two Blue Moons," Brooke added. "All together." She smiled at Conner.

The bartender poured the beers and set them on the bar, waiting for payment.

Conner pulled out his card and nodded to indicate how impressed he was by that move. Brooke and Darci picked up their beers and thanked him for his generosity.

"We'll meet you at the shuffleboard table," Brooke said before weaving back through the crowd. There was no reason everyone couldn't win. She wished for a moment she could have ever been that cool in front of James.

She and Darci set up at the shuffleboard table, and a minute or two later, the two guys walked up. Darci and Brooke lined up on the same side of the table, ready to begin.

"Wait," Conner said, "are you guys on the same team?"

They both said yes, and then the guys explained the rules of the game, which clearly neither of the girls actually knew. They found out that members of the same team actually stood on opposite ends of the table, so Darci walked around, and Conner took his place next to Brooke.

The first game went terribly. Both Brooke and Darci sent every single puck flying off the table. They set up for a second game and ordered another round of beers. This time around, they had a bit more of a match, and Stella and Kate showed up in time to see the game really heating up. Kate was alternating between texting Bryan and snapping pictures on her phone, documenting all the action, including a moment when Conner playfully put his arm around Brooke after he knocked one of her pucks off the table.

The game ended with Darci and Brooke winning, and the guys proposed one more game to break the tie. They were all having fun, so it was an easy decision. They reset, and the girls took the first shot. While it was Mike's turn, Brooke decided to check her phone, which had been making a noise in her purse for a while.

She scrolled through several Facebook notifications letting her know that Kate had tagged her in a photo standing next to Connor and several people had "liked" it, but the most recent thing to come in was a text from James. She unlocked her phone and opened the message.

"Hey – if you end up downtown tonight let me know."

Her heart rate picked up, and for a moment, she forgot entirely about the game. *Let him know? Why? Well, technically I am downtown. Letting him know isn't hanging out. And since we do have class together, he could very well ask me what I did this weekend, and if I mention I was downtown and he asks why I didn't respond to his text, it might seem like I was intentionally avoiding him. And I'm not, remember? I don't care, and someone who doesn't care would have no reservations about telling someone plainly where they are.*

"Brooke!" Darci broke her train of thought. "What are you doing? It's your turn!"

"Oh, right!" She couldn't not answer his text, though. "Um, I think I got some sand in my eye," she said, squinting one eye shut. "Stella, you're my alternate; take over until I come back. I'm going to run to the bathroom to look in the mirror."

Brooke grabbed her purse, walked into the bathroom and opened up the text again. She thought for a moment then typed back, "I'm already downtown actually. At Lavaca Street Bar." She hit send, confident with her decision. She decided to take a minute to look in the mirror so at least there would be some truth to what she told everyone.

She pulled her hair down from the ponytail and shook it out. She was a little buzzed from the beer, so she awarded herself a few mental compliments on what a good job she did on her hair and makeup. She really did look pretty.

While she was trying to put her hair back up, her phone buzzed on the countertop.

"I'm at The W with some buddies. A block away. Maybe I'll stop by there next and say hello."

No! He can't come here. It will be obvious to the girls that this wouldn't be the first time I've seen him and what if everything comes out? I'm not prepared to answer questions about why I haven't mentioned that. What do I do? I can't make the girls leave without an explanation, and I can't tell him he can't come for no reason.

She looked back at herself in the mirror. She supposed if she *had* to make a stop at The W to avoid James coming to the bar, at least she was dressed for it. Suddenly that idea started to make sense. All she would have to do was walk down the street, stop in, show him how good she looks, show that same coolness and confidence she's had all night, and walk back out to prove *she* could resist *him*. He'd won every match so far, but the game wasn't over yet.

She typed, "Lucky coincidence, I told someone I'd stop by The W." She rationalized that as soon as the next text was sent, it could, technically, be considered true. "I'll find you while I'm there to say hi."

"I like the sound of that," he sent back.

She pulled off the black T-shirt to reveal her skimpy top, touched up her lip gloss, then headed out the back door. She pulled out her phone and sent a mass text to the girls. "Bathroom light here is ridiculous. Left to go to The W. Be back soon!"

As Brooke had discovered in herself, a few rounds of

drinks will make anyone a little more gullible, so she was thankful when everyone accepted her reasoning without follow-up questions. She took her time walking down Lavaca Street, gaining more confidence with every step.

She strutted through the doors of the hotel and paused to fix her hair before entering the bar. She took a deep breath and walked toward the door, but then she saw James out of the corner of her eye in the lobby. He was downing a cup of complimentary water like he'd just run a marathon or, more likely, as if he'd been dancing up a storm with some girl. Her eyes rolled involuntarily.

It threw her off to run into him before she'd planned, but her unease turned to panic when he spotted her.

"Evening, ma'am," the man holding the door open for her said.

James couldn't see her before she could pretend to have met up with a friend. He'd know she was lying when she left without talking to anyone else. And now he was walking toward her. She could feel him getting closer, but she wouldn't look in his direction. Instead, she looked up at the man holding the door open.

"Hey!" she said to the doorman with a startling amount of enthusiasm. "Good to see you again," she glanced at his silver name tag, "Eric!" James was right behind her now, and she couldn't stop herself from turning around. "Oh, perfect, there you are. I didn't have to go searching for you at all. Um, James, this is my friend Eric that I'm stopping by to see. Eric, this is James." The two shook hands awkwardly as Brooke nervously danced in place.

"Okay, well, I'll let you get back to work. Do you want to head inside, James?"

James agreed to, still seeming slightly confused by the entire interaction.

"Eric, so glad I stopped by," she said as she pulled him in

for a hug. "I'll give you a call later!" She had to give herself props for committing.

"Uh, okay, um you have a good evening then, ma'am."

Brooke practically pushed James inside and around the corner. *Glad that's over*, Brooke thought. She reminded herself why she was here.

"Do you want to get a drink?" James asked.

Now that she'd acted so spastically uncool, she had to at least stay long enough to redeem herself.

"Sure," she said, taking the lead and hoping he'd follow.

She'd order some mixed drink and sip slowly, or maybe just get a water. They made their way through the crowd until she found a gap along the bar, barely big enough to fit both of them, but they managed. She didn't hate being pressed up against him, but if history had taught her anything so far, it was that it wasn't good for keeping a clear head.

"You feeling wild?" He looked down at her and asked with that same smile that had made her weak at the knees a hundred times before. Suddenly she was.

He ordered two shots of tequila and paid.

"To small worlds," he said as he raised his glass in one hand and a lime in the other. "What are the odds you were right down the street?"

"And to coincidences. Crazy how I was already planning on coming here." She tapped her glass against his, and they both threw back their shots.

They spotted an open couch in the corner and sat with a few inches between them.

"So you're telling me you wore *this* to Lavaca?" James said of her barely there top.

"I may have lost a layer," she said as coyly as she could.

"Ah yes, I've heard you have a problem losing clothes."

They both turned in a little, so now their knees were touching.

After a few more minutes of back-and-forth, their legs somehow became intertwined. They continued to talk, and his hand moved to her knee. She leaned further into him. His other hand began playing with a piece of her hair, working his way up toward her neck. When his hand reached just above her collarbone, she snapped out of it and stopped him. She'd nearly forgotten that this time she wasn't going to fall for it. He'd seen how good she looked, and now it was time to go.

She stood up from the couch. "I should head back," she tried to say coolly as she picked up her purse and started to walk away. James got right up and began walking with her, seeming surprised. She knew she couldn't go out the same way she came in and risk another terribly acted fake-friendship interaction, so she began heading down a dark hall with louder music, hoping that direction would offer an exit.

"Wait, you don't have to go yet. It's still early," he said from behind her.

"I told my friends I was stopping by to say hi to Aaron, not having an hour-long conversation with him."

"You mean Eric?"

"That's what I said. It's too loud in here," she yelled back toward him, trying to recover.

"Don't go yet," he said.

"What?"

He grabbed her hand to stop her before she turned the corner, and she spun around to face him.

"Don't go."

The hallway was dark and loud, and they were packed up against a ton of other people, but suddenly none of that mattered. She knew better than to look up at him, or to stay another second, but suddenly none of that mattered either. With one text to her friends telling them she was safely back at the dorms, she'd made her decision.

Hours later, Brooke stared at the ceiling in James's bedroom. *You fucking moron. All you had to do was stick to a simple plan, and now look at yourself.* She rolled over to look at the clock. It was nearly 4 a.m. James was dead asleep, but she still knew she couldn't stay there. She slid out from under the covers as quietly as possible and walked out to the living room. Her items were scattered everywhere, along with his. She got dressed piece by piece then grabbed her phone to call a cab. She saw a few texts that didn't make sense.

"Dude, why'd you leave?"

"Hey, you comin' back? We're still at Chupacabra."

"You say you were going to The W? Something going on there tonight?"

She realized it wasn't her phone. The names were only familiar to her because they belonged to UT football players. Now she was confused. If he and his friends were across town at Chupacabra, why would he have said they were at The W? How did he get there so fast then? She didn't have time to analyze this one. If she just caught him in a lie, she didn't want to know why. She just wanted to get herself into a cab and be back in her dorm room where she could get her head straight.

By the time the cab dropped her off in front of her building, she'd realized a few things. She didn't regret what had just happened. This wasn't a one-time thing, and this time, she'd know what she was doing.

Chapter 19

Since Brooke's cab-ride revelation after her second rendez-vous with James, she had continued to sneak off to see him. Clearly, staying away from him altogether was impossible, since they'd have class together every week anyway, so why should she torture herself every time she had a little fun with their circumstances? There was no point in sitting around and thinking about the consequences. Besides, how could there even be any consequences? She knew what this was, and she had everything under control. She could walk away from this anytime she wanted. They were casually hook-ing up, and that's it. There weren't going to be feelings and expectations this time. She was just having fun.

Occasionally, there was a small trace of fear that if he ended whatever this was, she could be a complete wreck all over again, but she had no intention of giving him a reason to do that. This time, she wasn't trying to be his girlfriend. This time, she *did* know better.

She'd never text him first. She'd meet him somewhere if he asked her to, but she'd never, ever call him or make it seem like *she* was the one who wanted to see him. Sure, it might seem like she was at his disposal, but she was getting something out of it too. Things were just fine. They were great, actually.

Wednesday morning while Brooke was getting ready for class, she heard her phone go off. She ran to it knowing it might be James. That part had never changed. She still grabbed her phone and read his texts like they'd disappear if she didn't. The only difference now was that they were fewer and far between, and they typically only came at night. She couldn't help getting excited when she saw it was really him—excited in a totally cool, casual way, of course. She read the message. "Can't make it to class today, not feeling good."

Her heart sank, accidentally.

It was okay, though. What did she care if he wasn't going to be in class? It meant nothing. Class would probably even be better without him distracting her the whole time with his stupid jokes and elbow bumping.

She walked to class, took her normal seat, and completely disregarded everything the professor said for the next three hours.

I wonder how sick he is? Maybe I should bring him soup! Um, Brooke, you aren't his grandmother. You're not bringing him anything. Oh, what about a movie? Stop it! You're not his girlfriend. You're closer to being his grandmother than you are his girlfriend. Ew, no you're not. That's a disgusting thought. Why would I think something like that? Man, I hope telepathy isn't a real thing. I'd be mortified if someone in this room was listening in right now. Hm, telepathy, I wonder if any of the psychology courses touch on that. I'd totally take that class. Remember to look into that later. Okay, so what's the plan? Just soup, a movie, and a chocolate-chip cookie? NO, dammit!

After her wasted three-hour class, Brooke decided to walk over to Java City and start begging people to let her take their shifts for the rest of the day. She could no longer be trusted when left to her own devices. She needed to be trapped somewhere so she wouldn't try anything stupid.

Thankfully, she managed to score a shift, so a few hours later she suited up to voluntarily serve time behind the counter.

Brooke was busy building a pyramid out of the cups for a fourth time when Kate startled her and she knocked it down. Jeff, who was also behind the counter, didn't even look up from the staring contest he was having with a cup.

"Brooke Aarons, where have you been lately?" Kate demanded as forcefully as she could muster. "I feel like I haven't seen you in years. I finally had to track you down here." Her tone was already back to being sweet.

"I know," she said as she picked up the fallen cups. "I've been so super busy lately… with school." She was still a terrible liar. "How are you? And how are *you and Bryan*? Catch me up on everything."

Kate laughed shyly, instantly forgetting she was trying to be mad. "Things are great with us! Really great, actually." A smile spread across her face. "He, um, dropped those three little words." She looked down at her shoes with her lips curled in as she waited for a response.

"I have chlamydia?"

"Hilarious." She shook her head, fighting a smile. "After that."

"Uh oh. *We* have chlamydia?

"Oh my *god*!" Kate interrupted. "He said 'I love you,' you cynical jerk."

Brooke laughed, "Kate! Really? That's huge! I'm so excited for you! When did this happen?"

"When he took me to dinner last Tuesday night at this restaurant…"

The sentence trailed off to Brooke. *Last Tuesday?* Brooke used to know everything about her friends' lives. Hell, she knew what they ate for every meal. How did over a week go by without her knowing that this major thing had happened to her friend? The guilt of all her lying started creeping back in. It was her fault. She didn't know what was going on in her friends' lives because they didn't know what was going on in hers. She'd been keeping this major secret for weeks, and in comparison to Kate's news, it made everything feel so cheap. It made *her* feel cheap.

Things with James were fine, really fine, but it sort of bothered her that she had never returned to being herself around him like she was in the beginning. She was always walking on eggshells, trying not to appear clingy or needy. It was like walking through a minefield. One wrong step and she could be catapulted back into that place of sweatpants, *Sex and the City* reruns, and barely enough energy to get a piece of chocolate to her mouth. That just couldn't happen. Maybe she should get out before that becomes a risk. Maybe it was already too late. She pushed the thought out of her head for a moment so she could focus on Kate. "Kate, I'm so sorry I've been a crappy friend. I let," Brooke paused trying to think of what to say, "one stupid subject in class get in the way of everything."

"What's the subject?"

She wasn't expecting the question. "A serious mental disease," she said, quoting the wise Plato line Professor Bornstein had shared with her.

Kate twisted her face, not fully understanding.

"Not important, though. That's going to change now. Things are going to go back to the way they were."

"Good to hear, since *someone* has a birthday coming up! And I'm planning your party, which is why I'm here. Plus, you have to make me a coffee."

"Fine," Brooke said, rolling her eyes, lifting the tip jar, and setting it in front of Kate.

Kate cracked a smile. "I so haven't missed you. But thanks for the quarters," she said, taking a few out and replacing them with a dollar bill. "Looks like it's going to be another cocktail-laundry night without you."

"Reschedule for tomorrow after my shift, and your order's on the house."

"Is he going to care?" Kate pointed toward Jeff, who Brooke had forgotten was still there. Brooke looked at him to see he was still staring at a cup.

"Uh, no. I don't think he's ever cared about anything."

The next day, Brooke took a seat in Professor Bornstein's class as he began his lecture. "All right, everyone, who can tell me the definition of *insanity*?" A good portion of the class raised their hands, and he smiled as he called on a boy in the back.

"It's doing the same thing over and over again expecting different results."

"Yes, that's Albert Einstein's definition. I'm sure many of us are familiar with it."

Brooke felt her phone buzzing in her bag next to her foot. She carefully reached down, opened it, and saw a new text from James.

"All better. Must have been a 24-hour thing. Still on for tonight?" *Tonight?*

That meant she'd be missing out on the cocktail-laundry night she made the girls reschedule. She checked the time as she did every time a text from James came in now. It was 3:12 p.m. *Okay, at 3:22 I can write back. He knows I always have my phone on me, so he'll think it's not a big enough deal to me to respond—perfect.* She set her phone on her lap and watched the second hand go around until her watch read 3:19. *Close enough.* She picked up her phone and typed, "Gross, I don't want your lingering germs."

She had just promised Kate she'd be around more, and that's what she was going to do.

He responded, "I'm 100% germ-free."

"Not buying it," she sent back. She was proud of herself for holding out. Although, the thought of passing on spending time with him made her painfully anxious.

"Hm, I recall you nursing me back to health once. That wasn't such a bad time."

Hook, line, and sinker, she thought as she waited 2.5 minutes before sending, "I'll see you tonight."

She wondered how it was possible for one person to feel disappointed, excited, and guilty at the same time.

Professor Bornstein faced the board, writing as he lectured. Brooke took notes until class ended, and like she did in everyone one of her psychology courses, she found herself or James in every single case or definition, no matter how obscure.

That night, Brooke paced in front of her door. If it hadn't taken her so long to get ready, she could have gotten out, but now the girls would definitely be in the laundry room. She had sent them all a text saying she felt sick and was putting herself to bed. Hopefully her line about giving them a chance to plan her birthday party would deter them from wanting her to be there.

Unfortunately, she hadn't really thought everything through. She watched the clock, debating how she would get past the laundry room without them seeing her. Several times she debated just joining them; her laundry pile was at an all-time high anyway. But what if they asked questions? Sending texts and avoiding them was so much easier than having to lie to her friends' faces, or worse, tell them the truth.

She couldn't sit down. She was already so tired, abnormally tired, that she didn't want to risk falling asleep. It was 11:30 p.m. when she finally decided she could pull it off.

She snuck out of her room, down the emergency stairs, and made it to her car without being spotted.

"Well, it took you long enough," James said when he opened the door. "Whoa, you don't look so good."

"Um, you're not exactly dressed your best either." An obvious lie, considering he wasn't wearing a shirt.

"No, seriously, you're kind of pale."

"I'm just a little tired. Long day in class."

"I don't know… I hope you're not coming down with what I had."

"I'm fine," she said, noticing suddenly how much more tired she was becoming by the minute. "I just… Can I just sit for a minute?"

"Why don't you go lay down? I'll grab you some water."

She started to argue, but lying down sounded so good. She followed along a wall until she made it to the bedroom and crawled onto the bed. She rolled onto her side and tucked her legs up into a ball.

James walked in a minute later with a shirt on and a glass of water.

"Your lingering germs act fast," she said.

"Yeah, like most things about me, they're pretty strong and manly." He leaned over and touched her forehead.

"Says the guy playing nurse."

"Hey! It's an equally respectable career choice for men."

She laughed and then moaned in pain. "Am I hot?"

"What?"

"Do I feel hot? My head?"

"Oh, yeah a little. Sorry, for a minute I thought you were taking that somewhere else."

She rolled her eyes at him. "If we're going to throw in role-play, I'm saying right now this isn't a scenario I'd agree to."

"Aw, really? Sickly, discolored girls have always kind of been a fantasy of mine."

"Shut up, I look phenomenal right now," she said sarcastically.

"You do." He paused for a moment. "But to help you avoid mirrors, I have movie choices." He picked up the Apple TV remote that was sitting on his nightstand.

"No, no, no. I just need five minutes. Swear."

Chapter 20

The sound of running water woke Brooke up. She couldn't believe she'd fallen asleep but was relieved to see it was still dark. That was until she propped herself up and saw light as bright as day coming through a thin slit where the curtains were drawn. It was morning. It was morning and she was still at James's place. She was still lying in his bed.

The bathroom door was closed, but she could hear the shower running. Talk about the ultimate sign of being in a committed relationship: a sleepover without sex. He had taken care of her too. That was sweet. But this was too much for him. It had to be. What was she supposed to say to him? Sorry? Thank you? It'll never happen again?

She decided then that she didn't want to have that conversation. She hopped out of bed with all the energy she could muster, despite how sick she still felt. Then she picked up her purse, opened his door without making a noise, and headed back to her car, tiptoeing even through the parking lot. She couldn't help envying Kate for a moment. Knowing that Bryan loved her meant she'd probably never have to sneak out of his place feeling like a criminal.

Brooke looked at the clock in her car. She had class in twenty minutes, but the closer she drove to campus, the more she realized there was no way she could go. She felt miserable. She parked her car and headed toward the dorms.

"Ahhh, zombie!" she heard familiar laughter and saw Bryan, Garrett, and Kyle walking out of the building and pointing at her.

"Nice look you've got going on today," Bryan said.

"Shut up," was all she could manage.

"Weren't you wearing those clothes yesterday?" Garrett asked in an accusing way.

"Weren't you wearing that shirt for the last three weeks?"

She poked her finger through a hole at the bottom of his shirt. "I'm sick. What's your excuse?"

"No, you can't be sick," Kyle said. "We're going out for your birthday tonight."

"My birthday's tomorrow."

"And tomorrow starts at midnight," Bryan chimed in. Brooke moaned and leaned against the railing. "Okay, just let me get some sleep, and I'm in."

"So you *were* up all night!" Garrett yelled.

"I'm sick!" She yelled back twice as loud before pushing through them with the last of her strength.

That evening, Brooke woke up in her bed just in time to see the sun going down from her window. She'd slept the entire day. She sat up and stretched, realizing she was actually feeling much better. Not one hundred percent yet, but definitely getting there.

She pulled the covers off of her and walked over to get her phone out of her purse. There were a few texts from the girls but none from James. Disappointment crept in, a feeling she'd become all too accustomed to but still didn't fully understand. How could she be disappointed by something she had no expectations for?

She texted the girls that she was alive then hopped in the

shower before meeting in Kate and Darci's room so they could all get ready together like they had so many times before.

They popped a bottle of champagne, played music, danced, drank, tried on clothes, and navigated around an obstacle course of curling irons, blow dryers, and straightener cords. Brooke invited Sophie, too, so she met them in the room. Kate and Darci did Sophie's hair and makeup, while Stella helped her pick out one of Brooke's dresses. South by Southwest was in town, so the city was packed, and they all couldn't wait to get into the action.

When Brooke was dressed and ready, she lay down on Kate's bed. Maybe she wasn't going to be able to go out. But what was she supposed to do? Go back to her bed and lie next to a phone that doesn't ring? No way. She had to be out. She wanted to be distracted. She just wished she felt better.

The girls all jumped on the bed around her. "You're okay to go out, right?" Stella asked.

"Yeah, definitely." She rolled onto her side. "I think I am, anyway."

"Do you want some ginger ale," Kate asked, "or some vitamin C?"

That wasn't what she needed at all. "I'm fine, really. I just want to have a good time."

"Well, you're not going to if you're sick," Kate said.

"I've got an idea." Darci got a strange look in her eyes that Brooke couldn't quite figure out. She walked around the corner to the bathroom then came back a few seconds later and held out her hand. Brooke stared at a small white pill in her hand. "Take this," she said with a wink. "You'll have a good time."

Brooke hesitated for a moment. Everyone was staring at her. What would it say about her if she took it? Everyone there knew her well enough; she wasn't really worried about being judged. It was more a matter of what she would think of herself. She hadn't exactly been a shining example of good judgment lately. Looking back at the last few weeks, it seemed all her decisions had been bad ones. So what was one more? She sat up, took the pill out of Darci's hand, and washed it down with champagne.

They grabbed the guys on their way out of the building, and the group hopped in two cabs. All that Brooke knew was that they were going to a place with a live band and a huge outdoor area where everyone could dance and drink.

Brooke didn't know the name of the place until Kate told the cab driver. It was Stubb's. They were going to Stubb's, the place she had gone to brunch with James that first morning when she knew she'd fallen for him. Back when things with them were normal and fun.

Her heart rate picked up a little as they filed out of the cab and Brooke grabbed Darci's hand. "I think the pill's kicking in," Brooke whispered.

"Feeling better?" Darci asked with a smirk.

Brooke smiled, "Let's go straight to the dance floor."

The band was amazing. They sang along to the country music and threw back shots, and Brooke danced like she'd never danced before. She felt wild, and fun, and unpredictable. She felt invisible. She loved it. She spun in so many circles dancing that she made herself dizzy. Everything was becoming a blur.

At midnight, they all did a toast to Brooke's birthday and clinked their clear plastic cups together in the air. It was officially her birthday.

She felt her phone buzz in her purse and fumbled around until she pulled it out. It was a message from James: "Happy birthday, kid." That's all it said. She didn't know if she was surprised to hear from him or not. She didn't know if she liked or hated his message. She finished off her drink and threw her cup into the trash can. She did, however, know exactly how to respond.

Chapter 21

The next morning Brooke woke up and looked around. She was in Darci's bed, and Kate was across the room sharing her bed with Bryan. She looked for her phone so she could see what time it was. When it wasn't in the bed, she assumed it was probably still in her purse, and since that was nowhere in sight, she figured it must be in her own room. She quietly climbed down the ladder of the bunk bed, walked down the hall to her room, and carefully opened the door to her room.

She looked up at Sophie's bed to see if she had woken her up.

"Oh my god!" Brooke yelled. "Kyle?"

Then she noticed Stella stirring in her bed. And she wasn't alone, either.

"Stella, who is that?" she whispered at the volume of a yell.

Stella opened her eyes enough and twisted to see who was next to her. "Oh crap," she said, smacking her hand over her face. "It's nobody. Look away."

"*Nolan?* You slept with Nolan in my bed! Why would you do that? In my bed?"

"Because I locked myself out and my roommate was at a rave," she said as she climbed out of bed.

"That doesn't answer the big question."

Nolan had woken up at the sound of his name and was starting to get up.

"Did everyone get laid on my birthday but me?" She turned away to avoid seeing any of Nolan's skin and spotted her phone on her desk. She picked it up and it automatically opened up to a text conversation she'd been having with James. As she read through the messages, her stomach suddenly dropped like she was on a roller coaster, a bad, bad roller coaster. This couldn't be real. The conversation she was staring at could not have actually taken place.

"Okay, Nolan, it's time to go. I need my best friend back," Brooke said, clapping her hands loudly. "You too, Kyle! Out, out, out!" Nolan was still almost completely asleep, so he didn't even argue past a few inaudible grumbles. She waited until Nolan was completely out the door before she turned back to Stella.

"We've got a problem."

Kyle was still working on getting down from Sophie's bed. "We're going to talk about this later," she said to him with her finger in his face. Sophie was still asleep somehow. Kyle walked out of the room and started down the hall. Stella and Brooke followed behind. They passed Nolan waiting for the elevator, and Brooke caught Stella giving him a smile and a discreet wave. Brooke set her shock and curiosity aside for the moment and grabbed Stella's hand to hurry her along.

After Kyle unlocked his door, Brooke pushed by him and entered the room. She had a feeling Darci was here. Sure enough, she was lying face down in Garrett's bed in a pair of booty shorts and a T-shirt. Brooke patted Darci on the butt a few times. "Wake up, beautiful."

"Five more minutes," she mumbled.

"How about you enjoy those five more minutes in your bed instead of *Garrett's*." Her eyes shot open.

"This is a reoccurring nightmare."

"Yeah, it is. C'mon, sleepy head."

They walked back into Darci and Kate's room, and just as Brooke was about to wake up Bryan, Darci stopped her. She picked up a marker off her desk and knelt down next to his face. When she stood back up, Bryan had a perfect mustache and a unibrow. "Okay, go ahead," Darci said. Brooke clapped her hands once as loud as she could right in front of his face and laughed as he jumped up.

"Bry-Bry, we love you, but you're going to have to leave."

Kate was awake now too. "What's going on?"

"He's on our spot," Brooke said.

"I don't know why you guys have to be so mean," he said in a whiney voice. They couldn't hold back their laughter at his new face. He turned over to say goodbye to Kate, and when she saw his face, she yelped and jumped back.

"What?" he asked.

Behind his head, the girls were waving their arms for her not to tell him.

"Um, nothing. Your breath is just really bad. Love you, though!"

"Oh, sorry," he said as he did a breath check in his hand. "I'll see you later. *You* guys suck," he said to the rest of the girls, but they kept laughing as they all piled onto Kate's bed. As soon as he was out of the room, though, Brooke remembered what was weighing on her.

Brooke: "Ladies, I have a crisis. I am a slutty, slutty texter."

Darci: "Oooh, I love a good slutty text convo."

Brooke: "Well the convo is slutty and then some, and the 'then some' is the crisis."

Stella: "Who's the lucky victim?"

Brooke: "That's the biggest part of the problem. It's… it's James."

The girls were all silent for what felt like forever.

Kate: "Well, how bad is it?"

Brooke turned her phone around to show them, and they all took a moment to read. Almost in unison they all leaned back and yelled, "Whoa!"

Stella: "Did… did he ask for that?"

Brooke scrolled up a little.

Brooke: "Nope. It looks like he was talking about some *Superbad* scene he was watching. But you know, without proper capitalization of a movie title like that, who's *not* going to assume they're talking porn?"

Stella: "And this is how you respond? You used emojis."

Kate: "What does the donkey mean?"

Brooke turned the phone sideways in Kate's hands.

Kate: "Oh. *Oh.*"

Brooke frowned and nodded as she fell into Kate's lap for comfort.

Stella: "I'm embarrassed *for* you, if that's possible."

Brooke: "Oh, there's enough to go around. It gets worse."

Kate: "How does it get worse than something that involves a pig and a cactus?"

Brooke: "Read the last message I sent. The one with no response."

Stella took the phone and read aloud.

Stella: "I wish you were here. I think I'm in love with you… thumbs-up."

Darci: "Whoa."

Kate: "Yeah, I've never seen the thumbs-up. Show me where that one is."

Stella: "Oh shit."

Kate: "Right, back on topic. *How* did this happen?"

Stella: "Wait, Brooke, you've been talking to him a lot! What is all this?"

Brooke: "He turned out to be in one of my classes this semester."

Darci: "What!"

Stella continued to scroll up and read.

Stella: "Have you been seeing him outside class too?"

Brooke: "Yes."

Kate: "Why wouldn't you tell us?"

Brooke: "Because I knew I shouldn't have been. But what am I supposed to do now? I was trying to be cool and casual, and I just completely fucked that up. Tell me how to fix this."

Darci: "People always send weird drunk texts. It's just part of a night out. He'll understand."

Brooke: "Kate, you and your stupid 'I love you's got in my head!"

Kate: "Hey, don't blame me. Ninety percent of the things people say when they're drunk is the truth."

Brooke: "You just made that up."

Kate: "Okay, I did. But it sounds true!"

Brooke: "So last night when Darci said that crack addict was Ke$ha, we should have taken a selfie?"

Darci: "Hey, I stand by my statement. Nobody knows the long term effects of glitter."

Kate: "You missed my point. Maybe you said it for a reason."

Brooke: "Oh my god. I did say it for a reason. I said it because I was fucked up on whatever drug Darci gave me! I knew I shouldn't have taken that stupid pill! How could I have been so reckless? Dancing around like that, everyone had to know I was on something. And now I have to figure out how to deal with this. I told him I loved him! I never would have said any of that on my own! This is a mess. And why are you smiling, Darci, this isn't funny!"

Darci: "It's a little funny."

Brooke: "Why's that?"

Darci: "You really want to know?"

Brooke: "Yes!"

Darci: "Last night, my wild, reckless friend, you were partying on baby aspirin."

Brooke: "What?"

Darci: "Yup. It's just a little something I call the placebo effect. You weren't feeling good. I gave you something that would virtually do nothing, but you believed it would make you feel better, and so it did! Damn, I'm a good scientist!"

Brooke: "It was a 24-hour bug. Of course I felt better 24 hours after it started."

Darci: "Okay. And the part when you stared at the moon and told me the colors were beautiful?"

Brooke: "That was… just… What happened to you being banned from performing psychological experiments on me?"

She fell back down into Kate's lap.

Brooke: "Well, there goes my excuse. Someone get the aspirin."

Darci: "Sorry, Brookey. It'd probably take about fifteen of those to even put a dent in your hangover. But hey, I have something else that'll make you feel better. Last night I convinced Garrett to put on my underwear and dance around the room because I thought it would be sexy. It actually wasn't; it just turned out to be really weird. But I took a video on my phone. Want to see?"

Brooke: "In no way would seeing Garrett in your underwear make me feel *better*."

Darci: "I'm texting it to you so you can watch it later."

Stella: "Oh, so that's why Sophie and Kyle came running into the room."

Darci: "Yeah, I know. I thought they were asleep, but I guess they caught the show."

Kate: "Poor Sophie."

Brooke smiled despite her circumstances. She hadn't realized how much she'd missed her friends until now.

Brooke: "So how can I make it up to you guys for being such a liar?"

Stella: "How else? Pass over your key. Your closet is ours for a week."

Brooke: "I can't dress all of us for a week! I haven't done laundry in weeks."

Stella: "You really should have thought about that before you lied."

They all recapped the best parts about the night, and after a couple hundred drafts, Brooke finally came up with a text message to send James.

"Just saw the things I texted you last night, and one, who-ever possessed me sounds like a lot of fun (or has serious issues with her father) and two, that last message, please understand I was drunk and what I said is entirely not true. Not at all, not even a little."

Okay, that may have been overkill, but she had to be sure he knew she meant it.

He wrote back a minute later. "It's cool. I figured you were drunk since you kept misspelling my name. Don't worry about it. I fell asleep before you sent it anyway."

As soon as he dismissed it, she thought she'd feel relieved, but she didn't. It was almost as if she wished she *had* meant it, or at least that he had taken it seriously. That was crazy, though. Why would she want him to think that?

She started to wonder if maybe for her it never was all that casual or within her control. Maybe she was secretly hold-ing onto hope that things might change somewhere along the line. She was stuck in Limbo. Maybe she was doing the same thing over and over again expecting different results. Yup, that's exactly what she was doing. She was insane. One hundred percent, by definition, certifiably nuts.

She was doing the very thing she was so against. But things weren't going to change. She'd dug this hole, she'd made this okay, and she knew she wouldn't do anything about it.

Chapter 22

A few hours later, Brooke was in desperate need of a coffee, so she walked out of her room and headed toward the elevator. Kyle walked out of his room at the same time, so they rode down together, exchanging some banter, and walked out of the dorms toward Java City. He was complaining about not wanting to work, but when he stopped for a moment, Brooke seized the opportunity.

"I heard you caught quite the show last night," Brooke said. "Some things you can't unsee."

"You want to explain to me what happened with Sophie?" she asked point blank.

"Nothing happened, I swear! We just fell asleep talking," he said, raising his hands up like he was surrendering. "But she is really sweet."

Brooke was pleasantly surprised. "You think you might like her?" She wondered why she hadn't already thought of them together before.

"Yeah, I think I do," he said bashfully, looking down at his shoes.

She debated a moment then reached over and grabbed the apron and visor out of his hands.

"Then take her to lunch. Go hang out with her for a bit. I owe you a shift anyway."

"Seriously, are you sure?"

"Yeah. Go. I'll see you tonight."

He thanked her a hundred times then turned and ran back in the other direction.

Brooke let out a sigh of disappointment when she saw Jeff behind the counter.

"Do you work every shift here?" she asked him.

He just shrugged his shoulders like it was an answer.

Nobody was on campus on a Saturday, so the shift was going by extremely slowly. It didn't help that her mind kept crazily overanalyzing the text conversation with James this morning. Then overanalyzing everything that had gone on with them this semester. Then overanalyzing every tiny detail of every moment she'd ever spent with him ever. She was sick of it.

She looked over at Jeff, who didn't seem to have a care in the world or a thought in his head. She envied him in that moment. If only she could have five minutes of feeling that peaceful.

"Hey," she said, getting his attention. "You wouldn't happen to have any, um, weed on you now, would you?" He pulled a brownie in a Ziploc bag out of his apron pocket then dropped it back in. She waved it away then started pacing behind the counter. "Never mind. I just had some stuff going through my head. I shouldn't. Forget I asked. It's just that, do you remember that guy I was telling you about? Well I…"

He held up his hand to stop her and pulled out the bag again. He'd prefer to sacrifice the last of his stash than listen to her apparently.

She'd never even smoked weed before, let alone eaten a pot brownie. But after hitting the baby aspirin last night, she figured she might as well move on to the hard stuff. Plus, desperate times called for desperate measures. She took the piece out of his hand and popped it into her mouth without another thought.

Half an hour later, Brooke was sitting on the counter next to Jeff with a can of whipped cream in her hand. "Dude, I was so wrong about you, Jeff. You're like a genius disguised as an idiot. You don't talk much, but when you do, you say some profound stuff. You're so right. Life isn't short. Life is long. I literally cannot think of a single activity that's longer. Class? No. Driving across the country? No. *Game of Thrones* episode? No. Still just living life that whole time. We need to write this whole conversation down and—whoa! I have an idea. Do you think if we told Del Taco how close we are, they'd deliver?" She lifted the can of whipped cream up and tilted it toward her mouth.

"What's going on here?" Brooke turned to see their manager standing in front of the counter. She just stared at him without being able to answer. "I asked you a question," he said. "What's going on here?" Neither one of them said a thing. "You're not *high*, are you?" He looked directly at Brooke.

Brooke gulped. "No. Wait. Yes. Wait, does yes mean I'm not, or does no mean I'm yes?" When she heard herself mess up what she was trying to say, she started laughing, then laughing harder, then laughing so hard she fell trying to get off the counter. "Wait, ask the question better. I'll get it right this time," she said, wiping tears out of her eyes.

The manager looked at Jeff and asked him if Brooke was high. He nodded, pointing to her on the ground.

Brooke gasped dramatically.

"Brooke, you're fired. Get out of here."

"What! No! Wait, but—"

"But what?"

"But… um… it's my birthday."

"You're fired, Brooke! Get your things."

Brooke stood up, despite how dizzy she was, pulled off her visor and apron, and slammed them down next to Jeff. The evidence was on her. His pockets were empty. It was his word against hers and he betrayed her.

"Uh. Happy birthday?" he said, as if that would make it any better.

"Idiot."

She stormed out and made it about ten feet before she ran for a trash can and threw up. She spent the next few hours lying on her bed with the spins, repeating to herself that drug free is the way to be.

Later that night, when Brooke had made a full recovery, she met up with the girls in Kate and Darci's room. Omega Chi was throwing a party to celebrate spring break. This time the theme was Stop Light, meaning if you're taken you wear red, if you're seeing someone but it's not official you wear yellow, and if you're completely single you wear green.

Kate put on a cute red dress. Darci slipped into a green skirt with a tank top in a completely different shade of green, just to make sure her status was clear. Stella wore a tank top that was so lime green it was almost yellow, but the second they tried to call her out on it, she turned strangely defensive. And Brooke reluctantly put on a green fitted T-shirt with some jean shorts. She had never disliked her favorite color so much. She knew she wasn't going to be interested in any of the guys at the frat house, but what choice did she have? She was in the green zone.

The party was up to the usual Omega Chi standard. They strung a stop light through the center of the courtyard, made street signs in every corner, and, of course, had plenty of alcohol stocked. They had gone all out with the decorations, and everyone looked like they were having a blast. As the night wore on, though, Brooke just wasn't feeling like herself. She watched Kyle introducing Sophie to all of his friends and saw Nolan and Stella making out in a corner where Stella thought no one could spot them—solving the lime-green mystery. Bryan had his arm around Kate sitting next to the fire pit, and even Garrett and Darci were sending dirty texts to each other as if no one could tell what they were doing. She decided she just didn't feel like being out anymore.

She was just about to leave the hallway when she heard a voice come from behind her.

"Hey, sexy." *Please no, not him.* She couldn't take talking to Stan. "You're going the wrong way, babe. My bedroom's this way." He slipped his arm over her shoulder to turn her away from the front door.

"Leave me alone, Stan," she said, shoving his arm off.

"What's your problem now?"

"Nothing. I just want to go home. It's late."

"It's 11:30." In college time, that was basically considered evening. She opened her phone to confirm that was the time and realized it was still opened to the text conversation with James.

"Oh, you've gotta be kidding me. You're not still into that guy, are you? You know, you were all over me before that dude came along."

"I say this with all due respect, Stan. I'd sooner die than even consider spending an ounce of my time with you voluntarily. I'm serious. I'd willingly jump into a shark frenzy."

"That's cute. You're funny. Look, just let me take your mind off whatever is bugging you," he said, this time forcefully trying to direct her the opposite way down the hall.

"Get off!" she screamed as she pushed him away.

"Fine, you're fuckin' stupid, anyway," he said with such

annoyance it got her attention. "If you're dumb enough to think you're the only one that guy's hooking up with, then you're a waste of time. Hey, I've got respect for the dude, he gets more than his fair share of ass around here, but don't act like you have something special when you're not even the only girl in the room he's screwing."

Brooke looked in the direction he nodded his head. Maddie was standing there, mocking her with a fake smile from across the room.

She felt like he'd punched her in the chest. James had been with Maddie? James is with Maddie? She suddenly felt weak and grabbed her stomach like she was going to be sick again. She was dizzy and felt like she was suffocating, so she walked farther into the hallway to be out of sight from everyone. She didn't want to believe it, but how could she not? This is exactly what she always knew would happen. It hurt more than she told herself it would but it was always going to be how it ended.

Stan's tone changed when he saw her reaction. "Hey, listen, I get it, that sucked to hear," he said as he followed her. "I'm just trying to look out for you. If he's out there doing what he wants, you should be too. Just come with me. Let's just hang out in my room where it's quiet and talk, maybe see where it goes. Maybe we'll get Maddie to join us then give that *boyfriend* of yours a call after. I'm sure he'd be glad to know you two can play nice together."

She looked up at him and he winked. Suddenly she wasn't weak, or dizzy, or confused. She was pissed. At Maddie, at James, at herself, at Stan. If she had a drink in her hand, she would have thrown it in Stan's face. But she didn't have a drink, she had a foot, so she pulled out of his grip, wound up and kicked him in what small bit of manhood he had.

He fell to his knees and screamed a list of profanities at her as she turned back and ran for the front door. Maybe he'd taken a hit there so many times he'd become accustomed to it because before Brooke could get out of his reach, he grabbed her by arm and pulled her back with more force than she could fight.

Just as she was about to lose her fell to the floor, she heard someone yell, "Hey!"

She turned just in time to see Sophie spray Stan in the face with a can of pepper spray and watch as he fell back to the ground. Brooke looked at Sophie, who blew at the can like it was a gun and tucked it safely into her back pocket. She mouthed, "Are you okay?" to Brooke, who nodded then shook her head in the other direction. She wasn't okay. "Go. I'll see you back in our room, okay?"

Brooke nodded and turned to leave, then ran back and hugged Sophie. Brooke still couldn't speak. Words couldn't come out if she tried, but she hoped Sophie got the message. She walked out the door and closed it behind her.

She walked all the way to the dorms, just putting one foot in front of the other, never slowing down. She didn't cry; she refused to cry. She didn't believe she had the right to.

She got back to her room, changed clothes, scrubbed her face until it was bright pink, and crawled into bed. But she didn't sleep. She just concentrated on breathing as images of James and Maddie with their nice cars and expensive things and thoughts of them laughing together at how stupid she was, or how she had to work in a coffee shop, or only had one good pair of heels, or even how she couldn't eat dairy played over and over again in her head.

She just stared at the ceiling, becoming angrier with every passing minute as the conversations in her head became more real. By the time the sun rose, she couldn't force herself to stay in bed any longer. She ripped the covers off, went to her closet, pulled out a sundress, and threw it on her bed. *Oh great*, she thought. She'd spent the last three Wednesdays in a row with James and forgot she hadn't done any laundry. She was completely out of underwear aside from one pair of giant granny panties she didn't even know why she owned. She pulled them on, threw on the sundress, and grabbed her keys.

She kept telling herself to stay calm as she drove all the way to James's condo and parked her car. She walked up the stairs and knocked frantically on his door. It occurred to her that this behavior could be considered crazy, but what did she care? She'd acted like a fool since she met the guy. Why try to change it now? She heard him walk up, turn the knob, then finally open the door.

"Hey, what are you doing here?" he said, rubbing his eyes. It was clear she'd woken him up. His eyes focused, and he looked at her. "Are you okay?"

"No."

"Come in. What happened?"

"*You* happened, and I hate you for it." She pushed past him into the living room.

"Good morning to you too."

"*Don't try to be cut*e. I had to hear from that fucking moron Sta*n ab*out all the other girls. And Maddie McCullerlance! Of all people, her! Why did it have to be her?"

"Okay. You're acting crazy right now."

Her look of sleep deprivation probably wasn't helping to counteract his claim. "And I can't stop thinking about all of the ways I've looked like such an idiot and felt like a fool and all the time and energy I've to put into pretending like I don't care. Being too cool to give a shit about anybody may come easy for you, but it doesn't for me, and I'm sick to death of feeling sick over this. I'm tired of wanting something I can't have and not feeling good enough, and feeling like a psycho."

"And acting like a psycho?" he asked, smiling, in an effort to lighten the mood.

"Stop trying to be funny, because I am falling apart right now, don't you get that? It's because of you I'm like this, and you can't even understand where I'm coming from because you've *never* had to feel like this. Everything is just a party to you. Living in your nice condo, getting as many girls as you want, whenever you want, and walking around campus like you own the place because you can catch a fucking ball. I hate football, and I hate you! And the worst part is I did this all to myself. I knew what you were all along."

"Brooke, listen, I don't know what you've heard, but I can explain. There were no girls."

"I don't know that! And guess what, I don't get to ask. You don't have to explain, because all this time I've been working my ass off to make you feel like you don't have to explain yourself to me. You don't have to explain because we're nothing to each other!"

"He made that up! Yes, there have been other girls in the past, but you can't believe—"

"Yes I can!"

"Why?"

"Because I need to believe it. Because if it wasn't this week, it'll be next. Because I need to be mad enough to just stay away from you!"

"Brooke!"

"What?" She looked at him, hoping he would say something to stop her from leaving, anything that would make her feel better than she did at that moment.

"I…" he started.

"*Wha*t do you want, James? Just tell me what you want," she begged, needing to understand him.

He shook his head and looked down at the floor. "Nothing." That was all he had to say. He wanted nothing.

She turned to leave and grabbed the doorknob. "I just wish I'd never even met you."

"Fine," he shot back, suddenly angry. "Go have fun with Stan. Oh wait, you've already done that."

All the air she'd been holding in her chest burst out. She couldn't even defend herself. She pulled the door open and slammed it behind her.

She got in her car and started driving back toward campus. The more she thought about the conversation, the crazier it made her. All the thoughts of what she'd done and what she'd said and what he'd said played through her head without any way for her to stop it. She was gripping the steering wheel so hard her knuckles were white.

Brooke was just about home when suddenly she heard a siren and saw flashing lights in her rearview mirror. She looked at her speedometer. She was going 85 mph. *Holy shit, I'm going to jail* was the first thing she thought. She slowed down as fast as possible without slamming on the brakes and pulled over to the side of the road. Of course it had to be right in front of Kerby Lane and a ton of people near the dorms. Sure, why not add public humiliation to the list? She suddenly remembered that she never paid for the last speeding ticket, which had now probably tripled.

She rolled down her window, and the officer walked up. "License and registration, ma'am." She knew with certainty she couldn't flirt her way out of this one today. It wasn't even worth trying. She did the familiar reach across the car to her glove box and pulled out her papers. "Here you are, Officer…" Oh god, no, "ugh… Officer Hurley." She didn't need to look at his name tag. She'd recognized that accent anywhere.

"Wait in your vehicle, ma'am." With that, he turned and walked back to his car. She let her head fall back against her headrest. She closed her eyes and took a few deep breaths. When she opened her eyes, she saw Officer Hurley in her rearview mirror already writing up the ticket. *Whoa, whoa, whoa*, she thought. *No 'Ma'am, you did this. Ma'am, you did that'?* He wasn't even going to let her *try* to explain? She sure couldn't flirt, but maybe if he heard about last 24 hours of her life, he'd understand. She'd put up with enough, and she was not going to put up with this. She decided she couldn't take this sitting down, not today.

She ripped off her seat belt, kicked the door open, and stepped into the open air. A car drove by inches from her body, blowing her dress straight up and making her really regret today's underwear selection.

Without even bothering to think about all the people who just got a show, she began her angry march toward the real enemy, Hurley. "Hey, wait just a minute! Where is the justice here? I demand to know wh—"

When she got within about a foot away from him, he stepped back, and in one swift move he opened the back door, ducked her head, and swiveled her around. The next thing she knew, she was seated in the backseat of his car. *Shit. I am definitely going to jail.*

"You trying to be roadkill?" he bellowed. "You mind telling me why you stepped out of the car when I instructed you to remain in your vehicle?"

"You mind telling me what I've done wrong here?"

"Well, ma'am, I'd be happy to. I clocked you going 87 miles per hour in a 45 zone. Nearly doubling the speed limit is a felony and—not even counting your outstanding ticket—I have every right to take you in, book you, and leave you sitting behind bars until someone takes enough pity to collect your sorry behind. You need any further explanation?"

She was fully aware she was about to see the inside of a prison cell and that the ticket was without a doubt happening, and though her circumstances were pretty bleak, she hadn't made her point yet, so she wasn't finished.

"See, that's the problem with the system. You're all fine and happy to tell me I was speeding, but do you even bother to ask *why*? No! There are a billion things that could cause a person to need to move a *little* faster than what's on a stupid yellow sign. Can you arguably say the speed limit is appropriate for every single situation known to man? No, you can't! What if someone was chasing me?"

"Is someone chasing you, ma'am?"

"No, no one's chasing me, but sir, you do not even want to hear about the week I'm having."

"You're right about that, ma'am. I absolutely do not. Sign here, please." The man was impossible. She signed the ticket and shoved it back at him. She was shocked when instead of closing the door, he stepped aside and held his hand out to show she was free to go. She exited his car without taking the hand he offered and strutted back to her own car in a calm, controlled fashion.

She got in her car, closed her door, and turned to see Hurley outside her window again. He handed her the ticket, tapped the top of the door with his palm, and said, "All right, Miss Aarons, drive safely now. Please obey all posted speed limit signs."

Brooke just sat in her car for a few minutes, then leaned forward to look out the top of her windshield. "Excuse me, universe," she yelled at the sky, "have I done something to offend you? If so, I take it back. Whatever it is, I take it back!" She rested her head on her steering wheel and stayed like that. Eventually she started her car and turned back onto the road.

When she got back to the dorms, she went straight to her room. After pacing around for a bit, she decided to log onto Facebook, and remove that ridiculous picture Darci had set as her profile. There was a new message. She clicked on her inbox to see who it was from. *Kevin Mitchell?*

"Hi. I was sitting outside the restaurant when you got arrested today, and I couldn't help but notice your underwear. You think maybe you'd like to see a movie sometime, when you're out of jail?" She slammed her computer shut. She had zero control of anything in her life anymore.

She lay down on her bed, and her exhaustion finally caught up with her. She felt horrible, guilty, embarrassed—every word found in a thesaurus under *bad*. All she could do was bury herself under her covers and hope the shame of it all would go away soon.

Brooke woke up in the middle of the afternoon when she heard a knock on the door. She knew it would be the girls. She thought about getting up to answer it. Hanging out with them would definitely make her feel better. But she stayed where she was. She wanted to feel miserable. She needed to feel miserable. Distracting herself from the pain wasn't going to make anything better. Pretending none of this happened wasn't going to make these feelings go away. And wishing things were different wouldn't change how it all turned out.

Chapter 23

Brooke stayed in bed until the sound of the lock turning woke her up. Sophie and Kyle walked in.

"Oh, hey," Sophie said sweetly. "I hope we didn't wake you." They both had their hands full of bags from the student store.

"No, it's okay."

"There's something in front of our door." Brooke got out of bed and stood up, mostly because she felt weird lying in bed with company over, but she was slightly curious, too.

"What is it?"

"I don't know. I couldn't look down with all the stuff in my hands."

"I think it's a game," Kyle said.

"We're just dropping this stuff off," Sophie said, "but I'll be back later."

Brooke barely heard her as she walked to the doorway, looked down, and saw in big, bold letters the word "SORRY!" She knelt down and picked up the box.

"See you in a little while, okay?" Sophie said.

Brooke nodded but didn't take her eyes off of the game as she brought it inside and set in on her desk. Sophie and Kyle closed the door behind them, and Brooke stared at the box for a minute longer before opening the lid. There was a piece of paper inside with a note written on it. She recognized the handwriting.

Brooke,
   I don't know what to say… but I'm sorry.
   —James

She put her face in her hands and closed her eyes. What did he even have to be sorry for? Of the two of them, he was the only one who had been honest about what he wanted. She was the one lying and pretending and messing up her own life. She went to her closet, dug out a shirt she'd buried in her bottom drawer months before, pulled it on, crawled into bed, and laid there until she finally fell asleep again.

She slept through the night and until the next morning, even later than she usually slept. She picked up her phone, turned it back on, and saw a text message from Darci.

"Hey Brooke, meet us at our spot at 11."

Brooke dragged herself into the shower, put on some shorts and a tank top, and let her hair air dry as she walked to the restaurant, reminding herself to act like nothing was wrong, like she had this thing under control the whole time. She was fine.

When she got to the restaurant, the girls were already at their table.

Brooke: "Hey, guys, what's up?" She said as perky as she could muster.

Darci: "Ahem. Brooke, this is an intervention."

Brooke: "What?"

Stella: "Sophie told us you slept all day yesterday and were acting weird."

Kate: "And you were completely out of it the other night

at the Omega Chi house. Plus we heard about some drama between you and Stan. We can't figure out what's going on with you, and you're not allowed to disappear or lie anymore, so you have to tell us what's going on."

Brooke: "There's really nothing to tell guys!"

Darci: "You're a terrible liar."

Stella: "And a really bad actress. If you think you're doing good job acting fine right now, you're not."

Kate: "We know you better than that, and we're worried."

D*arci:* "Last night you spooned with a board game while wearing a hideous beaver T-shirt. That's a red flag!"

Brooke was surprised she knew that.

Brooke: "You can't prove anything."

Darci pulled out her phone and showed her a picture of herself doing just as she'd described. "If you need anymore evidence, there's a drool spot on the letter Y. It's all wavy now."

Brooke put her head on the table with a thud. She told them about what Stan said, about James and Maddie, and about her psychotic rant at James. When she got to the part about getting pulled over, she could tell they were all holding back laughter, and recapping it now even made her laugh a little. Getting thrown in the back of a cop car was pretty much the icing on a really bad cake. Once she cracked a smile, they all just let it out. They were all in tears when she described how she got fired, and it took them all some time to catch their breath.

Brooke: "I was so stupid."

Kate: "No, you weren't stupid. We've all been there. Or will be there."

Darci: "There is no worse feeling than falling for a guy who doesn't feel the same. Why do you think I decided to be such -"

Brooke: "You're not a slut Darci. I don't want you to talk about yourself that way."

Darci: "I was going to say an independent woman."

Brooke: "Oh, sorry. I meant, you're just comfortable keeping things casual, which clearly I am not. I wish I was more like you. I wish I could take all of this back."

Kate: "Call it a learning experience. We're all going to have to get our hearts broken a few times before we find the right person. This was you just paying your dues."

Brooke: "And two speeding tickets. I'm just ready for a clean slate. I want to start all over and pretend none of this ever happened."

Stella: "Well, we can't erase your memory, but we can get close."

Brooke: "Please don't roofie me."

Darci: "God, you're messed up."

Brooke: "No psychological experiments either. I'm serious this time."

Kate: "Oh no, no. That lesson's been learned already."

Brooke: "Well what? What is it?"

In their best mock sorority girl voices, the three of them yelled, "Road trip!"

The girls told Brooke about a country music festival called Bayou County Superfest eight hours away in Baton Rouge, Louisiana. They'd decided a huge concert with Lady Antebellum, Zac Brown Band, and Brad Paisley was the best way to spend the rest of their spring break. Other bands were playing the first few days, but the best ones were on the last day, just when they'd be getting there.

Brooke heard her phone go off. She pulled it out and saw it was a text from James. She opened it up and saw a photo of a napkin from Stubb's with a smiley face drawn on it. The message read, "Grabbing a bite here, just thought of you."

She stared at it a second, not knowing what to make of it. How could she be so mad at him and still feel her stomach flip to know he was thinking about her? She couldn't be drawn back in. She'd learned from her history with James, and she wasn't going to repeat it again. Even though it broke her heart a little more, she took a deep breath, swiped her finger over the message, and hit "delete."

"Let's do it," she said to the girls. "Let's go."

Chapter 24

Brooke, Stella, Kate, and Darci ran back to the dorms to pack and met back downstairs. They somehow fit all of their bags into Kate's car and piled in.

"Okay, everyone I have a few car rules to go over," Kate began. "Number one: Stella, there is no picking up hitch-hikers, even if you think they're cute. Number two: Darci, if I find alcohol in your Big Gulp cup, I'll ditch your ass in whatever bum-fuck town we're in at the time. And number three: Brooke, you're not allowed to even sit behind the wheel or hold the map. Everyone gets one emergency bathroom break request, except for me because I'm driving, so make sure you use yours wisely, and if you get carsick and throw up, then you'll be responsible for getting my car detailed. Can we all agree to that?" The girls nodding to each other and agreed. Kate started the car, rolled down the top, and turned onto the highway.

They blasted music and rehashed their favorite memories from the year. They laughed about all their experiences with guys they'd met, with the exception of James, whose name was not to be spoken, and laughed at all the stupid mistakes they'd made when they were drinking. They stopped at a gas station to fuel up, load up on car snacks, and put the top back up.

An hour later when they were all high on sugar and getting a little stir-crazy, they decided to pull over and see if they could spot any alligators in the river. Kate pulled over, and they all jumped out of the car. Darci ran down first, and the rest of them took a minute to stretch and fix their clothing before turning to follow.

As they started down the slope to meet Darci, they saw her running toward them flailing her arms and screaming, "Get back to the car!"

They all looked at each other to determine why she was yelling, then back down at her.

"Run!" she yelled again, and as they all turned to run, they saw her surrounded by a huge swarm of mosquitoes.

They all screamed and ran back toward the car. "Get in!" Kate yelled. They jumped in the car, but hundreds of bugs had followed them in. Kate started the car and rolled down the windows. "We have to drive to blow them out!" she yelled over their screaming. She screeched onto the road and drove like a maniac, swerving as she tried to drive while being bitten. The car began to empty, and they all started to calm down.

"Okay, I think we got them all," Kate said, trying to catch her breath. Brooke glanced over at her from the passenger side to see she was looking a little pale. Kate looked back at her to ask why she was staring at her, and Brooke screamed as she saw a huge mosquito going to town on Kate's neck. She pointed to her neck, and Kate's eyes widened when she figured out why Brooke was screaming.

"Get it off!" Kate yelled.

"No!" Brooke said, shaking her head.

"Get it off!" Kate yelled louder and more desperate.

"I can't!" Brooke screamed in a high-pitched cry.

And in a voice none of them imaged could come out of her, Kate roared, "DO IT!" so loud that Brooke finally hauled off with a warrior cry and slapped her in the neck, killing it on the spot and causing Kate to make a choking swallow noise.

"Thank you," Kate said, returning to a sweet, but hoarse, voice. Brooke sat there wide-eyed, staring straight ahead out the window like she'd just been through a trauma.

All four of them kept shivering and slapping their skin just in case, trying to calm down, as big red welts appeared on their arms, legs, and faces. They were just beginning to breathe normally and start to laugh when suddenly there was a loud bang and Kate lost control of the car. The tires screeched, and they could smell burning rubber. They screamed as the car spun around two full times and finally came to a stop on the side of the road.

They all sat there catching their breath all over again, afraid to let go of each other. "Is everyone okay?" Kate finally asked, still panting.

"Yeah," Brooke answered as she looked down at Kate's hand firmly planted on her chest. "We're good. Are you okay?"

"I'm okay." She slowly unbuckled, opened her door, and stepped outside. The girls followed her lead and got out to look at the car.

"We got a flat," Kate said. Brooke and Darci looked at each other like they were going to die out there, then ran to Kate's side to comfort her. Not that they could offer any. They were covered with welts in the middle of nowhere.

Darci pulled out her phone. "There's no reception here!"

Brooke heard her phone go off inside the car. "I guess I've got reception."

"Call for help," Kate said.

Brooke pulled her phone out of the car and opened a new text. It was James again. He'd sent a picture of one of the plastic cats from Funny Nails waving its paw. Underneath it read, "Facing fears… P.S. Wasn't funny."

Normally his message would have made her smile, but today it just hurt. Nothing had changed. Just because he had taken on one minor fear didn't mean he had tackled his Mr. Big syndrome. She had to stop holding on to something that would never be. She felt tears welling up again.

"Tell whoever it is to save us!" Darci cried, pulling Brooke out of her own thoughts.

Brooke looked up at Darci to tell her who had texted her, but when she saw her face, she gasped and then burst out laughing instead. One of Darci's mosquito bites had swelled her left eye halfway shut. Her own laughter surprised her more than anyone, but she couldn't stop. It felt so good to laugh, really laugh, after so many days of feeling up and down.

While Darci ran to a mirror, Brooke finally caught her breath, then finally looked back down at her phone. She took another deep breath and deleted the message. She turned her attention back to their situation.

"Hey, guys," Brooke said to Kate and Darci, "I don't think we need saving."

She nodded toward Stella, who had opened the trunk and pulled out the spare tire and jack. Without saying a word, she knelt down and got to work. The three of them all stood there watching, too in awe to even comment.

Stella finished replacing the tire and brushed off her hands. "What? I had to learn something in auto mechanics."

When they finally recovered from the shock of their near-death experience—and the bigger shock that Stella could change a tire—they piled back into the car. Kate passed around a tube of ointment for everyone to put on their mosquito bites. They all looked hideous covered in swollen, goo-covered lumps: Kate's ear lobe was the size of a cherry, Stella's lips had swollen up on one side so much they could barely understand what she was saying, Brooke had a massive bump right between her eyebrows, and Darci's eye was now almost completely closed. They took pictures on Darci's phone to document the moment and made a pact that these photos would never see the light of day.

The sun had just gone down, and their sugar highs and adrenaline rushes had turned to fatigue. "Let's just stop in the next town and turn in for the night," Kate suggested. "I don't want to drive any longer." They all agreed with that decision. That was, until they actually got to the next town and saw their only option.

"Hell no. I'm not staying here. This motel is the setting for a horror movie," Brooke said, looking at the one-story building with a dirt parking lot and lights that flickered on and off.

"Well the next town's not for another 45 miles, and I'm tired," Kate said, trying to sound positive. "I'm sure it looks worse from the outside."

"Whatever," Darci said. "I'm so tired, I'll be able to sleep anywhere." Darci poked Stella, who was already falling asleep. They parked, and Brooke and Darci went into the front office while Kate and Stella unloaded the car.

Darci rang the bell until a clerk walked out from the back. His hairy stomach poked out from under a plaid shirt he was unaware had come unbuttoned, and his lazy eye was stuck staring in one direction.

Brooke shifted her eyes back and forth a few times trying to figure out which one to look at before taking her best guess and requesting a room with two beds. As he explained the amenities, which included a vibration option on the beds, Brooke noticed Darci looking behind her every few seconds. When she realized she was trying to figure out what the clerk's other eye was staring at, Brooke elbowed her to stop it. After a transaction that seemed to take ages on his archaic computer system with dial-up, he finally handed them a key and pointed in the direction of their room.

They walked cautiously along the building until they found the room number they were looking for. When they opened the door, they didn't go in. Instead they just stared at it for a while from the doorway. Darci started to laugh, presumably out of terror, but the others soon began to as well.

"This is the most hideous place I've ever seen in my life," Darci said, wiping tears of laughter from her eyes. They were all so delirious that everything was becoming funny.

They walked in slowly and set their bags down. Stella walked over to a closet, pulled the doors open, and screamed as a rat ran out and across her feet. She cried so loudly that the other girls screamed out of instinct, and they all jumped up on the beds. They watched the rat run out the front door, but they didn't stop shrieking and shaking for at least another five minutes.

"There's no way I can sleep here!" Stella said. "Not happening. Get your things. We're going."

"Not a chance." Darci said, pulling out her flask and tossing it to Stella. "We're all way too tired to get back on the road." They all took a few sips to calm down then passed it around while jumping back and forth on the beds until they all sat down and finally fell asleep—after locking the door and piling the chairs and their luggage in front of it, of course.

In the morning, they loaded the car up and hit the road, thrilled to put the creepy motel in the rearview. With the temporary tire on Kate's car, they were forced to drive much slower than they'd planned. They finally found a repair shop to replace the tire so they could pick up the pace, but the sun was already setting when they reached the campground.

"When I read 'camping,' I assumed everyone would be in tents," Stella said. "I didn't know everyone would be in RVs."

They pulled their tiny tent out of the trunk along with their bags, and Kate drove over to the grounds parking lot. Brooke consulted the tent directions, turning the papers different angles hoping one would make sense, while Darci just kept poking Stella with the tent poles.

Kate came back just as a man walked by and said, "Y'all heard there's a storm coming in tonight, didn't ya? Might want to hurry up and get that tent up," then kept on walking.

"Well, that was helpful," Brooke said while the man was still in earshot. Suddenly they all realized how humid it had become. There was definitely going to be a storm, and they didn't have much time. They worked together as fast as possible as the lightning came closer, and after only seven attempts, they got the tent standing just in time.

They crawled in seconds before the thunder roared and rain came pouring down. While they were still high-fiving and laughing at their close call, Darci reached in her bag and pulled out a deck of cards and a bag of Franzia she'd squeezed into her duffle. The rest of the night was spent playing cards, passing the bag around, and making hilarious tangent-driven conversation.

To their surprise, the tent survived the storm, and the next morning they walked over to the concert area. They spent the whole day buying tacky souvenirs, taking pictures, and dancing with strangers as they listened to the bands play. They knew every word of every song and danced around like fools, but they didn't care who saw. Being in a completely unfamiliar place was so freeing and made everything back in Austin feel like a distant blur. That was, until Brooke checked her phone.

It was the end of the night, and they'd gone back to the campgrounds to pack up their tent and load up the car. She pulled her phone out of her bag where she'd buried it and saw the message from James. She opened it and couldn't help feeling a little stunned. Why did he send a picture of her ribbon? Why did he even still have it? She'd forgotten all about it. The message read. "You left this in my car months ago. Can't believe I've held onto it all this time. Crazy, right?"

"Guys! Come here," she heard Kate call. Brooke walked over to Kate with her phone still opened to the message. "Look at this tree. Look how many people have carved their names in it." She held up her phone to shine the light on all the names. The tree she was talking about was huge. It had to be ten stories high and probably forty feet around. They all walked over and started reading some of them off. Brooke ran her hand over a heart with two names in it.

She looked back down at the message. She so badly wanted to answer. She wanted him to know it was killing her not to respond to him. But she didn't. It was probably just one of those tiny actions she could twist in her head to mean more than it did. She had, after all, done it so many times before. But she was past wishful thinking now.

"Okay, I have a really corny idea," Kate said as she pulled her keys out of her pocket and held one up. "Should we leave our mark on this place?" Without missing a beat, they all took turns carving their names into the tree before standing back to admire their work.

Stella: "Hey, highs and lows of freshman year. Who wants to go first?"

Kate: "Oh, I know! My low is getting a D in Spanish. And my high is the first time Bryan said 'I love you.'"

Stella: "Okay, my high was when we broke into the Omega Chi house and replaced Maddie with Fatty, and my low was any moment spent in the Omega Chi house bathroom."

Darci: "Well, my low was even letting those bitches give us a reason to put that picture on the wall in the first place, but my high? Hm, so many to choose from. My high was this weekend, definitely."

Kate: "What about you Brooke, what's your high?"

Brooke: "Kicking Stan in the balls."

They all laughed, but then she decided on a better one.

Brooke: "My high was that Saturday back in August when we all met for the first time. When we went to the worst, most disgusting party ever and then sat on the street drinking a bag of wine."

Stella: "Well, what's your low?"

Brooke racked her brain, but in that moment she was just so happy and at peace that not a single thing came to mind.

Brooke: "I don't have one."

Stella: "Oh c'mon, there has to be something."

Brooke: "Nope."

Kate: "Not even bombing that final last semester?"

Darci: "Or when you got fired?"

Stella: "Or when you barfed up a pot brownie?"

Kate: "Or when everyone saw your granny panties?"

Darci: "Or when you almost shit your pants after eating too much ice cream?"

Brooke: "Okay, okay! Geez! Not my finest year."

She knew they were only trying to distract her from the one thing they knew was her low, but jeez, did they really have to nitpick? She smiled to herself.

Brooke: "Yes, I did have a low point, but I'm not sorry it happened anymore. Mostly because you guys took enough pity on me to buy my concert ticket."

Stella: "Yeah, well, you're better now, so pay up! It was a loan."

Brooke looked at her phone again for a moment then clicked away from the text message. She held her phone up and took a picture of their names on the tree. They decided to take turns sleeping and driving on the way home so they wouldn't have to stay at another horrible motel again. Despite rule number three, Kate allowed Brooke to take the second shift, since it was only a straight shot for the next 230 miles, and there was absolutely no way she could get lost.

Brooke replaced Kate, who fell asleep within seconds. She looked in the rearview mirror at Darci and Stella sleeping in the backseat and then at Kate in the front, and she just couldn't help but smile. She couldn't imagine her life without these girls. They all had their quirks, but none of them would ever have to change a thing about themselves to fit in with each other. She didn't need anything else.

Chapter 25

Monday morning when Brooke woke up, she instinctively felt around for her phone. She pulled it off the charger and looked at the screen. No new messages. She told herself that's exactly what she wanted and continued to do so as she checked her phone throughout the day without change. There was nothing from James Tuesday either. By Wednesday morning she had come to terms with knowing that whatever she'd had with him was over now.

There were only two weeks left before finals started, and then her freshman year would be finished. She decided she just couldn't go to her class with James anymore—not until the final, at least. She'd been teaching herself the material all along anyway and had been doing well. All she wanted was a little time and distance.

Brooke spent all of the next week studying and the following week taking her finals. She felt good about all of them and was finally able to just crack down and focus. There was nothing to divert her attention.

Her last final was in her Wednesday class. After a morning full of stomach-wrenching nerves, she finally decided to show up seconds before 9 a.m. so she could see where James was sitting and position herself as far away as possible. When she couldn't find him, she just grabbed a seat in the back. She took her time on the test, reading everything carefully without ever looking up. She stood up, turned in her test, and walked straight out, feeling like she'd done the best she could.

When she got back to the dorms, she decided it was time to start packing up her room. Everyone else on her floor was planning to stay for another week, but she had to get home for Sarah's wedding. Her closet alone took the rest of the day, so she left out an outfit for the drive home and waited until the morning to pack up her bedding.

"Knock, knock," Brooke said as she stood in the doorway of the boys' room. "I'm taking off, guys."

"Get over here," Garrett demanded.

"Group hug," Kyle said in his corniest tone, as Bryan and Kyle joined the huddle.

They squeezed so hard Brooke was sure her ribs would crack.

"You two both better be good to my friends over summer," she said to Bryan and Kyle. "And Garrett, I'm holding you personally responsible for making sure they're respectful of them at all times, or else this," she pulled her phone out of her pockets and hit play, showing the video of Garrett dancing in Darci's underwear, "hits the Internet."

His jaw dropped, and he stiffened up. "Uh, um, yes, ma'am. Definitely, of course. Women deserve respect. There won't be any problems."

"All right then," she said, smiling and punching him in the arm to loosen him up. "Bring it in again." They hugged one last time before Brooke walked out and closed the door behind her. She pulled a piece of paper out of her purse and taped it to the door. Then she pulled out a sharpie and wrote, "Do not disturb. We're watching *Brokeback Mountain*!" then walked down the hall to Kate and Darci's room.

"Okay, ladies, I've got to get on the road," Brooke said.

"Did you hear the good news?" Darci asked.

"What?"

"Maddie McCullerlance will no longer be a problem," Kate said proudly.

"Oh really," Brooke said. "And how is that happening?"

"Apparently she's had a stressful year, which I believe we can help take credit for, and it turns out the girl's a stress eater," Darci said.

"Yup, Nolan said she gained like 15 pounds and didn't get reelected as president," Stella said. "Looks like her own little rule bit her in the butterpants!"

Maddie calling other people fat or telling her minions they had to be pin-thin to fit in with her was gross. Brooke wasnerpants!rularly proud of the method she took to send that message, but she hoped it helped end the cycle of excluding based on looks.

"Apparently she's no longer Omega Chi's Sweetheart either, but they've decided not to replace the picture," Kate said. "They're going to find a new spot for the Sweetheart photo because the one we made is a house favorite. Bryan said she'd been a bitch to a ton of guys in the house and other people, too, so they all think it's too funny to take down."

"Holy Kappa. That's probably the best thing I've ever heard in my life," Brooke said. "To Fatty McButterpants!" They all held up imaginary glasses to cheers, then group-hugged. "We're sticking to our plans to visit, right?"

"Definitely. San Diego in June and Miami in July," Stella said.

"Then right back here in August to do it all again!" Brooke said. They spent a few more minutes saying their goodbyes and hugging again before Brooke grabbed her bags and walked out of what had been her home for the last year.

The day of Sarah's wedding arrived, and she looked even more beautiful than Brooke had imagined. The strapless white sweetheart dress fit her perfectly, and her light-brown hair was pulled back into a bun with a veil flowing all the way down her back. Brooke had never seen her sister look so happy, and she'd never seen her mom go through more tissues.

The ceremony was by the beach at Port Hueneme just before sunset. The bridesmaids all wore long, light-blue dresses and carried white roses, and Brooke walked down the aisle with Dan's brother then took her place next to where her sister would be standing.

As the music began to play, Brooke glanced at Dan to see his face light up before turning to watch Sarah walk down the aisle with their dad. As she watched Sarah walk toward her future husband, Brooke's mind couldn't help but fill with all her insecurities. Her sister had found someone willing to commit the rest of his life to her. Meanwhile Brooke couldn't even get a man to commit to dating her for a while. All those feelings of inadequacy rushed back in, but she forced herself to keep up a happy face.

She truly was happy for her sister. She was also happy for Kate and Bryan, who had both found love for the first time in each other. For Stella, who finally admitted she had feelings for Nolan. For Sophie, who landed her first boyfriend, Kyle, and for Darci, whose confidence and independence were unwavering.

At the reception, Brooke sat next to Sarah, and they whispered back and forth about all the people neither of them had seen in years and the ones they had no clue why their mom had invited.

Brooke noticed Sarah glancing across the room at Dan, who was talking to their grandma. When he looked back at Sarah, Brooke saw a moment that made her realize she couldn't imagine either of them with anyone else in the world. Maybe there was such a thing as the one.

A photographer came by to snap a photo of Brooke and Sarah, and they learned in to pose together. "Okay, hold that smile when I tell you this," Sarah said, "but Mom invited Dr. Roberts for you, and he's sitting over there staring."

"What?!" Brooke said as the camera flashed. She glanced over and caught sight of Dr. Roberts's enormous smile. "Why would she do that to me?" She wondered if it was her mom's way of punishing her for asking her parents to help pay off those speeding tickets.

"Oh, she was just worried about you being dateless tonight, but don't worry…" Sarah started. Before she could finish whatever hopeful cliché she was about to say, the DJ called Sarah to the center of the dance floor for her first dance with Dan as a married couple. Sarah stood up, then paused for a moment. She opened a small clutch Brooke hadn't noticed and pulled out her phone. "Here, you left this in the hotel room," she said as she handed it over.

Of course she'd left it in the room. Why would she need her phone at the wedding? She set it face down on the table, leaned back in her chair, and let out a long sigh. She was actually glad Sarah didn't get to finish her first sentence. She didn't need to hear any more platitudes. She'd learned more about herself this year than she had in every class combined, and she finally knew what she wanted in life. She wanted a career she was proud of, friends she could always lean on, and—someday—a man who would do crazy things to be with her. And somewhere in the world, he was out there.

She watched Sarah and Dan dance and sipped her champagne, feeling at peace and in control of her life for the first time in a long while. She surveyed the room, taking it all in, but her eyes suddenly caught on an empty chair. She frantically searched the room until she spotted Dr. Roberts. He was on the move and heading straight toward her.

Her phone buzzed on the table, and she grabbed for it like it was her only chance at freedom. She scrambled out of her seat and darted out the door, happy to have escaped what surely would have been an awkward interaction.

Her phone vibrated in her hand, reminding her she had a massage. She slid her finger across the screen to see a name she hadn't seen displayed in a while: James Cartwright.

It wasn't like she hadn't been thinking about him all day— she had. It just caught her off guard to see a message from him. She opened up the text to see he'd sent a new photo. "Good morning from the East Coast," she read as she looked at the photo of a gorgeous sunrise. She could see a few skyscrapers on the sides of the picture and realized she was looking at the East River from a tall building in New York City. She stared at it for a while, taking a big breath in and letting it out as she leaned against a wall of the building. She forced herself to push every sweet and sad thought from her mind and decided it was just plain weird to send a "good morning" picture to someone at night. The sun was setting in California, so it was surely pitch black in New York by now. She let herself wonder what he could be doing over there for just a moment, when suddenly another photo came in.

She studied the picture. It looked like it was taken from the backseat of a cab. The driver was waving over his shoulder with a big smile, and the message read, "Who says New Yorkers aren't friendly?" This message was stranger and more out of place than the first, but the man's goofy grin forced her to hold back a smile of her own. It was one thing for him to send things that reminded him of her in Austin, but she'd never even been to New York. Why would he think to send her a picture of the East River and a cab driver?

Her phone vibrated again as another photo popped up. It was of a huge, angry-looking woman in a uniform. Brooke looked closely at her to see she was next to an airport scanner and staring at the camera as if James was about to pay for snapping that photo.

"About to feel very, very violated," it said underneath, causing her to finally crack the smile she was holding back and laugh to herself. She rested her hand on her chest and realized her heart had started to race. She hadn't even had a second to think about it when another photo came in. This one was a picture of keys with a green Enterprise keychain. "If anyone asks… I'm over 25."

For a moment she thought she might have been seeing a pattern, but there was no way she could be right. It was impossible. She knew it was impossible—until another photo came in. There was no caption, just a photo of a sign that said, "Ventura County." She pushed herself off the wall and started walking in a straight line to get away from the music so she could hear her own thoughts. Her heart was racing faster now. She grabbed the wooden railing of the pier and faced the ocean, taking in a few deep breaths. Was he actually in California? Her question was answered when one last photo came in. He sent the same view she had of the sunset. She studied the picture, then looked over her shoulder toward the building, and there he was.

Her heart felt like it was trying to jump out of her chest as she instinctively started to walk toward him. She stopped herself while there was still a distance.

"Hi," he said, looking so unfairly handsome in a black suit and white shirt with his hair brushed over to one side.

"Hi," she exhaled. Neither one said anything for a moment. She didn't know who should speak next. "What, no flowers?" she asked, instantly kicking herself for resorting to sarcasm after everything.

"Yeah, after flying across the country and showing up at your sister's wedding, I was worried it might look desperate or something." He took a few steps closer, then stopped.

"You know, my phone records would build a strong case for a restraining order." Again, she wished she could control her responses. She took another few steps forward.

"That'll hold up well coming from the girl seen jumping into the bushes outside my place, very far from home." He stepped closer.

"Maybe I went for a long run," she suggested.

"And tripped?" he interjected. "I guess that's believable."

"So how will you explain crashing a wedding uninvited?"

"Oh, I got an invite," he said confidently. She rolled her eyes and then realized he couldn't have known where it was without someone's help. "See, I had to talk to you, and I just thought if I could get your attention, you'd give me a chance to say what I needed to." Her mind raced to find examples, but he went on before she could stop him. "I thought bringing over a board game named after an apology would be enough, but when you didn't answer the door or call, I realized the only way I was going to be able to tell you what I wanted to tell you would be in class. Of course then you bailed, so there went that plan, along with my by that time perfectly thought-out speech." *He was waiting for me in class?*

"But I couldn't just give up there. So at the risk of looking like an actual stalker, I went back to your dorm room and Sophie told me you moved out a few days early to get to your sister's wedding. Would most people cut their losses at this point? Probably. But instead I talked Nolan into talking Stella into getting in touch with your sister. Stella got me her number, after she made me plead my case, and I called Sarah and found out where the wedding was. And with a little back story about who I am and how much you mean to me, I scored an invite." *There's no way my dad would have let...*

"Except at 85 bucks a plate, your dad said I wasn't allowed to eat, so I'm kind of starving right now. But I'm here, with you. I just . . . I showed up."

He caught his breath, and she just stared for a moment. "Because," she paused, trying to register everything he just said, "you had to tell me something?"

He looked at the floor and laughed before meeting her eyes. "Didn't that just say it all? There was no Maddie. There were no other girls. I lied once about being at The W when I got jealous seeing you in a photo with another guy on Facebook. Then paid for it when I had to haul ass to get there, but I've never lied to you any other time than that."

Brooke could think of ten lies she told just that night. Suddenly it became clear. It seemed so simple, yet so many things still didn't add up. She took a deep breath. "But why didn't you say something before?" she asked, finally finding her words. "Why didn't you stop me while I was having a meltdown? Why didn't you tell me this all those times we were sneaking around? Why didn't you say something months ago when you apparently caught me jumping into the friggin' bushes?"

"I did! Well, I mean, I texted you after I saw you, but you never responded, so I figured you still wanted nothing to do with me." She remembered the 212 number she deleted at breakfast and wondered why she didn't realize it was the same area code as his then. "And I don't know. I didn't know what we were doing. But I also didn't want to say anything that would make you run again. I can't explain it. I just wanted to be around you. So much I even flunked a psychology class I didn't need."

Didn't need? "Then why were you in it?"

"Brooke, I'm an architect major. Why would I need a 200-level psychology class? I registered for five of them, and it wasn't until the last one I went to on Wednesday that I found one you were in. That wasn't a coincidence."

She hadn't even thought about why he was in that class.

"I even had to go into the psychology office to talk to our professor about skipping the final. Actually, while I was waiting, this really old professor sat down next to me, we got to talking, and he told me this great one-liner from Plato… but anyway, our professor wouldn't let me make up the test, so I got a failing grade in the class because, thanks to you, I didn't do so great on the midterm either. Now I have to retake the course over summer to try to fix my GPA."

She never would have imagined he cared, not enough to go through everything he was saying. But he did. He does. She'd been so busy psycho-analyzing everything she hadn't even realized what was going on right in front of her. There was so much she wanted to say. She had so many more questions still, but all she could do was bite her lip to hold back a smile. "Well why didn't you tell me you were crazy?"

"I just found out," he said, making her laugh as she closed what was left of the gap between them.